THE 9 LIVES OF MARVA DELONGHI

THE 9 LIVES OF MARVA DELONGHI

JODY J. SPERLING

CREA8
COLLABOR8
PRESS

For Marv

I

1

I LEANED AGAINST THE BRICK FAÇADE OUTSIDE OUR office, drawing figures of infinity in the air with my favorite four-inch pocketknife. My thoughts were as stained as my shoes from wandering every dark alley in Omaha. Two voices spoke muffled words on the other side of the door: maybe love, maybe fear. I flicked my knife closed, dropped it in my purse, and turned the knob to see which. With the door open an inch, I paused. First impressions say so much. If I walked in on love, there'd be a happy ending. I didn't want to think about fear. I knew Lyle's gristly baritone anywhere, but my partner's guest spoke with an unfamiliar lilt. When I stepped into the office, the conversation paused.

Lyle pointed a ham and cheese hoagie at me. A smile formed around shreds of lettuce and a dribble of mustard. "Luke! We were just talking about you."

The tableau I faced wasn't love, though Lyle might've thought otherwise. The woman opposite him had yellow hair. She wore high heel shoes. Lipstick was everywhere. Some faces look made for bruises. I shook my head to shoo the lopsided thoughts.

Extended my hand. "Detective Mia. Some people call me Little Cancer, and not just because I was born in July."

A fat lip didn't stop this woman from showing a seductive smile. "You weren't kidding." She looked at Lyle. "Your partner's a real charmer."

He took his time chewing a bite of sandwich. "She grows on you."

"Like a tumor, I'm sure."

I patted my pockets. "I've heard that one before." My cigarettes were somewhere.

Before I found them, Lyle said, "Let me finish eating, huh?"

He hated the smell of smoke. I slipped the hard pack of Pyramid Menthol from my jacket and tapped the clamshell in my palm. "When do you think that'll be?"

He tongued a piece of ham lodged in his gums. "Maybe you should consider quitting."

I tossed my smokes on the office desk next to the rent bill. We were several weeks past-due and two lost cats from destitute. I gave Lyle the finger and looked again at his guest. "What'd you say your name was?"

"I didn't." She cradled her cheek in her hand like no one had ever loved her. "Marva DeLonghi. I was just telling Mr. Kuperchink how someone's trying to kill me."

I smiled. Death gives meaning to life. "Let me guess. You don't know who it is."

"I have a few ideas, but it seems I'm growing short on time."

It's almost endearing that Lyle won't correct a person when she butchers his last name. I spoke on his behalf: "It's Kuputchnik, by the way."

"I—" Tossing a fist-sized chunk of bread and meat into his mouth Lyle uttered a sound like a gut-punched boxer. I moved a step closer. If Heimlich Maneuver isn't a band name, it should be. He put his hand up to ward me off. A smear of mayonnaise shaped like a bear clung to his palm. We waited for choking or monologue, whichever came first. On both accounts we were disappointed. "Luke—" he swallowed hard—"Get us some drinks, huh?"

When have drinks not been a good idea? I've tweeted this question multiple times, and no one yet has posed an unreasonable setting. On my way to the kitchenette, I snagged my smokes. "Neat or on the rocks?"

Lyle and Marva answered in unison. I struck a match and walked it to the refrigerator. A moment later I returned carrying two highballs of Magdalene bourbon, neat, in my right palm, and one on rocks in my left. A cigarette smoldered between my lips, wisps of smoke drifting toward my face. I couldn't decide if my tears were from the smoke or because I'd glimpsed the future. One of us wasn't going to make it out alive.

Lyle tossed a handful of mixed nuts into his mouth, his expression half-vacant as Marva delivered the detailed account of the door that had put the hurting on her. He swirled his bourbon around the rocks, sniffed, drank, frowned, drank. Coughed.

Marva must've been president of some sorority back in college, because she treated her drink like bitter medicine. The glass thudded on the end table next to the armchair into which she'd retreated.

Her story came out a lot slower.

It started with a text message from a blocked number: *Any last requests?* The following morning, she woke to a text, picturing her, but in a bad way. Whoever wanted her attention got it in bold. She recognized her face, but couldn't remember the costume party when she'd worn a noose. It was tempting to admire the photo manipulation, except nobody liked seeing herself dead. Whoever the prankster was, they'd even gotten right the blood droplets dribbling from the eyes.

Lyle peeled the wrapper from a chocolate bar. "Blood from the eyes isn't typical with hangings. Only manual strangulations."

Marva traced the rim of her empty glass with her finger. "And you know that why?"

"I'm a detective, doll."

I'd dismiss any other man who demeaned women with pet names as often as he did, but no other man had spent the balance of a decade putting up with me. If he was the guy who grumbled when his favorite radio host was fired for preying on women staffers, he was also the guy who'd hunt a month for a lost child pictured on a milk carton, find the boy and decline the reward because the six-year-old's tears of joy at the reunion were payment enough.

I joggled my cup. "Refills?"

Marva asked if we had wine. I dug a dusty bottle from the closet, judged it gently-aged, and poured a glass. She dispatched the evidence, and I refilled her twice before she picked up her story again.

In the days following the troubling text messages, Marva began to think she'd overreacted. An Instagram follower with a bad sense of humor, a teenage prankster with a perverted definition of flirting. She fixed dinner for her husband, Ransom. He took her to a movie. They spent a morning at the Joslyn Museum enjoying a special Grant Wood exhibit. Marva obsessed over "The Perfectionist." Why was the second button on the woman's blouse half undone? What did it mean? The painting's title was more important than all the work Wood did before or after. And that button!

A few weeks later, walking to Jackson Street Bookseller, Marva's heel broke. She fell, spilling the contents of her purse. At the same time, a brick fell from the sky and crumbled on the pavement inches from where she'd fallen. It smashed her lipstick tube into a crimson splatter. If her shoe hadn't broken, the brick would've crushed her skull, sidewalk painted in brains.

Leaning from a window on the fifth floor of a loft above J's on Jackson, was the man with the pitchfork from "American Gothic": same wireframe glasses, same hollow cheeks. She blinked. When she opened her eyes he'd vanished. The windows were all closed. Hysteria? But there was the brick to consider. She retrieved it from her purse and handed it to me. It was stamped with the Riverfront Park Logo. As I corrupted any DNA evidence that might've lingered, she resumed her story.

At the bookstore a first edition of *Farewell, My Lovely*, by Raymond Chandler, caught her eye. She bought it for thirty-five hundred cash.

Lyle chewed ice cubes while a lime popsicle melted in his left hand. "As in, three thousand five hundred?"

"It might've been a little overpriced."

"Let me guess." I drummed my fingers on the arm of my chair. "Your hubby's a lawyer."

"Bio pharm. Emphasis in advertising and development."

I pinched my lower lip. "Must be nice, having all that money."

"Who knows? When you have it, you don't really think about it."

"Of course."

Lyle decapitated a blueberry muffin. He offered me the bottom half. I said I wasn't hungry and poured myself another drink.

Marva had returned home from the bookstore to find a package on her front porch. Inside the package was a bloodstained shirt. It looked familiar, though she knew she'd never owned it. And it wasn't the kind of thing she could call her girlfriends about so she did the next best thing, going straight to the cellar for a bottle of '85 Château Margaux.

When Ransom returned from work he found her on the

lounger, humming fragments of Miles Davis's "So What". The trail of bottles from the living room to the kitchen was ten thousand dollars long, and there at the end of it lay Marva. She wasn't much for conversation so he led her to the room, helped her into pajamas, tucked her in, and killed the lights.

The next morning he brought her breakfast in bed and asked if they needed to look into a local chapter of AA. She laughed a migraine laugh meant to mean no but that felt a little like yes. *Anything*, she was thinking, *to get my head on straight.*

She asked him to leave her alone, and when he meekly retreated, she threw off the duvet, walked to the bathroom and cranked the shower full-hot. The water burned her skin and cleared her head. She marched down the stairs robed, her skin lobster red. Ransom was folding white cheddar into scrambled eggs. She asked him what she should do if someone was trying to kill her. He said the only person trying to kill her was herself. With booze.

She wanted to show him the text messages, the brick, the bloody shirt, but instead she said. "Would you call the police?"

He plated his eggs, cut sprigs of chive and sprinkled them on top. "Is someone trying to kill you, honey?"

She lost her nerve. "Yours look better than mine did."

"Want a bite?"

"No." She thirsted. "I'm just embarrassed."

He rubbed her shoulder and reminded her she was his morning star, his white daisy. "What we need is a good vacation. You're absorbing all my stress from work."

Lyle sprung from his chair. "Why don't you trust your husband?" He buried his hand in a bag of potato chips. Crumbs sprayed from his mouth when he said, "Won't he believe you?"

Marva's eyes cleared from the fog of memory. "He's always so busy."

I lit another cigarette. Butts overflowed from the ashtray next to me. A haze of smoke tickled the ceiling. Lyle lacked a certain knowledge about women. He appreciated their bodies, usually managed to get their phone numbers, but he'd never known one more than sheet deep.

"Go back to the brick." I lifted it to eye-level. "Doesn't it seem strange that it came from the riverfront? I mean, every building downtown is brick. Hell, the streets are paved in bricks. Why lug one from a mile away unless you're sending a message?"

Marva folded her legs beneath herself on the armchair. "I hadn't thought about that."

I was teasing at angles to justify this object, lost in thought, hunting a trail, and when I came to the conversation had wound back to Ransom.

"His company's finishing human trials for a sleeping med. They're calling it Vivifica, and it's going to make everyone a lot of money. I don't need him worried about me."

Lyle groaned. "I'd think he'd want to know some creep's trying to scare you witless."

Marva seemed enchanted by the empty wine bottle: code for *I didn't come to discuss my husband's deficiencies.* All we had left was Magdalene, and I said so. She nodded. I poured her three fingers. "You want us to solve this without involving your husband?"

Lyle had scratched up a fried chicken leg and was savoring the crispy skin. The air conditioning compressor kicked on. Marva had something to hide but wouldn't show it straight on so I asked her to finish her story and listened for cracks in the narrative.

During the previous month she'd almost been mown down by a car that ran a red light; she'd narrowly avoided falling into an elevator shaft when the door opened to an empty lift; hours before she'd come to visit us, the aforementioned door had knocked her unconscious. These all could've been viewed as bits of bad luck if it hadn't been for the accompanying text messages. On the morning she'd almost been run down, she'd received a picture from a blocked number of a speeding car with a skull and cross-bones for its hood ornament. The night before the elevator incident, late, as Ransom tossed and turned, fighting wakefulness beside her, her phone vibrated. She opened the message to a picture of a cliff: no words, just a rocky precipice. Hours before the door bloodied her nose and blacked her eyes, her phone had buzzed, *Knock knock?*

I put out my cigarette and leaned back in my chair. "I don't mean to sound insensitive, but do you think this mystery person is more into scaring you than killing you? Why all the forewarnings? Wouldn't a gun be quicker?"

Marva pinched her nose and sniffed. She asked for a tissue. "I started wondering the same thing, after the door this morning, but then I got this." She unlocked her phone and passed it to me. The most recent message read, *Start planning your final meal.*

I gave her phone back. "You ever reply?"

"Dead end."

"Filet mignon," Lyle said. "Garlic mashed. Asparagus in chive butter." He rubbed a green apple on his shirttail.

"You won't tell your husband, and you refuse to call the police." I hesitated. "Why?"

Lyle popped a cheese puff. "Your cross to bear, huh?"

"Something like that."

The bourbon had permeated to the tips of my fingers, fogged my eyes, and swollen my tongue. I stared dumbly at Lyle as he chomped the last bite of apple and licked his fingers.

I picked a hangnail from my thumb. "Let's talk money."

Marva laughed. "Got any cigarettes left?" I checked the pack. There were two. I handed her one, offered a light. Smoking with someone forges an instant bond. As she dragged and exhaled, my empathy grew. What must she have felt? How had loneliness shaped her? She tapped ash into her cupped palm. "Five grand every day I wake up."

I passed her the ashtray. She emptied her palm into it and set the tray on the chair's arm. I tend to negotiate, but then again, most widows and cat lovers don't start by offering a month's wages as a daily rate. "Won't the hubs notice all the debits?"

Marva smoothed her skirt. Her legs were muscle, milk and honey. "Not your business."

Lyle stood, walked to the window behind our desk, and looked over Maple at the shops in Benson. "Your husband might be rich, but anybody's going to notice that kind of spending."

"He hasn't looked at our books in ten years."

Suddenly I couldn't stand the smell in our office. "Suppose that changes tomorrow."

"Nothing changes with him."

Bad practice to empathize with a client, but her loneliness splashed all over me. "We'll see what we can do." I told her she needed to forward any of the text messages she'd received from the blocked number. If Marva was right about time winding down, we needed everything we could get to put us on the trail of her stalker.

She stood, dug an envelope from her purse and tossed it on the desk atop the rent bill. "What about the bloody shirt?"

I rose from my chair on wobbly knees and made for the desk. I'm small, but I hold my liquor, and the zig-zags were for show. "Everything."

Marva started for the door. She rested her hand on the knob and looked back. "You're right, Mr. Kupershack, Miss Mia does grow on you."

I sneered at Lyle and the bag of cheese puffs in his hand. When I turned Marva had gone. Lyle snapped up the envelope from the desk, tore open the flap and fanned out a stack of Benjamins. "Looks like we got rent money, huh?"

2

WE DROVE MAPLE STREET TO RADIAL HIGHWAY AS IT curved and turned into Saddlecreek, stopping at QT for gas and smokes. The street lamps seemed half again as dim as a normal night. The city meets your mood as only a loving mother can. "There's something just a little too convenient with this damn brick." I hefted it in my hand.

Lyle dispatched a box of Cracker Jacks. He dug a kernel from his gums. "That, and I got money on this broad's husband being the type to shell out on fundraising souvenirs just like it."

"That *woman's* husband has narcissist written all over him, maybe more."

"Something's funny about him, for sure, huh?"

I cracked my window and tapped out a smoke. Lyle shook his head. I ignored him and sparked a flame. Through smoke, I said, "Funny *haha* or funny *look out*?"

Lyle peeled an orange and flung the rind onto the street. "Yes."

I gave him the you-should-be-ashamed stare.

"Biodegradable."

I shook my head. "You still haven't told me how you two met."

He chewed an orange segment, juice misting between his teeth. "Nothing much to tell." He said he'd gone to Jake's on the Benson strip for a couple beers, to absorb the nightlife. She came in not long afterward, looking around like she was expecting to find someone. Lyle tipped his glass to her. She smiled, approaching him, said she was looking for Lyle Kupnuchip. He said she'd come to the right place. She said she needed his help.

I laughed. "*Your* help?"

"I'm telling a story, huh?" He pressed his palm to his forehead.

"So tell."

"We talked. I ordered her a glass of wine. Annie was working. God she's a sight. What I could do with those pigtails, huh?"

"Stay on topic."

"So Marva says she's being followed and I say, 'As in, we're being watched?' and she says, 'Maybe,' and I say, 'By who?' and she says, 'Whom?' and I say, 'Yeah, who?' and she says she doesn't know, and I say, 'You don't know who's following you, but you know you're being followed,' and she says that's pretty much the long and short of it, and I ask why she thinks she's being followed, and she says someone wants her dead, and I say her situation sounds pretty serious and doesn't she think it'd be better to call the cops? and she says, 'The cops won't believe me,' and I say, 'Don't matter. They have policies and procedures when someone reports suspected crime,' and she says even so they won't help her come morning, and I start thinking certain things so I say, 'You're looking for around-the-clock protection,' and she says, 'Not exactly,' and I say, 'Then what?' and she says she wants someone who won't stop digging when they hit bedrock, and I say I don't exactly get her metaphor, and she says, 'My situation is unique, I think, and not many people are going to give me the time of day,' and I ask why, and she says I'll just have to trust her, and I say—

pardon me, but it's true—I say, 'You don't have to worry about me trusting you, but my partner's never met a person she doesn't doubt. She's got a bad case of cynicism no medicine can clear up.'"

"Christ! You said that about me?"

"Only the truth."

"Go on."

"So I say, 'Maybe we should go back to my office,' and she asks why, and I say, 'Even if my partner's a cynic, she's my partner and we don't work alone,' and she says, 'Not even if I pay you for two people's work?' and I say, 'As tempting as it sounds—'"

"Don't lie to me. You're lousy at it anyway."

"Fine. She said she wanted a woman's perspective."

"I *said* don't lie to me."

"I was going to give you your cut."

"We're getting closer."

Between cheese puffs, Lyle said, "Can I help it if the lady wanted me and not you?"

I started into a third cigarette just as Lyle was pulling up to the riverfront, the souvenir brick being our only decent lead. "Doesn't matter what she wanted, because she got both of us."

He angled into a parking space. "All for the best."

"Even if you don't think so." I opened my door. "You could've had this one all to yourself if you hadn't brought her back to the office for a seduction."

"She's married, I—"

"When has a diamond mattered to you?"

"Hey, I admire all the legal mumbo jumbo behind 'I do.' Respect the court papers."

"My ass."

He opened his door and we stood. "Plus. You're the brains of this operation."

14

3

Behind the Gateway Boathouse, at Riverfront Park, Charlie and Rube and a few dockers I didn't know were tossing crumpled bills to the center of a shipping crate outfitted with a plywood tabletop. Charlie was making splinters of a toothpick. He treated women like auto repair shops: a necessary service where everything is overpriced. Rube gnawed a mostly smoked cigar. Get him talking and you usually learned something you wanted to know, and a lot you'd rather not. The air smelled of skunk, sweat, and tobacco.

"Uh oh." Rube spat tobacco leaf. "The cancer's back."

Charlie laughed big as a blank check. He needed a new set of teeth or a zipper for his lips. The three unknown dockers looked up startled from their cards. "Who died, blondie?"

I pushed my hair out of my face. Men never let a natural blonde forget it. "No one yet."

"See boys." Charlie flicked his toothpick away. "Told you I needed a new baseball bat."

Rube wiped his lips. "Who you extorting tonight?"

Lyle flipped an empty produce box upside down and sat. "Deal me in, huh?"

Charlie snapped. "No one plays on credit, bud."

It was a mistake letting Lyle hold Marva's fee. He punched a clean hundred on the plywood. "No hole too deep tonight, fellas."

Some nights I feel like taking it in the teeth. I stepped up to retrieve the bill, but one of the dockers brought a blade to my wrist. "Money on the table stays on the table."

"Easy does it, Slice 'N Dice." Charlie lifted his hand. "We're all friends here."

Rube relit his cigar. "Rules is rules."

Some nights I feel like taking it easy. I pulled my arm back.

One of the other dockers dealt the cards. Charlie asked us to what he owed the pleasure. I showed him Marva's brick and asked if he knew anybody who had the funds to buy one. Lyle cracked a pistachio shell with his teeth and asked to change for a fiver, but Rube said no change in the middle of a hand, "No choice but all-in for you, pal."

Lyle grinned. He pushed. Charlie folded. One docker followed suit, then Slice 'N Dice. The last docker called. So did Rube.

While the three remaining players bet, Charlie examined the brick. "Didn't they sell these for that bullshit drive to save the plovers or whatever?"

Rube shoved a small mound of crumpled bills to the center of the makeshift table. The other guy tapped his knuckles on the plywood.

"You can't check a raise, dumbass." Charlie looked at me. "I'm not sure who'd drop coin on something that retarded."

Dumbass blinked. "I wasn't—" He moved his hand toward the pile of money.

Slice 'N Dice showed his knife. "No drawing back a bet."

Dumbass pushed all his money forward.

Rube called. "Someone's gonna have a short night."

Dumbass blew a snot-rocket. "I'm sticking with hookers from now on."

"Head's up," the dealer said.

In our line of business, informants never let us forget how ignorant people are of prejudice, "retard" being standard jargon, and hookers a common topic. You can't be a woman working in a testosterone-saturated environment without losing some of your outrage reflex, but it doesn't mean you don't boil beneath the surface.

Lyle mowed down a jar of neon green pickle spears, smiling. "My lucky day." He licked his fingers and flipped a pair of aces. The flop had given him trips.

Dumbass's face slackened. He showed a pair of eights, Rube a King and Jack, suited: diamonds. The diamond on the turn gave Rube a shot at a river ralph. Lyle had three or four ways to win the pot. The dealer burned and sailed the river card. A mess of silence followed when the five of diamonds landed.

The dealer whispered, "Jesus! He won. Jesus."

Rube slapped the kid upside the head. "No kidding, Shit For Brains. Detective Munchies used all his worldly luck on a full house." He pushed Lyle's stack of cash away. "At least Dumbass gave me first loser."

Lyle scooped his winnings, nurturing a dull, satisfied grin.

Charlie started on a new toothpick. "No one-'n-done or you're a first-rate pussy."

Lyle smiled. "I'd think you'd like first-rate pussy, huh?"

I thumped him on the back of the head. "I don't appreciate the language."

"If you can't hang with the boys—" Rube started, but I shut him up with an icy glare.

"Give Dumbass a chance at redemption." Charlie said. "I'll spot you, kid."

I knew how it went but couldn't help myself. "You said no credit."

Charlie sprung from his veggie crate and clenched his fists. "I make the rules, around here." He cracked his neck and sat. "Deal, Slice."

Rube named the stakes: five/ten, no limit. Lyle tossed in his blind and received his cards. Charlie dealt. The bets circled. Four players paid to see the flop. Behind them, the Missouri roiled. I slipped my phone from my pocket and opened Twitter, posted something about the river at night: just a way to document wasted time.

I told Rube about our interesting night, how someone had tried to brain our client with the souvenir brick Charlie was fondling. Rube asked if the girl in question had nice tits. I said her breasts were none of his concern. He said he just couldn't find it in himself to care about a dead broad with anything less than C cups. I called him a misogynist pig. He oinked and said he could go for a good massage. Charlie won the hand and passed the dealer button.

Dumbass shuffled, offered a cut and dealt. Shit for Brains said, "Rich chick? Probably ordered her tits in a doctor's office, if you know what I mean."

I wanted to test a theory. "What's your name?"

"Was Hey Kid. Guess I'm Shit for Brains now."

Sometimes you can do a person a favor. "I like Hey Kid better. Now listen up. Women aren't just skin and holes. Show a little respect."

Rube raised. He laughed. "Hey, Kid, let it ride. She thinks her turds don't stink."

I slipped my pocketknife from my purse and used the blade to trim a hangnail. "You've got it wrong, Rube. I think my crap stinks bad, just as bad as any man's. That's the point."

Slice smirked. Hey Kid folded. Charlie said he'd once occupied with a chick who claimed she farted in public. "We didn't last long."

Lyle lost twenty on the river, but shrugged and revisited his pretzel sticks for consolation. "So, Charlie, if you don't know about any bleeding heart brick collectors working down here, maybe you heard something about a guy who likes to send threatening text messages to random women before knocking them off?"

"Hell, sounds like me if you ignore the 'knocking them off' part. I flirt rough."

I folded my knife blade. "Is that why you did a two to five for rape, Charlie?"

Rube snickered. Charlie said, "No thanks to you."

"Could've been ten to twenty if you hadn't agreed to give me The Panda."

Charlie spit a toothpick splinter. "I hope that piss-ant's rotting in solitary."

Dumbass shrugged. "The Panda?"

Rube ground out his cigar. "Little chubby bastard worked down here some years back. Survived on a diet of onions and vodka. Liked to fuck chicks unconscious then shave their heads and float 'em bald down the river on shipping pallets."

Charlie winced. "He was a foreman, actually, and we all knew how he liked it, but still, no one's paid us so well since."

I dropped my knife in my purse. "Money for silence."

Lyle bet big. "I'm bluffing this time." His lips wrapped around a corndog. No one believed him and he collected thirty in blinds.

Slice ran a hand through his hair. "Maybe The Panda got a phone snuck in jail."

Hey Kid smiled. "I knew The Panda. He owned a coin laundry over on Vinton." It was his deal again. He forgot to burn.

Charlie punched him in the eye. "For fuck's sake, you really got shit for brains. Shut up and deal."

I liked Hey Kid after that. Most guys would've retaliated and ended up disfigured in a puddle of blood with empty pockets waiting for an ambulance that wouldn't come. He apologized, accepted the misdeal, paid the penalty to the next pot and passed the button.

"Maybe talk to Laser." Rube contemplated a fresh cigar. "Mean son-of-a-bitch. Kind of guy who shaves with a butcher's knife. Don't treat ladies too good, and unless I'm remembering wrong that fucker reads the New York Times. Maybe he's your John."

Lyle finished the last of a hard-shell taco and wiped his fingers on his jeans. I lit a cigarette and smoked as he won deal after deal. The guys around the table were starting to fidget too much with their hands under the table. I tapped Lyle's shoulder, leaned into his ear and suggested he bleed some cash.

On Lyle's deal, he bet low, but enough to get money on the table. He filled his mouth with cinnamon bears and called every raise. When the river card sailed, he cursed.

Rube laughed. "Gotcha now." Lyle raised, Rube reraised. Lyle folded, pushing his cards to the center. Rube punched the table. "Uh uh. Your bitch-ass is playing this one out."

Lyle said he didn't want to, and in a beat Slice's knife was at Lyle's neck. Lyle said Rube could have it his way, pulled his cards back and called. Rube flipped two pair: kings and aces. Lyle was slow to show his hand. He'd caught a third two on the river. He'd played a ten/two, which never should've won.

"God damn it all to hell." Charlie stood. "We work for this money, and you disrespect us by trying to throw a hand. You better cut out before Slice loses his temper."

Rube flicked his lighter, passing his finger through the flame. "Sweating green, mother fucker? Don't ever disrespect us like that again. Cash out, Doyle Brunson. You're done."

Lyle nodded. "I guess we'll see you around."

Charlie fingered a line across his throat. "Better not for a while."

I stepped between Charlie and Lyle. "You said we're looking for Laser?"

Dumbass said, "Wear something low-cut. He won't talk to women who don't show skin."

I crossed my arms and puffed out my chest. "He'll talk to me. I guarantee it."

4

THE NEXT MORNING THE HEADLINES WERE FULL OF reports about a woman who'd been murdered in Regency. I showered, smoked, dressed, ate a banana, and fixed a Bloody Mary heavy on the Magdalene. They say you're only an alcoholic if you drink alone. I'm not the marrying type so I can't see how that means I should join a recovery group.

My phone rang. Either a concrete mixer dialed the wrong number or Lyle had a bowl of cereal to one ear and his phone to the other. "Hear about the Jane Doe?"

"I bet people'll think twice before shopping at William Sonoma next time."

"Can't help laughing when the shit hits the upper crust, huh?"

"I'm out of smokes."

"Already?"

I cast a suspect glance at the limp celery stick in my glass and wondered who I was trying to fool. "Hey!"

"I'll pick you up in ten?"

"You're the best." I hung up.

After tossing the celery in the garbage, I shuffled to the pantry for more Magdalene. The ratios on my Bloody were skewed. Maybe because it was that time of month. I dumped in a little more bourbon, and tested the results. It squared things nicely. I figured on just enough time to pay a few bills before Lyle showed. Less those, I had just over three bucks in my bank account, and was expecting Marva to call us about her payment plan.

Thirty minutes later, I phoned Lyle. It rang to voicemail. I texted: *You better be dead*, because I hate people being late. It's a control thing. I hopped on Twitter and posted a picture of a barreling wave with the meme, *This is how I like my bourbon. #Magdalene*

Lyle showed two hours late. He handed me a couple packs of Pyramid Menthol, dumb grin on his face. "Buy-one-get-one." Purple juice rimmed his mouth, a half-eaten plum cradled in his hand.

I stepped aside, because it was clear he wanted in. "What took you so long?"

He sucked the plum pit clean. "Glad you asked." He aimed for my dining room and took a chair at the table. "I could use a beer."

I dug an MGD from the back of the fridge. He cracked it and sipped. "The Cereal Burglar strikes again."

My feet tangled with impatience. I tapped my toes. "Don't we have somewhere to be?" If I hated anything more than Lyle's hobby investigations, I couldn't think of it. Unlike me, he was always running a side game, but the problem with his pet projects was no one paid him. He'd skim the news for some bank fraud or Ponzi scheme, theory being if he hit on a clue and broke a case, someone'd pay him handsomely. I wondered if he hadn't calculated Marva's fee.

"Catch this." He slipped a cheese stick from its wrapper. "I'm at Walgreens, huh? They've got BOGO on your smokes, so I'm trying to decide if I should double down when the clerk's eyes wig out. She pulls her shoulders back, and I'm thinking how nice her body is when she stands up straight, but then she makes this nasty sound in her throat and I think, *no way*, but there's not much time for a pros and cons list—you know when it comes to bedability—because someone shoulders me aside, and I stumble into the makeup counter.

"This dude in a red and black plaid pushes by me, and he's wearing a black felt fedora, a facemask, and a pair of sunglasses so only his nose is showing. He's smaller than I thought he'd be, and a whole lot less, I don't know. Just little all around. He's got a cart full of Cookie Crisp and he hands a box to the cashier. She reads it and gulps. I want to say something, but there's a lump in my throat. Not cause I'm scared, but I can't even believe it's happening. I know I can take him down, but suddenly I can't imagine a world without him in it."

I'd unwrapped one of the packs and tapped out a smoke. "There's easier lies to explain why you're late."

Lyle swallowed the last of the cheese. "If I'm lying, I'm dying."

"So you let the Cereal Burglar go?"

Lyle guzzled his beer and sat back heavily. "He's been at it for so long. It was like meeting Brad Pitt or something."

"Did you ask for an autograph?"

He slipped a bag of licorice bites from his pocket, tearing a corner off the wrapper. "Guy walks out the front door with his box full of cash, and on his way out he looks straight into the security camera and pauses. Then he's gone. I ask the checker if she's okay. She says she's just a little shaken. I tell her she better call the cops. She says she already tripped the alarm. By the time I buy your smokes, the police are there. They wanted my statement."

It was seeming like we weren't going to head out so quick, and

I fixed another Bloody, hold the blood and celery, extra Magdalene. "OPD is the most useless heap-of-trash department."

Lyle picked at his gums. "They were all laughing at the box the burglar left behind."

Always using a box of Cookie Crisp, the burglar had staged upwards of seventy robberies over three years. The messages grew more elaborate over time: *Give me all the money in the register,* or, *You know the drill,* or, *This is not a roleplay,* then, *I'm holding a gun in my left hand. Made you look!* and, *The world will end in flames so what does it matter if I take a few bucks off your hands?* and, *You work for a company that collects more cash in its register in one hour than you earn in a week of work so don't tell me you're not secretly excited at the thought of me robbing this drawer and paying forward a little karma,* and more recently, *When I was a child I used to eat this cereal two boxes in a sitting, in front of the television, watching old* Gilligan's Island *reruns while my parents slept till noon. I think it's something about this routine that eventually caused me to start robbing cash registers. But then again, maybe I just love the electrifying joy of holding up a silly cashier like you and watching the look of terror on your face.* Even the longest notes were written with incredible penmanship, suggesting the burglar perhaps smuggled in a cereal box with the threatening note ahead of time. On one occasion the news reported that the burglar had copied such an extensive note that a magnifying glass was given to the cashier for him to read. Always, the outcome was the same. The checker emptied the drawer into the open cereal box that contained the note, the burglar snapped a photo of the cashier holding the box, then left by the front door, tipping the black fedora at the security camera. A few days later the photo would arrive at the World Herald office by anonymous tip.

In all the time the Cereal Burglar had been pulling jobs, no security camera had ever identified a suspect. It was known that whoever had been pulling the jobs was walking into the chosen stores without the plaid or the mask, but not only had no store ever isolated a suspect, no store had even found footage of a person changing into the burgling outfit. One moment there was no one of interest, the next the burglar approached a cash register dressed in fedora, plaid shirt and the ski mask, pushing a cart full of Cookie Crisp.

The magic appearing act fascinated Lyle more than me. "Did you see the note?"

Lyle popped a donut hole in his mouth and savored the powdered sugar, cleaning traces of it off his lips with his thumb. "Cops wouldn't let me."

"You had your chance, and you blew it."

Lyle smiled. "But I had an epiphany, huh? I don't really want to catch the guy. I'm putting this one to bed. Whoever the guy is, he's an artist, I'll tell you. The world needs people like him."

"What makes you so sure it's a *him*?"

Lyle looked askance at me, ate another donut hole. "Not again, huh?"

I sparked another cigarette. "You said the burglar was smaller than you expected. And there's the fact that no one's ever been able to identify a suspect. Maybe the police are too busy looking for a man to realize they're dealing with a woman."

Lyle sipped his beer. "Listen, I know you believe in the superiority of women, but sometimes I think you get all twisted trying to prove a point that can't be defended."

"I'm just saying maybe the Cereal Burglar might've enjoyed such a strong run because no one suspects a woman. I've got a hunch if you could watch all the footage from the robberies, you'd find a familiar lady starring in every episode."

Lyle rolled a slice of bologna and bit down. "You think the cops are only watching the security footage for men?"

"I bet they are, yeah." I stabbed my cigarette into the ashtray and stood. "Hey, we better get going if we want to talk to Laser."

Lyle polished off the rest of his beer and pushed back from the table. "If the Cereal Burglar's a woman I'm going to seduce her and film us doing doggy style."

"Wow." I stood. "You're a real catch."

5

THE DOCKYARD RAN LIKE A LEGITIMATE BUSINESS during the day. Men drove Bobcats and forklifts in frenzied lines, moving pallets full of produce, potted meats, canned fruit and catfish to bays for transport. The river is an artery between Omaha, Kansas City, and St. Louis.

Lyle parked, and finishing a slice of cold pizza, shut off the engine. "Guess it would've been too hard to take a little advice and wear something a bit more revealing, huh? You know you got the body for it, but of course you'd do the opposite of what anyone says."

My t-shirt came from a gift shop at the Pittsburgh airport. In yellow lettering, *CITY OF BRIDGES* underlined a graphic of the 16th Street Bridge. The narrow neck pinched at my throat, and the sleeves hung to my elbows. My jeans had come from Lyle's own drawer, the pair he'd given me years ago after I slipped in blood chasing the Walnut Hill House Breaker from the scene of his final murder. I swam in the jeans, and had to cinch the waist with a cloth belt, but they were worn and comfortable in all the right ways. "By the sound of it that would've been a recipe for rape. So thanks, but no thanks."

Lyle popped a handful of M&Ms. "Maybe a tank top. Short-shorts. A holster thong."

We walked to the security shack and I showed my badge. "A *holster thong*? What the hell would that even look like?"

The security guard stepped away from the window and ruffled through a file cabinet. Horseflies swarmed my head and bit my ankles. The air stuck to my skin like phosphorus to match flame.

Lyle slapped at his neck and cursed. "Just a string of fabric, you know. Kinda, 'Hey, baby, you like?' and then, Blam! 'You *like* my gun, asshole.'" He flashed his best imitation of a gang sign. "HOLSTER thong."

"That's the most ridiculous thing I've ever heard."

"All I'm saying," he picked a wilted grape from the bunch in his hand and tossed it aside, "is you could be sexy *and* dangerous. Sigourney Weaver. Give me a break, huh? Sandra Bullock. Lotion and gun powder are a perfect team."

"You know you're talking about Hollywood, right? It shouldn't come as a surprise that men directed the films you're referencing. I hope you don't think the actresses actually bought into that shit."

Lyle returned to cheese puffs. Little flecks of puffed corn leapt from his jaw as he spoke. "What's wrong with dressing a part? Laser enjoys tits and ass like art collectors dig Picasso."

I slapped at the air in front of my face. The flies wanted blood, and their mood was contagious. "Last I checked, no one exploited an entire group of people because of fine art."

The security guard returned to the window. He handed us visitors' badges. "Keep these around your neck, and visible."

I slipped the lanyard over my head. "You're a peach."

The security guard pointed toward a small tin-sided building. "Head over there with these and tell Mike you want to talk with

Laser." He winked and clicked his tongue. "And ma'am, if I may, be careful with Mr. Laser."

"I'm not a—"

Lyle hooked his arm around my shoulder. "I'll keep an eye on her." He pulled me away and guided us through the opening gates toward the tin building.

As we walked, Lyle finished his bag of cheese puffs and crumpled the empty foil into his pocket. "See. There. There's my point, huh?"

"Go fuck a chainsaw, would you?"

He dug a box of chocolate covered raisins from his jacket pocket and offered me a handful. I sucked the coating and spat the raisins on the concrete. "What's our play with Laser?"

Lyle tugged my t-shirt sleeve. "I take it you're not wearing a tube top under that thing."

I shoved him. "Ten bucks says the guy'd lose his shit if I was bad cop."

"Don't they say you catch more flies with booty?"

We came to the tin building, and I motioned to the man standing out front. "We're looking for Mike."

He cracked his knuckles, "Who's asking?"

I showed him my visitor's badge. "Need you to take us to Laser."

"Great. He's in it with the law again?"

Lyle popped a handful of gummy bears in his mouth and pushed them into his cheek. "Not that we can prove."

Mike dragged a palm down his leathery face. "He's over at the docks. Hop in, I'll drive you. Asshole was late for work this morning."

Mike led us to a golf cart around back of the metal building. Lyle and I squeezed in on the rear-facing vinyl bench. I'd seen the docks one other time during working hours, a mess of sweat and anger. The whole operation seemed like punishment: low pay and heavy lifting. It made you appreciate arugula side-salads in a new light, knowing some guy risked melanoma for minimum wage so you could have something to drizzle balsamic vinaigrette on.

The golf cart pulled into a bay where men were tossing twenty-pound catfish, flopping and screaming—the fish and the men—from hand to hand. A giant, thin bodied, but full of muscle, wearing round, wire-frame glasses stood fourth in line, holding a wood-handled axe. Tattoos bulged on his neck, and tendons twitched. He had a familiar air about him, one I could almost place, like he was pulled from some TV show or a painting.

When the third man in line caught a fish, he spun it, slapping the body on a chopping block. The axe man cleaved the fish head clean off, and a fifth man slung the decapitated fish into a netted wheel-cart. A sixth and seventh man traded places with an eighth and ninth, six and seven wheeling the cart elsewhere while eight and nine positioned a new, empty cart.

Mike shouted over the workers' grunts: "Phil, take over for Laser."

Phil took the giant's axe. Laser stepped back and looked at Mike. I couldn't remember the last time I'd felt so small. Laser was the kind who ducked through doorframes. With his arms relaxed the tips of his fingers extended almost to the tops of his knees. His face was chiseled stone and hollow cheeks.

Mike jerked a thumb in my direction. "These here detectives want to speak with you."

Laser folded his arms across his chest. "I didn't do it. Now can I get back to work?" He scratched a cut on his brow.

We'd stood when Mike parked the cart, and I had approached Laser as he spoke. "Charlie told us you might know something about a client we're working for."

"Charlie, eh?" He pushed his glasses up the bridge of his nose. "That asshole has hash for brains. Hope you didn't take him too seriously."

Lyle shoveled potato salad into his mouth. "We got a client says she's getting death threats by text message." He licked the spoon clean. "We hear you have a mean streak."

Laser rolled his shoulders, laughing. "I aint never done anything to a woman she didn't ask for, and Charlie knows it."

That pissed me off. Laser landed on the concrete with a satisfying thud. I pinned my elbows to his back and my knee in his ass. Mike laughed, and the sounds of workers working quieted. "Listen close," I leaned into Laser's ear. "You may think violence toward women is particularly funny. Plenty of men seem to, but understand if you don't cooperate we're going to push every charge in the book at you. It won't take me ten minutes to dig up all the shit OPD has rolled over on you. Take a breath and *understand*: you're *our* bitch. It doesn't matter how big you are, and it sure as hell doesn't matter how angry you are. You're our bitch. So tell us what we want to know."

His chin scraped the cement. Blood dripped from his lip. He groaned. I let up the pressure so he could talk. "You dress like that and call yourse—"

I pressed my elbow into his spine until he had no air left. "Try again."

He sucked a breath when I eased off. "I'm a human guillotine six days a week. These lowlifes who employ me pay half what I'm worth, and yet I show up with a smile every day. Doesn't matter what you think. I got nothing to do with your stupid client."

"Why's Charlie pin you for it, then?"

"Because Charlie spends his night smoking dope and gambling. He has too much time to cook up bullshit conspiracies."

I pressed my elbow deeper to remind him who had the power. "A woman named Marva DeLonghi's one blind corner from a bad break. You know something, you need to help us."

I rolled off Laser and let him stand. He dusted his pants off and spat. "She was your client? Shoot. If I would've known. I killed the bitch this morning."

Lyle paused with a fluffernutter halfway to his mouth. "Excuse me?"

"Between you and me—" he straightened his glasses—"It was too easy."

Lyle looked at me. "You hear from Marva this morning?"

I looked at Laser. "You're confessing to murder?"

Laser slapped the side of his head, rolled his eyes. "I'm not the one you're looking for. The fish are already dead when they come to me."

Mike stepped back: his smile fading.

Laser jabbed my chest with his finger. "I got a job swinging an axe, and I take it seriously. Fuck with that and I'll be your biggest problem. When I say you got the wrong guy, you got the wrong guy."

Lyle was somewhere in the middle of a bag of fried onion rings when he said, "If we're so off target, maybe you'd like to tell us who we should be talking to, huh? Or is that kind of thinking too hard for a lamebrain like yourself?"

Laser shaped his hands into fists. I stepped back. Lyle moved closer. He didn't stand a chance if the giant lost his temper. It's one thing tackling someone unaware. They call it a cheap shot. I make the most of them.

The standoff lingered a beat. Laser cleared his throat. "Talk to Nelly down at Showgirl. Sees a lot of twisted shit, and she's something of an expert on the topic of recreational violence."

I didn't like the term *recreational violence*, but I didn't like much about Laser. "If you're wasting our time, I'll scrape the tattoos off your neck with a rusty spatula."

Laser rolled his eyes, shot a glance at Lyle. "Why don't you muzzle your dog, pal?"

I lunged. Lyle caught me by the elbow. "Careful, buddy. You haven't seen her mad yet."

Laser ran his thumbnail across his front teeth. He examined whatever he'd scraped off, wiped it on his jeans and spat. "Nelly'll take good care of you. Don't worry."

6

WE STOPPED AT BLOCK 16 FOR A LATE LUNCH. I ORDERED a burger topped with a fried egg, blue cheese, ham and mustard. Lunch is serious business, and like any work worth doing, eating it makes me sweat. Lyle drank two beers. He said he wanted to get sloppy drunk.

After paying our tab, we drove Farnam to Saddlecreek and up the diagonal. We had a few hours to kill before any semblance of nightlife emerged so we ran back to my place for a little five-o'clock-somewhere. I never tired of scrolling Twitter, even when my drunken eyes doubled the feed. At dusk, we stumbled back out.

20's Showgirl had run down over the years. The billboard outside had large script on one side: the number twenty. All its light bulbs were blown. A storm had destroyed the opposite side of the billboard, which the owner never bothered to repair. The building stood windowless, an eroding, rust-colored brick fortress surrounded by a potholed blacktop parking lot. The wrought iron canopy surrounding the entrance represented the last common-sense barrier between those outside and those in.

My father used to spend Friday nights entertaining his coworkers at Showgirl when it was Omaha's premiere topless club. My mother protested at first, teaching my childhood self that women can accept anything: our great strength and shame.

Some rumored the joint was closing. I doubted it. Objectification of the female body generates more money than every professional sport combined. And even if Showgirl went under, its dancers would find stages elsewhere.

When we walked through the front doors, a bright neon sign behind the stage blinked, *Dance! Dance! Dance!* and a small woman melted down a brass pole. My feminine instinct wanted to focus on the woman's face, but that denied the purpose of her dancing. She wore red sequined heels and a white bikini bottom. Her breasts swung, marvels of cosmetic surgery, full to bursting. The discs of her nipples were pale as salmon and wide around as baseballs.

Lyle's eyes dilated. He breathed slow and shallow. A churro hung from his lips. We took a table near the rear of the club. I ordered two Magdalenes, mine neat, and a glass of water. When the server left I seized Lyle's elbow. "It's like you never saw a naked woman."

"Always feels like the first time."

The server returned with our drinks. I thanked her and asked if she knew Laser.

"Big guy?" she said.

"Giant."

"He comes every night. Emphasis on *come*. Asks Nelly to marry him more often than he orders drinks."

"A loyal customer?"

"You could say that." She shimmied for Lyle. He smiled. "Guy likes to buy private dances and recite Henry Miller while he gets off." She adjusted her bikini top. "Kind of weird if you ask me."

I sipped my bourbon. "He sent us here, looking for Nelly."

The server eyed the stage. "You're looking at her."

I was afraid of that. "Can you let her know Laser sent us?"

"You cops?"

"Private detectives," I flashed my badge. "All we want is a scoop."

The server said she'd do what she could. Lyle's eyes followed Nelly's every gyration. I kicked his shin under the table and said, "Business, remember. Not pleasure."

He nodded, his jaw slack. The song droned on for minutes before fading. A woman's clean deep voice came over a loudspeaker: "Give it up for Nelly Fretittes."

Not counting us, there were a dozen or so people watching the stage. The men voiced their pleasure, lobbing folded bills and handfuls of change at the stage. Several women applauded. Nelly squatted low with her feet close, flapping her knees like a bird in flight. The triangle of her bikini reflected the stage lights, a halo promising the other-worldliness of her sex.

Drops of sweat formed on Lyle's brow. The churro dangled from his lips like an unlit cigar. I finished my drink and signaled the server. She nodded and raised one finger. I showed her two in reply even though Lyle hadn't touched his.

When Nelly had collected the money on stage, she sauntered behind the red velvet curtain and the noise inside the club tripled. A guitar-heavy song blasted, and those nearest the stage who'd been silent in captivity began to jaw and laugh. I wondered what people enjoyed about such an atmosphere.

The server returned with drinks. Lyle had belted his churro and bourbon. The server said Nelly agreed to meet us after dressing. Lyle nodded, a small smile parting his lips. He sipped his second drink, and after the server collected our empties he said, "This place is filthy. I don't even want to know how thick the grime on the walls would be if we saw it in full light. And it smells worse than a locker room."

"You didn't seem to mind a minute ago."

"Don't confuse arousal with pleasure."

"Oh?"

He shoveled a handful of candied nuts onto his tongue and chewed deliberately. "Remember when we went to your aunt's place for Thanksgiving. Don't think I'm disgusting, huh? but your brother's kids were all piled on top of me when we were horsing around, and I got—you know—I felt pretty gross, but it was like, just, pressure and friction. I don't know what I'm saying."

"Come on." I socked his shoulder. "That's natural. Nothing deviant or weird. I've had cats sit on my lap and bring me so close to climax I had to flick their nose to shoo them."

Lyle poured the ice from his drink into his mouth and crunched. "I once fell in love with a beer at a baseball game. So cold between my legs. That's pleasure *and* arousal."

"Gardening gives me a lady-boner."

"Now you're just fucking with me."

That time at Thanksgiving, Lyle and my uncle had spent the entire afternoon one-upping each other. My uncle rode dirt bikes and he told the story about how he broke his collarbone jumping a three-hundred-foot gorge. Landed hard on the other side and cartwheeled at sixty miles-per-hour. Lyle told a story about how he'd fractured his skull trying to dunk a basketball, but instead caught his brow on the backboard. My uncle said a whiteboy like Lyle probably couldn't jump two stairs. Lyle wanted to know where this three-hundred-foot gorge was.

It felt like we were family, and I held Lyle's eyes in mine until Nelly approached our table followed by a one-ton-truck of a man. She'd changed into tennis shoes, and wrapped her shoulders in a white fur coat open in front to show her white bikini. "I understand you wish to speak to me."

The guy, clean-shaven, wore an enormous Hawaiian shirt, a

tan fedora, and had three tear-drop tattoos below his left eye. He folded his arms across his chest where they rested comfortably on his thick, round belly.

Looking at the Hawaiian, I addressed Nelly. "Laser sent us."

Lyle struggled to keep his eyes focused on Nelly's face, as she writhed with the pleasure of his effort. She was a woman who had accepted her role and played to it with every movement of her body. As if on cue, she shifted her weight to one leg, bending the other slightly at the knee so her jacket parted, giving a clear view of her tapered waist and flat belly. The faintest trace of stretch marks striped her hips.

"How many kids do you have?"

Nelly laughed. "I didn't realize this was going to be a personal interview. I don't really do that."

I shrugged. "Fair enough."

Lyle was losing his battle. His lips hung slack as his eyelids drooped.

"What we want to know—" I knuckled the tabletop—"is whether you're aware of any person or persons who send threatening text messages with graphic images to rich women. Maybe extortion. A personal grudge. We've got a client who's afraid for her life, and our best lead says you might know something." I summarized Marva's claims and shared her husband's position in the community. "Whoever's doing this to her has no problem with graphic violence."

"Don't forget the bloody shirt." Lyle almost sounded convincing, like he could actually think about something other than sex.

Nelly stood tall, pulled her coat closed and sat in the booth next to me. I slid toward the wall, elbowing the napkin dispenser and spilling the saltshaker. Lyle righted the salt, tossing a pinch over his shoulder. He moved the napkin dispenser to give me more room.

The Hawaiian stepped up to our table and turned his back to

us, his body an ominous wall. "Thanks, Bruce," Nelly said and turned to us. "Here's the deal. Laser warned me about you. You embarrassed him, and he hates sassy—"

"Watch it—"

"Let me finish. You're on Laser's naughty list so he sent you to me for a little playtime, which I guess is a way of saying I don't sell private dances. There's nothing you can do about that now. Doctors have labeled me a sadist, but I think its worse. I enjoy torture in the most unnatural way. I need the release, and I'm grateful you're here."

Lyle's eyes were wide and clear, his jaw set. "What are you saying?"

"Exactly what you think I'm saying."

Lyle fished in his pocket and came up with a package of fruit snacks. "Let us up."

Bruce turned slowly to face us. "We'll make it fun." The tendons in his neck twitched. "Hate to send you off without a bit of pleasure." Lyle moved to stand, but Bruce pulled the table into his ribs, pinning him to the booth. "Sit!"

Lyle doubled over, gasping.

Nelly adjusted her fur wrap. "At some point, you're going to ask yourself what would've happened if you'd trusted your gut. But I've owned this place for two decades and change. No one's caught me yet. You're not exceptional." She kissed Bruce's enormous hand. He showed no delight in the affection—if affection is what her kiss could be called.

"It was a trap." I felt stupid. It's one thing to speak the obvious and another to speak the insultingly obvious.

Nelly reached for Lyle and took his arm in her hand. He froze. An asterisk of pudding clung to the side of his mouth. "But here's the interesting thing. I actually do know something about your Marva DeLonghi."

My skin prickled. I breathed to gain composure. "You're lying."

"Wrong." Bruce nodded his chin. "Mrs. DeLonghi's a trending topic today."

I considered the knife in my purse. With a few strategic swipes I could end Nelly's career. Who would want to watch a one-breasted woman with a glass eye dance on a pole beneath yellow spotlights? But that left me to deal with Bruce, and even Lyle and I against him were outmatched. "I've got a hard head." I reached into my purse for a toothpick.

Bruce eyed my hand digging in the purse. "Maybe so."

"How about we pretend we never met, huh? You forget we came, and we forget you know anything."

"Doesn't work that way." Nelly licked her lips. "Plus, I'm going to enjoy your reactions when you hear what I know."

I rolled my eyes. "You're not going to strike me speechless. I've seen it all."

Nelly leaned close so the warmth of her breath moistened the tip of my earlobe. "*Someone* cut Marva DeLonghi into twenty pieces this morning."

My instinct was to stab Nelly then and there, but her rebuttal had, in fact, left me speechless. "You're lying," I managed after a moment.

Bruce scratched his cheek beneath the tear drop tattoos. "Do you have daddy issues? You seem to be fixated on lying."

Nelly produced a phone from the cup of her bikini. She swiped and tapped and typed on the touchscreen before sliding it toward the center of the table. The headline read, *Wife of Prominent BioPharm Executive Slain*, with a photo of caution tape strung across the entrance to Borsheims at Regency. I read on. The article detailed what it called *a murder too graphic to describe* and named Marva DeLonghi as the victim. The breath caught in my throat.

Nelly wrapped her arm around my shoulder. "It's been all over the news today. I'm not sure how you missed it."

I wasn't either. Sure, the morning headlines hadn't included the victim's identity, but I should've been smart enough to do the math. I couldn't raise a word in defense.

Nelly curled a long fingernail under my chin. "I'll save you for last. You've got that special hatred that makes you just too much fun." She turned a hungry stare at Bruce. "Let's show them the basement."

Lyle tried to speak, but Nelly shot a fist across the table and relieved him of his front teeth. Bruce covered Lyle's mouth with his bear paw of a hand. Blood trickled between the big man's fingers. What Bruce's hand didn't muffle of Lyle's pain, the overhead music masked.

They escorted us across the floor toward a door to the left of the bar. I scanned the area for witnesses. The bartender, polishing pint glasses, smiled at me. I knew then it was hopeless. I opened my mouth to scream, but Nelly kneed me in the back where my kidney lived. The pain ripped the voice from my throat and filled my eyes with white stars.

Bruce opened the door beside the bar and shoved Lyle. He held the door for Nelly who guided me down a flight of stairs. Lyle lay on the basement floor, trying, and failing to stand.

I'm not given to panic, but I understood our dilemma, and we hadn't even found justice for Marva. We'd come hunting a lead and stumbled into a trap. I don't know where I got it in my head that I would at least die a hero's death, but the reality of my misunderstanding made the situation more bitter than it might've otherwise been.

It's probably best I keep details to a minimum, because what we found when we reached the basement was anyone's worst nightmare. The concrete floor sloped toward a single drain. Metal rafters hung from the ceiling. A half-dozen pair of handcuffs dangled from pegs in the walls. A single steel table stood over the drain in the center of the room, various tools strewn across it: heavy chains, steel hooks, several whips of various lengths, a leather-wrapped switch with a knot at the end the size of a golf ball, and yes, it's true, there were dildos, several larger than I imagined any company would manufacture; two long knives sat next to a cattle prod; a horse bit, a bridle and a saddle hung from hooks on the bottom of the table.

Bruce walked to the far corner of the room, where a single bulb in the basement dimly shone. He was obscured in shadow. Nelly slapped my face. I flinched. She tugged my arm. I stumbled. Her strength astounded. She collared me. I clawed at her hips, skin gathering under my fingernails, but she only tightened her grip. "Don't turn me on. I'm not ready to love you yet." She squeezed my throat in the crook of her elbow until my vision ran dark.

When I came to, I hung, suspended from the ceiling by handcuffs. Lyle lay on the table gagged and naked. "Stop this, now!"

Nelly turned, wearing a smile like a slug wears salt. "Ever heard about the post mortem tumescence?" She thrust her hips. "I bet not. Men are such exquisite creatures that they'll ejaculate even after they've been dead for twenty-minutes. They stand atop the evolutionary pyramid. I can't express how much I adore them." She raised a whip and slapped Lyle's cheek. "You're not the strongest specimen, I'll admit, but we'll have fun."

Lyle groaned. Nelly praised the art of necrophilia, speaking at length on the pleasures of joining with the recently dead. She said a man's soul lingered for a time after his body was dispatched, and that that window in time provided "certain opportunities." "What I do—" she went behind Lyle and wound a towel around her fists, placing the excess under his chin and pulling back—"is I take this towel. It's going to cause his blood pressure to spike." He writhed, but his hands were bolted to the table in manacles. His legs windmilled. "Some people think it's about oxygen depletion, but what you really want is to stop up the blood. That way it all pools in his body, engorging the tissues. See?"

A sob jumped from my throat. "No." I kept repeating it. "No, no, no." Hot tears carved my cheeks. The scene defied reason. You're not supposed to die pointlessly. Lyle kicked until he didn't, and when he stopped, Nelly hung her weight from the towel until a popping sound said something irreparable had broken.

What I'm not going to describe is how Nelly satisfied herself with his body. I'm also going to skip the part where she graphed my breasts with my own knife, and how she used the other equipment in the basement to shame me. But I do need you to understand: I did die. I died and died—I think, because I was too stubborn to return to the scene of my humiliation. Perhaps Marva signed a contract with the devil, if you believe in that kind of thing. Maybe the universe fell in love with her long long legs, and it couldn't bear to see her taken by violence, but every time she was murdered Lyle's death followed soon after, then my own.

Nelly had the most perverse desires. I'm convinced she wasn't human. Bruce remained in shadows, a voyeur, a foreboding presence, the suggestion of strength, but Nelly had the strength.

When she had finished with me, she drew a deep cut from the center of my right wrist to the elbow. My consciousness percolated, until, like coffee brewing, it hissed and steamed to an end. By that time, the knife aroused me. I can't explain it. I've died enough to say that that death was the only one that aroused me. But Lyle was right: there's a difference between arousal and pleasure.

1

I LEANED AGAINST THE BRICK FAÇADE OUTSIDE OUR office, drawing figures of infinity in the air with my favorite four-inch pocketknife. My thoughts were as stained as my shoes from wandering every dark alley in Omaha. Two voices spoke muffled words on the other side of the door: maybe love, maybe fear. I flicked my knife closed, dropped it in my purse, and turned the knob to see which. With the door open an inch, I paused. First impressions say so much. If I walked in on love, there'd be a happy ending. I didn't want to think about fear. I knew my partner's gristly baritone anywhere, and his guest spoke with a vaguely familiar accent. When I stepped into the office, the conversation paused.

Lyle pointed a ham and cheese hoagie at me. A smile formed around shreds of lettuce and a dribble of mustard. "Luke! We were just talking about you."

The tableau I faced wasn't love, though Lyle might've thought otherwise. The woman opposite him had yellow hair. She wore high heel shoes. Lipstick was everywhere. Some faces look made for bruises. I shook my head to shoo familiar thoughts. Extended my hand. "Detective Mia. Some people call me Little Cancer." My arm ached from wrist to elbow. A faint purple scar mapped a wound I didn't remember, burning like slow-dying coals. I drowned every distraction to massage the pain. When it subsided I said, "Have we met?"

A fat lip didn't stop this woman from showing a seductive smile. "Um—" she looked at Lyle. "Your partner's a real charmer."

He savored a bite of sandwich. "She grows on you."

"Like a tumor, I'm sure."

Throbbing still-frames shot across my mind's eye. "You're Martha? No. Marva." Where had we met? I flung a nervous glance at Lyle. My brain told me he was the worst kind of dead, but the bolus of sandwich in his gaping mouth spoke life.

I felt for my cigarettes. When I had one lit, despite Lyle's protests that I wait until he finished his sandwich, my pounding heart calmed. I blew a long cloud of smoke over my shoulder and squinted at Marva. She was coming into focus—or more like, someone who had been chopped into a thousand pieces reassembling.

"Since you're up—" Lyle winked at me—"mind getting us some drinks?"

I raised my hand in a fist. "I don't want to hit you, but when you bring a woman back to our office to seduce her, you deserve what you get."

Marva chuckled. "He didn't—"

I interrupted. "Try again. His dick does all the thinking for him, and it sure isn't private." I felt like the cigarette was smoking me. "Now, listen. You're here because someone's threatening you. Text messages? You believe time is running out, and your husband hasn't stopped long enough to realize it's real. He'll regret that."

Something was channeling through my veins, speaking to me from outside the script, a flash of something, then silent. "If you want help, you need to give us a lead with teeth. We can't wait for the morning to get copies of those texts."

Lyle stood and showed his displeasure with a loud sigh. "Fine, I'll get the drinks, huh?"

"Mine neat. Marva likes wine."

"We don't have wine."

I shot my thumb toward the closet. "In there." But I was sure we didn't have any.

"Geez, Luke. What's got into you?"

A faint breeze blew into the room after Lyle went into the kitchenette. Perhaps he opened a window. I wanted to lighten the mood. Slow myself to see where the fortuneteller act was coming from. "How do you like Jake's?"

Marva was playing with her fingernails. "Never been." She looked at me.

"Isn't that where you and Lyle met?"

She paused, showing that bad actor's approximation of a thoughtful expression. "Oh. You mean the bar down the street?"

"The one that says Jake's in neon and has a big cigar underlining it."

"Yeah." She straightened in her chair. "Say, how about a cigarette?"

I obliged. Some alternative history bombarded my brain.

She exhaled smoke. "It's a cozy place. Not my style, but nice enough."

"Not too many places let you smoke indoors anymore, so you can guess I'm a fan."

Lyle returned with the glass of wine and an eightball of bourbon on rocks. "Last pour."

"What a gentleman." I jumped to my feet, trailing a cloud of smoke. "I guess I'll get it myself." Drinking from the bottle I tried to coax the witch from my brain. What did I know? Did it matter? After several slugs, I reentered the fray. I slammed the bottle on our desk and turned to Marva. "Someone tried to bludgeon you with a souvenir brick from the riverfront, but your high heel broke and saved your life. Maybe you pissed off some construction foreman down at the Heartland of America Park redevelopment? Though, I've got my money on the dock workers."

"Neat trick." Marva tugged a lock of her hair. "You have the office bugged."

Lyle stood. "You told me your story at Jake's."

"So the bar's bugged. Probably offers kickbacks for scheduling client meetings there."

Lyle unwrapped a peanut butter cup and popped it in his mouth. "You came looking for me." His brow, working overtime, creased and smoothed to rival any metronome. He glanced at me. "Where you hiding your crystal ball, huh?"

Marva stabbed her cigarette on our end table. "I don't know how you did it. Don't even care. But I do care that you stop whoever's after me."

She'd emptied her wine glass as soon as Lyle handed it to her, but he'd left the bottle in the kitchenette. I let it ride. "Maybe I can post a bulletin on Twitter: Damsel in distress threatened by crazed killer. Tips appreciated. Hashtag reward offered," I drummed my fingers and paused for dramatic effect. "Or how about you tell us where to start, cause I'm pretty sure I know where a trip to the docks will lead." A shiver sped from my toes to the crown of my head, a nauseating aversion to the Missouri River. "Have you recently argued with anyone? Have you come into any sensitive information about something that could get someone in trouble?"

Marva evaluated my question, no play-acting. She pinched the bridge of her nose and winced. "Honestly, it could be anyone. My advocacy work doesn't exactly make me the most popular. And with all the publicity Ransom's—he's my husband—with all his you know—"

"Wait." I knew enough to know I'd been talking to a potential client, but I couldn't remember about what. No doctor I'd heard of would diagnose selective amnesia. I motioned Lyle to join me, and stood, aiming for the kitchenette.

Lyle tapped my temple. "You fall down some stairs, huh? Maybe drink too much with lunch? You're acting weird."

My knees felt weak. I sat, pressing my hands into my closed eyes. "Marva."

She looked me over. Her body stiffened. "What I was saying was that ever since Ransom started his clinical trials we've been plagued with celebrity status."

Lyle opened a bag of pork rinds. "Clinical trials on what?"

The thread of memory snapped back in place. "He works in Bio Pharm, right? Developed some kind of sleeping med?"

"Vivifica." Marva asked for another cigarette. "Do you usually research clients this much?"

I handed her a cigarette. "Never."

She asked for more wine. Lyle jumped up. Sometimes he approximates generosity. It comes at such rare intervals that what for most people would be common courtesy is for him a heroic deed. He's always had a knack for drawing attention to the little things. It works. His slightest gesture of kindness leaves me feeling indebted and grateful.

Marva belted the wine and settled in her chair with the cigarette half smoked. Ash littered the carpet. "Ransom was working on a hair growth product. But you probably know all this."

I shot a longing glance at the bottle of bourbon across the room. "No. But go on."

Marva took the bottle Lyle handed her. "To think, more men pay for elective surgery to have hair transplants each year than women for tummy tucks and breast implants combined. Anyways, his formula wasn't going anywhere fast when he started observing trial mice passing out. Hundreds of little rodents all just snoring away." Marva's cigarette crackled as her cheeks hollowed. "I don't know. I'm probably explaining it all wrong, but basically the drug's active matrix didn't do shit for hair, but it had a profound impact on sleep patterns. Lemonade from lemons kind of thing. Now his company's all over him to rush the formula to market, because whether you're hairy or bald you need sleep."

Lyle licked the cream filling from a cookie and studied the flavor on his tongue. "Who got the shaft?"

Marva eyed him. "Pardon me?"

"Your husband." Lyle popped the cookie wafer in his mouth. "Maybe the Ambien folks don't like competition, huh?"

"If that's the case, why go after me?"

I stood, walking to the desk for the Magdalene. "Makes sense to me. Direct attacks usually make people bolder. Go after something the guy loves and he's pudding in the knees."

"My husband's pudding in the knees no matter what."

I studied Marva like an impossible puzzle. "Struggling marriage?"

Lyle forked a bite of key lime pie onto his tongue. "Strong women have a way of ruining marriages, from what I hear."

For a moment Marva and I were on the same side of an issue. We glared at Lyle.

She stabbed her cigarette on the end table. The smoke died a sudden death. "Ransom's loving, supportive, honest, and hardworking. He's also cautious. Anyone who wanted to shut him up could."

Why was I thinking of Laser pointers? "You're saying this has nothing to do with him?"

"I can't even tell him someone's messing with me. No it's not about him."

Just when we were getting somewhere the witch flashed in my brain. A sudden image, more like the imprint of a voice. It's hard to explain. I didn't exactly see Borsheims, but the impression of the fine jeweler surfaced in my memory. "We should talk to him just in case."

"No."

"He might have valuable inf—"

"I don't want you talking to him."

If memories of headlines proclaiming Marva's bloody end hadn't surfaced, I might've pushed harder on her resistance to involve Ransom, but as it was I showed a slug of bourbon a nice dark place to rest and relax. "Anyway, stay away from the shops at Regency."

Marva tilted her head and stared at me. Lyle was unwrapping a package of cake doughnuts. A police siren howled outside our window.

"I have an appointment at Christian Nobel Furs tomorrow morning."

My head shook violently like my body knew something my brain didn't. "Cancel it."

"It's been on the books for months."

"Yeah. Well, you're not the only one who's looking forward to that appointment."

She dug in her purse and came out with an envelope. Anger accenting her face, she stood tossing the envelope on the desk next to the bottle of Magdalene. "Flat fee." She walked toward the door. "Five grand a day. You draw your own expenses from that. If you don't have good news for me in two weeks, you're fired. If you get this monkey off my back before then, I'll pay you an extra one fifty. But I'm not changing my lifestyle. I'm paying you to keep me safe." She opened the door. "Someone told me you were good. I'm trusting him."

When the door closed behind her a drugged calm settled over the office. Lyle finished his doughnuts and I sunk into the leather armchair where Marva's heat still radiated.

Lyle dug his phone from his pocket. "She never gave us those text messages."

"Something tells me she doesn't care so much about dying, but needs to look like she wants to live."

There was a mess of quiet between us. I waded through an assault of odd impressions, like a film of another life crowding my consciousness. A trip to the boat docks. A game of poker. A giant and his bloody machete. Rape and torture. Then, pressing against those odd sensations that read a lot like memory were questions. Marva said someone told her we did good work. I knew one person who'd recommend Lyle and I. Not that we weren't good, but we'd worked our share of cases under strong influence, drink mostly, though there had been the case of the stolen cattle when Lyle had come across some magic mushrooms. We both ate a handful and ended up hiding behind an oil drum at a construction site just off I-80 in a standoff with a one-armed octogenarian who spent bullets like pennies but aimed like a blind toddler.

We'd run ourselves out of well-paying jobs with a reputation for excess: unfair since except for the time Lyle zonked on a stakeout and slept through the weapon's transaction he'd been hired to film, we solved every case our clients came to us with. The last several years our only jobs came from missing pets fliers and spouses wanting to catch a husband's indiscretions. Sometimes— more often than you'd believe—a cheating husband would come asking if we'd setup a seduction for his wife: frame her. I wish I could say we'd taken the high road, but chances at paying work were scarce enough, and we lived perpetually within days of defaulting on our debt. This all made Marva's cash more welcome, and I knew who to thank, but that didn't change that we'd taken a client who gave us a little more than nothing to go on. Too, I should've been grateful for the sudden gift of clairvoyance, but I lacked key details, like who was going to kill Marva, or where to find that person before the bloodbath the next morning. I knew the deadline, but not who we'd meet when we got there. With just under fourteen hours to thwart the attack at Regency, including the dead of night, we had a lot of work to do.

A jag of snoring jolted me from my ruminations. Lyle blew a spit bubble from his mouth. Melted chocolate dripped from his hand. He was a good partner, but one who needed his sleep.

8

Philipe Ruskov lived in a penthouse at the top of the Old Market Lofts in downtown Omaha. He'd come from Moscow as Uncle Sam's protected informant. Secrets he'd shared with the CIA spoiled a planned chemical weapons attack on American embassies in Kazakhstan. In exchange for the information, Ruskov received two million dollars, US citizenship, a theatre projector, and a 400-volume library of 16mm reel-to-reel films.

When I called, he answered on the last ring. I'd never witnessed him taking a call, but I suspect he intentionally waited to engage the line until the last moment. I could imagine him listening to the ringtone and waiting. He relished narrow escapes. If he told the unembellished truth, he daily slept less than two hours, ate one small meal, and walked ten miles.

He'd supplemented his initial payment from the government by cementing his reputation as an informant. Ignoring his sources, every American, law-enforcing, alphabet soup paid Ruskov handsomely for his information, which was always right unless it was spectacularly wrong. When it was wrong it was wrong in the way that made people think he'd shared fake news because someone deserved a toe tag.

Lyle and I met him in '07 after the Watson twins robbed First National Bank's central vault. A burnt orange Bentley Continental cut Lyle off on westbound 17th near the bank tower. He'd been returning to our office from a rendezvous with a woman he picked up at The Dubliner Pub over lunch. Lyle swore lunch was the best time of day for seduction. Lady professionals, as he called them—despite my pleas for him to see the sexism in such a label, as if "professional" was inherently a masculine word and needed a clarifying modifier—businesswomen were at their most vulnerable around noon. Emerging from hostile office environments, they felt contentious, willing their coworkers violent deaths, needing a break from the grind.

After the Bentley cut Lyle off, he wanted to bend the guy's fender, but he'd learned from a defensive driving class the city assigned him after a speeding ticket that the best way to combat road-rage was to let others prosecute bad driving. Copy the offender's license plate: report traffic violations to the police. Doing that not only defused anger but also kept roadways safe. Police frequently ticketed drivers reported through nonemergency lines. As he was preparing to call on the Bentley, its driver fired a handgun. The bullet lodged in Lyle's shoulder.

Shock numbed him. The driver sped away. Lyle pursued. The chase led across the Iowa border, through Council Bluffs and onto country roads. Dizzy from heavy bleeding, Lyle lost the Bentley on a two-lane. About then his phone rang. Philipe Ruskov announced himself, introducing that familiar nasal tone, the thick accent, the strange practice of apparent familiarity.

"I see you run detective agency, Mr. Kaptrapernis."

"Kuputchnik. I've also got a bullet in my shoulder, if you wouldn't mind calling ba—"

"Is shot by driver of orange Bentley, I believe."

"Okay. You got my attention."

Ruskov identified the driver as Amos Watson, the elder twin of a bank robbing outfit. "I would call police myself and receive reward, but more money available if handle privately."

"So?"

"Do I misunderstand you? You are not wanting a revenge."

"I'm not a vigilante."

"Private detective. What is difference?"

"What kind of deal?"

"Seventy percent."

"Sixty."

"This not negotiation. I am having information. You not."

"Huh."

"Bring monies to this address. I would like be meeting in person." Lyle's phone buzzed. An address populated the text message bubble. "Your johndoe—" he pronounced the J like in Dijon and spoke the name without space between words—"he and brother will be at Court and Hamilton. Big white house. What you call hideout."

"What about the bullet in my shoulder?"

"Make stitches. Alley Doctor. Lesson learned. Be smarter." Ruskov hung up.

Lyle had called me from his house. His place reeked of formaldehyde. He'd given me the rundown on the phone, but I'd expected hyperbole. His breath smelled of cheap rum. Shirtless and pale, he was worse than he'd let on. The wound on his shoulder was stitched with copper-colored thread. His eyes darted, milky and distant.

"We need to get you to a hospital. That thing's going to get infected."

"I'm fine." He coughed. "Get me my jar of olives." He spat out the pimientos. "We need to go, huh? Big money. Tight deadline." He slugged a flask of Magdalene. "See. I'm reborn."

58

Weekend traffic clogged the roads. Groups of college kids collected around Blackstone bars. The sky darkened with storm clouds, one of those summer downpours that flood the streets and clear in twenty minutes. The rain fell so heavy with the first crack of thunder I couldn't see the front of my bumper. As the storm passed, we converged on the address Ruskov provided. I tried to persuade Lyle to back out.

He said I could go. "No time to debate, huh? I'm seeing this through."

As if he truly had been reborn, he leapt from the car, stalked up the walkway onto the porch, knocked on the door, then ducked out of sight. A stalky fellow with a short red beard peeked out. His eyes locked on Lyle's car, and he stepped out tenting his hand over his eyes against the streetlight glare. Lyle slipped a wire over the guy's neck and dropped him with a knee to the gut. He frisked the guy's belt and came up with an 8mm. Dragging the guy's flailing body, he flung him against the truck. "You shot me, you son of a bitch."

I dug cuffs from the glove box, tossing them to Lyle. "I hope you know what you're doing, cause this looks a lot like armed robbery."

He showed me a half grin, simultaneously the most and least confident I'd ever seen him. He handed me the 8mm. "Be ready." He raised up, turned toward the house and cupped his hands around his mouth. "I feel you watching, huh? Come out, asshole." I did what he asked, as if he were still talking to me.

A nearly identical man to the one in our backseat emerged, hands held high. A black duffel bag hung around his neck. "You want this? Give me my brother, it's yours. Tip off the cops tomorrow. You collect a small reward for your efforts, but we'll be long gone."

"Not a cha—"

Lyle interrupted. "How do we know you won't come around

to recoup your losses?"

He started to lower his hands. "This bag's one of ten. Call it a finder's fee. You're were smart enough to collect."

I turned the 8mm on him. "No dea—"

Lyle cut me off. "You got it."

I looked to him. "I'm not taking a bribe."

Lyle spoke loud enough for all to hear. "This isn't a bribe. It's a gentlemen's agreement. I have a hunch Mr. Watson knows Philipe Ruskov."

"That asshole's gonna get his."

Lyle tossed a grape in his mouth. "Looks like he already gave you yours."

The twin said we'd better hope we never got on the wrong side of the Russian bastard. "Dude's got more eyes than a shit-eating fly."

Lyle raised the handcuff key. He tossed it in the yard. "Walk me the bag. Keep those hands high. You try anything, she puts one between your eyes. Understand?"

Even as the twin cooperated, he laughed. "You talk tough, bud, but I know a creampuff when I see one."

I whispered into Lyle's ear, "Coercion. Really?"

While I kept the 8mm aimed, Lyle lifted the duffle over the twin's head. He backed around the side of the car, knelt, opened the trunk, tossed the bag inside, kicked Amos to the curb, and brushed his hands. He nodded at Amos. "Lay down beside your brother."

That done. Lyle jogged to the driver seat. "Get in, Lu." He never let me drive again.

Fleeing with a bag full of cash, I felt utterly out of control and afraid. "He was wearing my best pair of handcuffs."

"He paid plenty for them, huh?"

So did we, I thought, but I said, "Who are we?"

Lyle opened a bag of tortilla chips. "Opportunists."

9

I STOOD WHEN RUSKOV APPEARED. BURKE'S PUB WAS nearly empty. He stopped on the doormat and scraped his shoes. Dried mud clung to the cuffs of his pants. The knees were darkly soaked. He shrugged off a pea-green trench coat and folded it over one arm.

The bartender nodded at Ruskov. Ruskov tipped an imaginary cap. He approached, kissing my left cheek like an apology. After we sat and Ruskov ordered a drink he tented his hands on the table and sighed. "The question you want ask is only one I not answering."

"What's in it for you?"

"Perfect marks for predictability, little Lukey." He mimed zipping his lips. "You will be finding out soon enough."

"I called because you recommended me—"

"I am understanding why you call, and you are correct. I put Mrs. DeLonghi in touch with partner of yours. Having not come across genuine mystery since I leave the land of Russia." He laughed. "Ah! Crafty dealer of stale breads. Outwitted my mother's landlord. You will have never been seeing so much money in one place."

"What happened?"

"As I say. Is mystery."

"Unsolved?"

"Only kind."

I imagined a world where people could profit selling stale bread. "So you're saying Marva's circumstances are similar to what happened with your mother's landlord?"

Ruskov rubbed his thumb back and forth across the tips of his fingers in the universal gesture meaning money. "Is missing that situation what this one need: persons with high integrity and low scruples."

"I wouldn't say Lyle or I have high integrity."

"You not give yourself credit enough."

I listed cheats and bribes and blind eyes. Ruskov called those examples of low scruples. He said Lyle and I operated with gross loyalty. When we accepted a case we gave everything: all give and no take. If there was a solution, we solved with disregard to our well-being.

I couldn't argue.

Ruskov ordered a dry gin martini. "You and Mr. Kuperchini are something like good people."

"Hardly."

He shrugged. "Details bore me." He said he couldn't help with Mrs. DeLonghi. It was rare for Ruskov not to have the scoop, and it worried me. If he'd known why someone wanted Marva dead, he couldn't have held back.

He'd first met her at a fundraising dinner at the Hotel Deco while speaking with Magnus Adderpaine, a friend of the DeLonghis, and the conversation steered toward intrigue, as always. Threats. Perhaps blackmail. Ruskov worked the angles hoping for a nibble. Magnus said someone apparently despised Mrs. DeLonghi's advocacy projects.

The room where they dined was hot and humid. Guests shed sport coats and shawls. The owner of the hotel wheeled in silver basins of ice and blew fans across them. He apologized for the inconvenience of the broken air conditioner and treated the guests to caviar.

Ruskov delighted in sturgeon eggs. "First rate," he recalled. He learned later in the conversation with Magnus that Marva was in attendance. Magnus pointed to her.

Ruskov introduced himself. In the way he had, which is a way I've never seen but only overheard, he ingratiated himself to Marva and learned the intimates of her situation.

"And you recommended she speak with Lyle."

Ruskov had a fist like a ham. He pounded it on the table. "No jump ahead, Lukavonovich. You spoil suspense." He said Marva had cried, and he spent time describing the perfection of her waterproof mascara.

"Maybe I'm misjudging the woman, but I don't peg Marva as the crying type."

"We all manipulate."

"Fair enough."

He marveled at her eyes. He said her cheeks were perfect for slapping, the kind that shade rosy but not apple-shocked. "I envied the husband." Marva had drunk two bottles of wine on his tab, two bottles in twenty minutes. "And still, she stand upright. Good Russian genes, that one."

"Is this all necessary?"

"You wanting story or no?"

"Whatever."

"Poor, Luluchik. Is not knowing pertinent details when whacking her on side of head."

"Upside the head."

"That too."

"Please." I raised a cupped palm. "Carry on."

Marva, he said, wanted a meaningful life. She scowled at her husband as he wove through the crowd. He told stories to strangers, laughed at their responses, shook hands, hugged, ate and drank, all like a man enchanted by money. If she'd had half his influence, Omaha would've been a hub for socio-economic and environmental progress. But even as her jealousy boiled, anyone watching would've thought her the perfect helper for a man building a coalition. When guests at the event gushed praise on Ransom, she swelled, called him a visionary, expounded on her luck at having married him.

"Is first thing," Ruskov said, "that is make me crazy in nerves. Not every day I am meeting person can hate so quietly. This is person with much intelligence. I respect."

"I got the sense, when I met her, she was holding back."

"And you would not be wrong." Ruskov sipped his martini. "Marva lives secret life, so secret even I cannot guess it. Nothing small time like love affair, and nothing vile such as participate in a secret society." He nibbled his lower lip. "This is what I want, Lukala. To read her secrets in news. Is making jealous brat of me. Someone hiding from The Great Ruskov."

He was the only person I knew who could title himself "The Great" and not come off arrogant. "So you fed her to us because you don't like that she's got the jump on you?"

"Your Mrs. DeLonghi have wit to gut opponent, while making feeling of friendliness."

"Yeah, and someone she's run into sees through it and wants to kill her."

"This unrelated, I am thinking."

"What? A random stalker?"

"Not."

"Are you done with your story? Can we talk about Marva?"

"What have we been talking about, Lukachik?"

"The thing is, I don't think we have time." I didn't want to let on about my strange clairvoyance from earlier that night. No one needed Ruskov digging around in her brain. "I have a feeling whoever's after Marva, they're imminently ready to knock her off."

"Is why you perfect for case."

"You say you want to expose her secrets, but you sent her to Lyle."

"Ah!" Ruskov swung his hambone arm in the air. "You are jealous."

"Not jealous. Curious. Lyle's great. No one could accuse me of undervaluing him—" it could be said I overvalued him—"but he's never been the investigator between us. He's the pilot light. Something like that."

"And suppose I send you pretty woman who not wanting give up why she has stalker, but want solution to problem anyway."

I saw his point. I'd've tossed her from our office in twenty seconds. Lit a fire under her ass, stewed her, and served her to the dogs. It almost went that way even with Lyle involved. "So you made sure we took her case." I'd held off on smoking but my nerves shivered. I needed nicotine. "Step outside with me."

Ruskov dug up a wheeze, "Am trying to kick second-hand smoking. Go on. I wait here."

While I smoked I prowled Twitter for nonsense to retweet, and composed a senseless missive about the transcendental nature of nicotine and onion rings. Social media is just another addiction that distracts from the meaninglessness of life. I highly recommend it.

When I returned, Ruskov was cleaning his teeth with a drinking straw. I checked my eyes in a compact mirror. "Here's the deal." I sat. "Someone's going to tell me what we got ourselves into—really tell us—or I'm going to walk."

"You can't."

"What do you mean, 'I can't'?"

What Ruskov said next should've sounded alarms, but I was too delirious to care. "You are being like cat. Coming back and back and back, no? Only way out is through, Lukenka."

"I don't understand."

"You do."

"Why'd you meet me here?"

"Am wanting to see how quickly you get desperate."

There was more. Small talk mostly, between Ruskov and I. I learned Marva liked fresh strawberries, that Magnus Adderpaine was a cult celebrity. Marva had difficulty sleeping. Ruskov seemed to draw insomniacs to himself—which if I haven't explained yet, includes me. Marva sat on a board in town for wildlife preservation and advocacy. She'd even appeared in the news to oppose the Millard Police Department after an officer there fatally shot a mountain lion that wandered into city limits. The poor cat, I remember, had come in search of food, was starving, and had discovered a dumpster behind Hy-Vee before finding a patch of shade to digest. The patch of shade happened to be the awning of a middle school. Instead of tranquilizing the cat, the city decided once a predator had found a food source as abundant as a city dumpster, it would return and threaten people's safety. Perhaps the logic was correct, but that no other solutions were tried was, in the eyes of many—me included—proof of police brutality.

Perhaps the detail about Marva's hobbies softened me to her obstinate side. I spent considerable effort plying Ruskov for information, but he maintained she was a mystery. We closed Burke's, both sober, both sparking with wakefulness. I walked home. He sped off in the back of some Rolls Royce, as always was the case with him, and I drew a bath. I shaved my legs and smoked my last cigarettes. The rest of city wouldn't wake for several hours, yet. I texted Lyle to bring me cigarettes when he came that morning,

THE 9 LIVES OF MARVA DELONGHI

and no sooner than I'd hit send, a flash of the witch in my brain told me I'd tread in the tracks of a previous life.

The sensation, the almost-but-not-quite déjà vu nearly convinced me to call off Lyle's errand, but a stronger sense persuaded me to compose a simple addendum: *Get an autograph.*

I didn't know what I meant, but I knew he would.

Then I opened my music cabinet, leafed through my record collection, selected *Far From Over* by the Vijay Iyer Sextet, dropped the needle and fixed a Magdalene with lemon juice and sea salt. Somewhere along the way I got sleepy enough to doze, and when I woke, it was to knocking on my front door.

10

Lyle said he'd met the Cereal Burglar. It took a hammer and ice to prepare my Bloody Mary, which fixed my brain. I asked if Lyle remembered to buy cigarettes. Walgreens had had a buy-one-get-one, he said, and he felt generous. He set his sausage and egg bagel on my kitchen table and slipped six packs of smokes from his jacket pocket. "If you hadn't asked me to get you these, I would've missed the action."

I peeled the cellophane from a pack and tapped out a cigarette. Occasionally, the landlord harassed me about smoking in her building, but she liked a detective living on the premises and said I kept crime rates down. I doubted her impressions, but no one argues special treatment.

Lyle said he needed a beer to calm his nerves, but even before he'd opened his mouth I'd raided the refrigerator for a High Life. It's impossible to convey the sensation of precognition. "I'm betting you didn't take her down?"

Lyle cracked the tab and drank. "Take who down?"

"Your Cereal Burglar."

"For starters, we've gone over this: we're not dealing with a

68

woman."

"That why she's smaller than you expected, just small all over?"

Lyle guzzled his beer. "Did I already tell you this?"

I skipped the fixings for another bloody and filled my glass with Magdalene. That was a tough question, because maybe I was suffering a mental breakdown. "Never mind."

Lyle said he'd apologized to the cashier for standing dumbly by while the Cereal Burglar cleaned out her register—a detail I was sure hadn't existed in the previous encounter.

What previous encounter? My brain told me I wasn't crazy, and I told it to shut up. "As much as I'd love to dissect this chance meeting, I think we need to get to business."

Lyle shook a handful of bacon bits into his palm and popped them like pills. "So I just met the most famous thief in Omaha's history and you want to glaze right past it, huh?"

"I want to save it for later." I slugged the bourbon, clenching my teeth. "Marva dies today, and I don't know why. But I know where."

"Pardon me?"

"She's headed for Regency now, and the only thing I don't know is if she goes down before or after her appointment at Christian Nobel."

"You know this why?"

Crazy or not, I had all the memories of living and dying. Why not see it through? "Believe it or not, this is my second life."

Lyle laughed. He dug a package of caramels from his pocket, unwrapped one and offered it to me. "Are you speaking literally here? Because if you are you need to swear off the bottle and schedule an appointment to see a shrink."

"I don't know what I mean." I declined the caramel. "I know I met with Ruskov last night. I know Marva found you on his recommendation. I know he thinks she's untrustworthy, which is saying something given who he is. And I know he warned me someone was going to make a move on Marva today." My conclusion contained a lie, and I hoped Lyle wouldn't resist.

He rolled a handful of jellybeans in his palm before selecting a neon blue specimen and placing it on his tongue. "What is blue raspberry anyway?"

"Can you please just trust me?"

"I do trust you, Lu. Always. The problem is, I don't understand the point. We aren't bodyguards. It's our job to dig up the why."

"We don't have time for *why* right now."

Lyle squeezed a packet of mayonnaise on a slice of thin-cut turkey breast, rolled the meat into a cigar and folded it into his mouth. "So what? We go and thwart this assassination or whatever, and then the thing's done."

It didn't seem likely. "Don't know." I slapped the table. "Maybe. Can we go?"

Lyle fished his keys and a handful of candied mints from his pocket. "You said you met with Ruskov. Why wasn't I invited?"

Because Lyle and Ruskov together were like a cheap slapstick routine. "You nodded off." Because I could only stomach about five minutes of the dick-measuring competition between those two. "I decided you needed the rest."

"You? Worried about me, huh? That's rich."

We all bluff sometimes. "I wanted you there."

Lyle looked across his shoulder at me. He pursed his lips and shook his head.

I followed him to the car. He turned the wrong way out of my apartment parking lot, and I asked where he was going. He said if we meant to break up an attempted murder, we needed more than bare-knuckle boxing. I nodded. He rolled the two blocks to our office, parked up on the curb, told me he'd be back in a jiff, and disappeared into the building. I considered leaving with his car, because for reasons I couldn't justify I felt certain he'd trade his life for Marva's, and I didn't consider the swap fair, but before I'd summoned the nerve to drive, Lyle returned.

The 8mm we never used poked from the waist of his jeans. I don't trust guns, and we don't use them. Clients have asked why I don't carry, and I always quote the stats. What it comes to is that if you're smart you can always swing a hostile situation in your favor with planning and preparation. The one time we'd used the gun, we'd walked away with stolen money and guilty consciences. All I can say is you'll spend stolen money as fast as you'll flush a gram of blow down the toilet if the police bust up your party. And when the money's gone, you won't have a nice new home or a decent car or a trust fund for some rug rat's future education. What you will have is a closet full of clothes you never wear and a gut rotten from a months-long bender on expensive scotch whiskey. And where gut rot is concerned Magdalene is just as reliable at a fraction of the cost.

Lyle parked in front of the Bonefish Grill and cut the engine. "What now, Cleo?"

Clouds had rolled over the morning's blue sky and a heavy humidity dropped, wrapping its fingers around my nose and mouth, making it hard to breathe. I searched a map of the Regency shops on my phone. Christian Nobel Furs was situated by Borsheims on the opposite side of the court from where we parked. We couldn't be sure where Marva would enter or exit, but given there were four entrances and two of us, we chose to station ourselves near the indoor fountain, which had a view of all four escape routes. Lyle caught a glimpse of Marva inside the store. She was pointing animatedly at a clerk who had mascara trails running down her cheeks.

It made sense. I'd pictured Marva trying on mink coats or a coon tail hat—crude representation of the actual inventory, I know—but she hadn't made her appointment for means of purchase but to spend a scheduled fifteen minutes cursing some retail clerk for exploiting animals for financial gain. I could almost reconstruct the scene, and in the wake of the verbal slaughter, I wondered why she'd waste her venom on someone who only drew a paycheck. Why not save it for the owner?

"I suppose it's too much to ask that you'd know who we're looking for, huh?"

I considered my fingernails for a moment. "Someone brazen enough to hack a victim to pieces with a machete in broad daylight."

"So we stop anyone wielding a machete?"

"Pretty much."

"Should be easy enough."

"But also someone smart enough to escape the scene of a gruesome murder without being caught by the police."

Lyle pointed to an elderly woman adorned in pearls of various sizes. She wore a heavy wool coat, absurdly overdressed for a summer morning. The coat's shoulder pads stood stiffly out of proportion with the woman's hips. "Wrong time of year for a coat. Take her down?"

I wasn't in the joking mood. "She's not our perp."

Lyle shook a handful of Boston Baked Beans into his palm. "Except maybe she is. You said it had to be someone no one would expect."

"I said it had to be someone smart enough to evade the police. Plus, can you see her being strong enough to cut through bone?"

Lyle's hand was stained red from the candy. "Depends how sharp the knife."

"Enough jokes. Keep your eyes peeled."

Lyle saluted. "Yes, sir."

"Cut the shit."

"Somebody could use a drink, huh?"

I walked several paces away, my back to Lyle. Someone shouldered into me just as I was settling my weight on my hips. My first thought was that Lyle had followed behind and was trying to drive me crazy. "Would you..." but it hadn't been him.

An overlarge man, a giant of a man—I'd seen this man—strode past with strong intent. The bald head, hollow cheeks, the tattoos on his neck.

Then Lyle was at my shoulder. "What's a guy like that doing in a place like this?"

The witch in my brain had a seizure, foaming at the metaphorical mouth, hissing, writhing. Something was wholeheartedly wrong. *Give me a name!* The man wore a loose-fitting denim shirt and heavy denim pants with steel-toed boots. He reached behind his back and adjusted something tucked into his waistband. "Laser!"

He turned his head far to the side and smiled, hesitating slightly. I grabbed Lyle's elbow. "Shoot him."

"What?"

"Shoot him. That's him."

"Ask questions later?" Lyle reluctantly drew the 8mm. "What's going on?"

"Laser," I said again, but with force instead of desperation. I knew he couldn't be two places at once. In purgatory there are hallucinations and ghosts. The world is laid over other worlds. There is also mental illness and fear. I couldn't guess how we'd missed it. If we met Laser at the docks, he'd gone straight from killing Marva to decapitating catfish.

I slapped Lyle's shoulder. "Shoot."

Lyle raised the pistol and told Laser to freeze. Laser spun, put his hands behind his head, winked, pulled a long-handled axe from behind his back and threw it. Blood sprung from Lyle's cheek. The pistol clattered to the ground. A shot fired. Screams issued from all sides. People scattered for cover.

Laser clomped across the floor, tackled me, regained his axe from Lyle's face and sprinted toward Christian Nobel. Was it shock? Disbelief? I rolled left, scooped the pistol from the ground, leapt to my feet and ran.

Laser lifted the axe over his head as he loped toward the entrance of the store where Marva was just turning toward the ruckus, away from a clerk whose face had contorted in paralyzing fear. A nagging string of neurons crackled, begging me to wake, but I knew better.

I jump-stopped, spread my feet like two anchors of a tripod, lifted the gun to eye-level, exhaled, aimed, fired. At the same moment Laser fell forward a crimson fist of blood bloomed from his lower back. The axe slipped from his hands: the head flipped backward. He tumbled, stiff-kneed to the ground. My ears rang from the gun's report. A vine of silence sprouted from my ears and wrapped around my body.

The bullet I'd fired passed through Laser's stomach, exited his belly at a slight incline and struck Marva at the center of her throat. In her right hand, she held a plastic bag. She saw me seeing her, then looked to the bag as it slipped from her fingers. It plopped on the stone tile.

Marva's knees crumpled. She slumped and fell. Not a moment later, a voice commanded me to "Drop the gun."

Hot breath filled my mouth and the ringing vine in my ears crackled. I swung my arms in the direction of the voice, the gun still aimed, but nothing, just nothing, made sense. My right eye was gone before I registered trouble. Don't let anyone tell you a gunshot to the head doesn't hurt. It's excruciating. Upon the bullet's passage, your brain holds on to time because it knows dying is a mistake.

I died anyway, but as a parting gift my one good eye locked on Lyle, the two halves of his severed face, the curve of his dead body on the tile floor. I thought, *He's a good man who doesn't deserve to die.* Dying is sentimental that way.

11

I LEANED AGAINST THE BRICK FAÇADE OUTSIDE OUR office, drawing figures of infinity in the air with my favorite four-inch pocketknife. My thoughts were as stained as my shoes from wandering every dark alley in Omaha. Muffled voices spoke on the other side of the door: Love? Fear? I flicked my knife closed, dropped it in my purse, and turned the knob to see which. With the door open an inch, I paused. First impressions. If I walked in on love, there'd be a happy ending. I was afraid. I knew my partner Lyle's gristly baritone anywhere, but I couldn't remember where I'd met Marva or how we knew each other. When I stepped into the office, Lyle and Marva turned.

Lyle pointed a ham and cheese hoagie at me. A smile formed around shreds of lettuce and a dribble of mustard. "Luke! We were just talking about you."

Lyle thought this tableau was love.

Marva had yellow hair. She wore high heel shoes. Lipstick was everywhere. I rubbed my eyes to punish the pain swimming in the fishbowl of my skull. "I think I have cancer." A headache throbbed behind my eyes, the remains, I imagined of a dream in which I'd been shot through the eye. I breathed deep to crowd the aching with oxygen. When it subsided I offered my hand. "Detective Mia. Have we met before?"

A fat lip didn't stop her from showing a seductive smile. "Um —" she looked at Lyle. "Your partner's a real charmer."

He took his time chewing a bite of sandwich. "She grows on you."

Throbbing still-frames pummeled my mind's eye. "What's your problem with 20's Showgirl?" It didn't matter where we'd met. I knew bad news when I saw it. I felt for my cigarettes. When I had one lit, despite Lyle's protests that I wait until he finished his sandwich, I felt slightly centered. I blew a long cloud of smoke over my shoulder and squinted at Marva. She was coming into focus—or more like, her story was bleeding into my mind.

"Other than that topless clubs are a microcosm of everything diseased confronting this world, nothing I guess. Why do you ask?"

I strode to Lyle, ripped the sandwich from his hand, wolfed it. Déjà vu awakens a woman's hunger. I spun on my heels and studied Marva. After a long drag on my cigarette to dull the ham and mayonnaise, I said, "Don't ask me how, because I'm one small headache from aerating my skull with a hollow-point bullet, but I know you make a game out of pissing certain people off. If I had to guess, I'd say you schedule frequent appointments at Christian Nobel Furs under various aliases just so you can raise hell over supporting the murder of animals for the trade of pelts. Something tells me you've got a similar gig at topless clubs around town. And where else? Omaha Steaks? Are you vegan? I guarantee you hate for-profit hospitals and colleges. A rich woman like you. You've got nothing better to do than protest all the businesses in town that don't operate like you think they should. I bet you're halfway to a heart attack about the new chicken plant opening in Fremont. Well, I'll tell you one thing, you might've been having all kinds of fun with your champion protests, but you really pissed someone off." The name was on the tip of my tongue. Kill him. Problem solved. I smoked my cigarette to the filter and coughed rancid fiberglass. "When'd you meet Laser?"

Marva's smile vanished. Her face cycled through a catalogue of expressions so quickly not one could be read. She asked if I minded getting her a drink. I told her to help herself to the bottle of wine in the closet. Lyle said we didn't have wine. I told her she'd learn a lot about what was what and who was who when she checked the closet.

She uncrossed her legs. "Some hospitality."

"Glasses are in the cupboard by the fridge, though the way you drink I doubt you need one."

Lyle made like a spurned lover and shouldered past me, flinging the closet door open. "What's gotten into you, Miss Huffy Pants?" He poked around on the shelves before saying, "Told you. No wine."

I pushed him aside, dipped my hand into a paper bag on the floor and pulled out the Shiraz. Some stereotypes are founded. Lucky for Lyle, his skills in detection were of human motive. Like all men, he couldn't find a glowing hearth in a Thomas Kinkade painting, but he did have a knack for untangling motives. Where it concerned the why of a criminal mindset, Lyle ran circles around me.

Marva cleared her throat. I wiped the neck of the bottle on my shirt, unscrewed its cap and walked it to our lovely-legged damsel in distress. "Skip all the shit about the text messages and focus on what you were doing the first time a threat came through on your phone. I'd bet you any amount of money you had just finished dressing down some poor woman at 20's Showgirl."

Lyle offered Marva the armchair. He pointed a thumb at me. "Get me a Magdalene, would you? On the rocks."

"Last I checked, I'm not Alice, and this isn't The Brady Bunch."

"So I guess you want me to toss your ass to the curb?"

Truth was, I felt petty, jealous and confused so I hurled the first dumb thought my brain churned out. "Alas! Chivalry died of testicular cancer." I gave Lyle the finger.

I knew Marva, yet I'd never laid eyes on her. But I also seemed to remember her dying, some image of her throat bleeding in fingers over her blouse. The whole predicament had me twice sideways and spinning. Was it memory or paranoia? You don't just say, *I know how you die, because I'm the one who kills you,* and psych hospitals don't treat the insane with dignity.

When I returned from the kitchen with Lyle's bourbon and a jelly jar for Marva's wine—the latter a formality best ignored—I said, "Let me start over. My name's Luke Evelyn Mia, and I've worked with Lyle 'The String Bean' Kuputchnik for twelve years. We met in college at a hotdog eating competition Tri Delta hosted. You wouldn't know it to watch him eat, but I can put away more food than he can in fifteen minutes any day of the week. I have a higher tolerance for alcohol too. But he's a better driver." I drank my drink and walked the glass to our desk. "Stop me if I'm wrong now, because I'm under the impression you met Philipe Ruskov at a charity dinner. The Hotel Deco, I believe, and you told him—"

Lyle jumped from his chair. "Thank god! I was starting to worry."

I scowled at him. "Excuse me?"

"Your mental telepathy shtick. I was starting to think you'd gone insane. But it makes sense, now. I should've known Ruskov was involved. So he called you, huh?"

I almost contradicted him, but maybe he was right. I'd probably taken Phil's call earlier that night, drunk, and stumbled down one of my alleys on a bender that led me to our office. Don't put that hypothesis under a microscope. I went with it because the alternative made my skin crawl. "Mental telepathy is redundant." I lit a cigarette, pointing the smoldering tip at Mrs. Sexy Legs. "I'll tell you what: you're probably already too late. I don't know why you waited so long to get help, but the people you pissed off aren't playing games. A man named Laser knows you have an appointment at Christian Nobel, and he's going to meet you there to deliver a message with a long-handled axe. If you know where I can find him, you need to fess up, and don't tell me he works at the river docks, because I already know what he can do to a catfish with a machete, and in his eyes all you are is a really big, severely annoying catfish."

Lyle peeled an orange and slipped a segment into his cheek. He savored the pulp, ignoring a dribble of juice down the left side of his chin. "Can we call a timeout? Huh? Marv. How much of what my hotheaded partner is saying is true?"

Marva was pouring the last of the red wine into her jelly jar. "Since I can't see the future, I don't know how to answer that question. I do know our little fortuneteller's done her homework. My protests against the most deplorable businesses in our city are tireless. I've made a number of enemies along the way, though I'd be surprised if my actions actually put me in harm's way. I've thrown enough money at my efforts to know I can't buy sympathy or hate."

She drank the last of her wine and asked if I would give her a cigarette. "From time to time—" jets of smoke shot from her nostrils—"I upset someone enough that they threaten me, but usually it's harmless. I remember one time I turned in information about Cargill polluting ground water, and the company's president told my husband he'd like to string me up to a tree."

"Yeah, but this time someone's not blowing smoke." I did, and dragged on my cigarette.

Marva stood walking to the window. She looked over the crowds milling around Benson. "I hate to pour water on your fire, but I haven't done any protest work against topless clubs recently. 20's Showgirl already filed for bankruptcy, and it's closing for good in December. Why waste my time on a dying business? Plus, the name Laser doesn't ring a bell. I think I'd remember a name like that."

She was holding back, but what? Why? I closed my eyes and focused. A fully-formed vision of Lyle and I parking out front of 20's, of sitting at a booth as an aging dancer defied gravity on a brass pole, of being ambushed and escorted into a dark basement, of having our bodies raped and discarded, it all rolled like film. I remembered eating lunch earlier that day at Block 16. Lyle won several thousand dollars in an ill-advised poker game with Charlie and Rube and their dockhands. The details were clear as if they'd happened days ago, but instead, here I was with Lyle and no one had subjected us to any torture. My whole body hurt in the way a late-stage alcoholic might hurt coming off the bottle. I thought 20's Showgirl was where I had to go, and I thought I never wanted to step foot in that place again. "If you didn't protest Showgirl, then why does someone there want you dead?"

Marva turned and fixed me with a glare. "Hey, honey, maybe you forgot, but you're the detective. Now, I'll say my piece to Mr. Ruskov when I see him, because he had no business prepping you about my situation. I didn't even tell him I was going to see Lyle, but what's done is done. It's your job to figure out who's after me. That's why I came." She dug in her purse and retrieved a stuffed envelope. "Everyday you keep me above ground you'll get one of these. Figure it out, will you?" With a flick of her wrist, she tossed the envelope on our desk. "My husband's scheduled to receive the Innovator's Award from the mayor at the end of the month. I'd like to be by his side. Make sure I get there. If you can take down the sick son of a bitch who's been leaving me nasty text messages, great. If not, at least keep him from following through on his threats."

She crossed the room with five powerful strides of her satin legs, opened the door and fled. Lyle followed. He lingered halfway out of the office and sighed. "What's gotten into you?"

I ignored his question, instead chasing Marva. She'd probably taken the elevator, since most people think stairs are for emergency use only, but down in the main lobby, there was no sign of her. I pushed through the doors to the sidewalk. A group of stumbling youths laughed, parting their merry crowd to pass me. A car engine fired across the street. Marva sat behind the wheel of a BMW sedan, bathed in apricot light from the flickering sign of the thrift store. She fastened her seatbelt, checked her mirrors and pulled onto the street. All the traffic signals down the strip are synchronized, and as one, they turned red before Marva had driven a block. I turned to go for Lyle, sour desperation in my stomach.

He'd already snuck up behind me. "Where are you going, huh?" He poured a handful of M&M's onto his palm. A kid riding a bike pulling a rickshaw with two girls in tow rang his bell as he pedaled past. Overhead a plane cut a trail across the humid night. Aromas of warm beer and fried food wafted from somewhere down the street.

12

Marva's Beamer had sped away when the signals turned green, but I still had a bead on her, six blocks ahead. She picked up speed by the elementary beyond Kremer Funeral Home.

I thumped the dash. "You're going to lose her."

"Remind me again why we're tailing our own client."

The problem with a guy like Lyle is he's willing to give attractive women benefit of the doubt. The way he saw it, if she looked good, she must be good, which didn't work so well for him a couple years back when Lani Boots invited him to her place for cocktails and an icepick through the ear. Don't ask. Before the first snowstorm each winter, he swears he hears Boots cackling in the northerlies. "Something tells me Marv only gambles with loaded dice."

He unwrapped a root beer Dum Dum and wedged it between his teeth and cheek. "Then we better not press a bet for the outside numbers."

"Not with the house edge."

He accelerated as we passed the post office, and when Marva

turned left on 72nd, he floored the gas, punched the roof of his car and squealed a hard left across traffic through a red.

I'll fault Lyle for a thousand things, but in loyalty, he's blameless. I could practically see steam chugging from his ears as his brain spun, trying to understand why we were in pursuit of this woman who'd sought us in hopes of protection. He worked a bag of sunflower seeds to keep his mouth in check. I didn't exactly have an answer myself, and if you would've asked me that night, I might've told you I was halfway down the road to insanity.

Flares of recollection kept clawing at the nape of my neck: The center of emotion? The seat of logic? No one knew. Sometimes you don't know what you know, and you need a baseball bat to dislodge a stubborn hunch.

At Dodge, Marva's BMW hung right. We made it through on the same green arrow. I told Lyle to back off. "We don't want her to know she's got a tail."

Lyle cracked a can of RC Cola. He offered me a sip. I said I needed something stronger. He dug in his jacket pocket and produced a flask. "What about this Laser?" He took a nip, then passed me the flask.

I drained it. Magdalene burn on an empty stomach is unlike anything: better than making love and more satisfying than a hot shower. I rolled the window down to smoke. Lyle asked me not to, and I was in the mood to consent. I propped the unlit cigarette between my lips, the menthol filter cooling my mood.

We took the Dodge overpass. Everything in me wanted to wrench the steering wheel from Lyle's hand. Since childhood I'd had a recurring dream. I'm seated in the passenger seat of a driverless car. Or it's not exactly driverless, but I can't turn my head to see who's behind the wheel. The shopping centers and streetlights and road markers are barreling by in a blur. In the passenger side mirror sirens flicker red and blue. A single car paces us. The eight-story First National building whizzes by on my left, and a golden eagle shoots past, perpendicular to us. A gaping hole opens in the road. I want to scream but can't. It's no use trying to grab the steering wheel, and in an instant the car plummets through the hole in the road and nosedives for the underpass. At impact I awaken with a jolt and a severe headache. A lingering scent of burning rubber hung in my nostrils each time the dream visited. No matter what I tried, I could never alter outcome.

What's most disturbing is the dream began visiting me before the Dodge overpass had been built. My therapist could confirm this, since in 1992, the first year I had the dream, plans to construct the overpass hadn't been drafted. But if you ask him today he'll say he's pretty sure the road in my dream changed *after* the overpass was built, that the road before the overpass was built might've been the I-680 interchange or somewhere similar. I would tell him it had to be Dodge and ask him to describe his notes. Hadn't I mentioned the First National Bank building? 680 isn't close to that building. No matter how many times I told him I was destined to die on the overpass, which wasn't built for another fourteen years after I first had the dream, he and everyone treated my dream as nothing more than a metaphor for my fear of losing control.

My parents jumped at the chance to describe what a control-freak I was. If I didn't want to eat steak at Caniglia's Venice Inn, instead sitting in my chair with a glass of water and nothing else, my dad would ask why I thought I had my dream. When I scissored the grass around the raised flowerbed in our front lawn instead of weed whipping because I hated the stain the trimmer left on the bricks, my mom would ask if I didn't think I had control issues. Don't get me started on how people would've treated me and my dream differently if I'd been a boy.

But listen, private investigators don't have pasts, especially not pasts that reach to their youth. Part of the mystery of a good PI is that no one knows where she comes from. She appears on the page with five seconds of prior history, the notion of a leg kicked up on a table or a knife pulled from a purse or the trace of tobacco on her breath. PIs do have futures, though, and the dream was meant to prepare me for mine.

Marva took the exit for 156th Street and bore south. By then, I couldn't control the urge and lit a cigarette. Lyle offered his standard rebuttal, "My car," and I ignored him as always. Next, we turned right on Pacific. We meandered through suburbia: winding sidewalks at either end of the streets, green lawns, concrete retaining walls cut to resemble stone, smatterings of cloned, two-story houses with blue-gray asphalt shingles, and the occasional strip mall with restaurants, coffee shops, knickknack stores, and corporate businesses. I opened my phone and checked Twitter. @ADDiane posted something about #MeToo, which bored me enough to close the app.

Lyle turned left into a subdivision. I missed the sign that marked the entrance, but Marva continued on, left here, right there, left again before parking in the driveway of a two-story brick home with brass address numbers nailed to the trim above an oak-plank garage door.

Million dollar homes are an exception in Omaha. There's a patch of them in the Dundee neighborhood, some in the heart of Westside, a handful on the outskirts of Bennington, and a few in Bloomfield Hills by the Westroads Mall. Lyle voiced what we were both thinking. "She's got money to burn."

"Money only matters if you're alive to spend it."

Lyle parked a half-block away. At moments like these I wonder how people don't know they're being tailed. How often have I been on an innocuous errand, noticed a car in my rearview, tracked it matching me turn-for-turn and concluded I was being followed only to shake it at a turn into a grocery store parking lot? The mind conjures danger and intrigue at all the wrong moments. Ask any woman who's willingly accompanied a first date to his apartment for a drink. Too often, it's the ones we don't suspect who force us into places we fight not to go.

The garage opened and Marva pulled her BMW inside. It closed behind her. Lyle cut the engine and killed the headlights. He peeled a banana. "What now?"

My mind said, *Find Laser*. I shook off the thought. In all likelihood he was at the topless club, and I knew where he'd be in the morning, or I was going insane. I didn't want to believe I was too scared to return to a place I dreamed I'd been murdered. In the meantime, I might learn a little more about what we were dealing with. "How about knocking on her door?"

"Oh, yeah." Lyle devoured half the banana in a single bite. "Like, 'Hey, we forgot to ask you a few questions.' Maybe she'll invite us in for drinks. 'Help yourself.'"

"Don't be an ass."

He crumpled the banana peel in his fist and chucked it into the backseat. "I'm an ass for thinking it's strange that we just followed our client like she's a suspect, but you're just fine keeping me in the dark."

I massaged the bridge of my nose. Across the street a possum waddled through a lawn to remind anyone watching that we had stolen its habitat. "We're both in the dark." I wanted to explain the nagging sense of déjà vu. I wanted to call it the witch in my brain. "Look, you have to agree Marva gave us nothing to go on and—"

Lyle stretched his jaw around the first bite of a runza sandwich. "She gave us nothing to go on because you treated her like a terminal disease."

I wanted to say I'd seen it all, but knew he wouldn't understand. "Bullshit. I pressed her because she wasn't willing to say what was really bothering her."

He unwrapped a chocolate snack cake. "You didn't give her a chance. Just because Ruskov gave you the scoop doesn't mean you had to shake her down, huh? Since when did you decide dictating the situation to a client was a good idea? Aren't you the one who always says we're different because we actually listen?"

"*Listen*?" I opened the door and stepped into the night. "She's not talking." The possum that had stopped to explore an exposed tree root in a nearby lawn fell on its side and played dead. I crossed the street.

Lyle came up at my shoulder and wrapped his hand around my elbow. "You're out of your mind."

"Tell me something I don't know."

He popped a circus peanut. "Look. You don't want this broad, with all her money, to give us the boot."

"Women don't like being called broads."

"And men don't like women to be cold-ass bitches, but some things never change, huh?"

There's a good chance we might've had a cleansing, knock-down-dragout there in Marva's neighborhood, the kind of fist-fight, hair-pulling, eye-poking wrestle that would've led to a temporary forgiving and a shared emotional bond if, at that moment, an old woman hadn't stepped onto her stoop and asked what we were doing.

Lyle turned on a cheesy grin and dropped the package of circus peanuts in the grass: half surprise, half performance. "Your neighbor hired us to investigate a stalker."

I elbowed Lyle in the ribs because he had no business telling a stranger ours. The first rule of private investigation is simple: always ask questions. The rule implies every other important skill a PI needs. If you're always asking questions, you're not answering them. Asking questions means looking for answers. If you're always asking questions, you're never accepting details at face-value. By breaking the first rule of private investigation, Lyle set in motion every terrible consequence Marva's case would bring into our lives.

13

Mrs. Stefevater had a face like a half-eaten apple dried in the sun. Her spine curved slightly forward, and she walked with a limp. She'd watched the world evolve, she said, for seven-decades and change. Her fascination with the microwave—she called it the pivot on which the great human machine tottered—set the tone of our conversation. "You can clearly trace all of human thriving in relation to the microwave. Thousands of years, folks cook over fire, then one day some bright-eyed bucko comes along and says, 'Why spend hours stoking a fire when you can pop dinner in the old box and eat in minutes?' and I'll be goddamned if every dollar spent since hasn't been to save a person minutes. It's why we live longer. We're saving time. Save it now. Spend it later. My lans! Just think how old we'd be if we weren't saving all this time right now. And there's the personal automobile and the personal computer, and the personal telephone. Nobody's got to waste a precious minute calling a landline and asking for Suzy or Joe cause Suzy and Joe have their own phones. That's more time saved. My grandson created a Facebook page for me. Can you believe it? Says, 'Grandma, you can write me a letter on Facebook any time you want, and you don't even have to wait for the post-man. You can save all the money you spend on stamps.' And I say, 'God bless you, Samwise,'—that's what I call my grandson Sam— but anyways, I'm thinking everyone's saving time and money. Just look how old and rich I am. I got more time than I know what to do with, and money to burn. Mircrowaves and Facebook, count me in."

Lyle was swooning over Mrs. Stefevater, because she had a big bowl of cut fruit she'd pulled from the refrigerator. He mowed through cantaloupe balls and watermelon balls and honeydew slices. I figured the honeydew was sliced to save time, but maybe that's just context and conjecture.

I enjoyed listening to Mrs. Stefevater's ramblings. Her house was a museum of flea market knick-knacks. The late Mr. Stefe-vater had built parallel shelves that ran the length of the living room at eye-level, and Mrs. Stefevater had filled those shelves with carved figurines from indigenous tribes: grazing buffaloes the size of a fist, miniature canoes, cranes and herons, bullfrogs. She'd collected glass figurines from small towns where Swedish pride and German heritage were still robust topics of conversation. Above the shelves of knick-knacks were painted portraits of prairie landscapes. If it all sounds tacky for a woman of wealth, I suppose it was, though somehow the clutter harmonized. I could've studied the cream tones in her wallpaper and the copper tinged lighting for hours, but my sense of urgency egged at the edges of my nerves. My luck seemed reasonably well-assured in that the old lady was a smoker and offered us each a Lucky Strike. I accepted, and savored the smoke. "You said you saw a big SUV stop in front of Marva's house last night?"

"Oh, dear. Did I say that?"

"Yes." Lyle wore a contented grin and dribbles of juice on his chin. "And you said Ransom came out and spoke with the driver for a while."

I shaped the ash on my cigarette. "You said you keep a close eye on the neighborhood and that that SUV didn't belong to anyone living around here."

"That's right. Yes. My brain's maybe not saving as much time as it used to. I remember. A big gold abomination, it is. Stopped in front of Ransom's house three nights running. Sat there in front of the driveway and just coughed exhaust. No one ever got out of that big damn car, and when I called Ransom, he said not to worry because since he was working on some highfalutin medical breakthrough a lot of admirers wanted to pay their respects."

I finger-traced a figure-eight on my palm. "But you didn't see it that way?"

Mrs. Stefevater stabbed her cigarette into a porcelain ashtray with sleepy kitten figurines tracing the rim. Smoking made adorable. "No admirers I know have to pay respects three nights in a row. Not to mention them tinted windows. Lordy no! No self-respecting citizen of America tints their windows."

Lyle finished the melon and eyed the bowl like it was enchanted and might materialize a new supply. "You said the driver had mean intentions. What makes you think that?"

"Aren't you listening, sonny? The car had tinted windows."

I yawned. "You didn't see anything specific to make you think the driver meant harm?"

"Like the barrel of a rifle sneaking through a cracked window?"

I needed a drink to rouse me. "Sure or—"

Mrs. Stefevater interrupted, "Honey, this aint the movies. I'm just saying a car that big at that time of night."

"Did you happen to notice any details that might help us identify the car?" Lyle opened a box of melba toast. "Like a license plate, or the car's make and model?"

"CRNHSK1. Something like that. Chevy Suburban. Gold paint and tinted windows."

I snatched my phone and copied the details into its notepad app. "You're sure on that?"

"Honey, there's a million Husker fans in this damn city, but I'm gonna guess there's only one gold Suburban matches those plates. Now I'd bet my whole personal fortune he aint no admirer, and Mr. DeLonghi's only trying to be brave, acting so calm. No ma'am. Someone's got an axe to grind. Way I see it."

That term *axe to grind*... "How long did they talk?"

Mrs. Stefevater coughed smoke. "Five, ten minutes each go around. Not more."

Lyle said, "And Ransom sounded calm when you talked to him?"

The proper procedure from there would've been to ask more questions. How well did Mrs. Stefevater know the DeLonghis? Had she ever noticed other strange events surrounding her neighbors? Did she report any of what she saw to the police? I asked none of these questions. A driving urgency pulled me toward the door. I stood, thanking her for the cigarette and her time. Lyle shot me a wounded glance. He wanted to linger.

Mrs. Stefevater smiled. "Thank god for the microwave. Because elsewise I mightn't have been able to afford you a piece of my evening to chat." Her eyes rounded in mock seriousness. "You think Mr. DeLonghi's in danger?"

I meant to give her the standard, *It's hard to tell*, shtick but Lyle took up her question: "It's Marva who's in danger." He came right out with the details, how Marva had been receiving threatening text messages, how she'd had a series of near-misses that read a lot like planned accidents, how she'd come to us confused and afraid.

"Oh my." Mrs. Stefevater tugged a ringlet of her hair. "That's terrible." She pinched Lyle's ear and handed him a small bag of jellybeans. "At least Ransom's not in danger. But I sure hope you can stop whoever's behind this mess, Mr. Kupchoonik. I'd hate to see that dear man grieved by a tragedy to his wife."

14

After our visit with Mrs. Stefevater a stakeout had lost its appeal. Lyle wanted a six-pack of cold beer and a plate of tacos. I wanted a solid Twitter binge and a hot shower. An uncharacteristic cool front had pushed across the city, and I envied Lyle his perpetual jacket. Most of the time I had to bite my lip to keep from harassing him about wearing a coat in ninety-degree weather. He'd said, years ago, that his body ran colder. I ragged on him to exercise. At the very least he should've seen a doctor and gotten on blood pressure meds.

We drove across town for Dos De Oros. Lyle ordered a dozen chile verde tacos and two bottles of Jarritos Mandarin. He spiked the soda with Magdalene. I ate until my teeth numbed and cold sweat beaded on my brow. Lyle's eyes dimmed to a dumb milky glaze.

We called The Shotz. "Hey, Mikey. I've got you on speaker here with Luke."

From his side of the line an echo like sticks breaking fed back. "Who died?"

"Nobody, Mikey. But we need a solid."

"*A solid?*"

I leaned into the speaker. "How you doing, Shotz?"

"Just bought a Playstation 5 with my citation quotas so I can't complain."

I gave Lyle a friendly nudge with my elbow. "Speeding tickets?"

"Actually popped a chick driving nude. She couldn't understand why that was a problem. On the DL, neither can I, but laws are laws. Eight hundred bucks."

Some chick! At times I withhold comment. "How about you run a plate for us?"

"A license plate?"

"No. A plate of spaghetti." Lyle licked his lips. "Yeah. Dipshit. A license plate."

"Watch your tone. I might arrest you. City always needs revenue."

"You'd be doing me a favor. Putch could use a few hours behind bars to cool his heels."

Lyle reclined his seat a notch and closed his eyes. "Last time I sat in a cell I ended up dating a hooker for three months. Mind if I skip, huh?"

"Seriously," Mikey said, "you just need me to run a plate?"

I crossed my fingers. "That's it."

"My lucky day."

Mike Shotz would never forget when we asked him to help us bury Dickie Hollars. The police could never pin Dickie for the big one. His name came up with every grisly murder: the blood and guts, the mass shootings, the concrete shoes. They even tried the old Al Capone, but the guy's taxes were Irish Spring clean. Then Lyle and I ran into a city engineer who'd gotten in a bit of betting trouble. The little man's book grew a few lines too long, too much red, and some goons came along to sell him a plot in the cemetery. Stupidity and luck saved the engineer's life at the cost of a broken femur. Not many people know this, but doctors will attest, when the femur bone cracks, a person often loses consciousness. At that moment, the heart will skip about five beats. Doctors refer to it as a resurrection injury. A couple kinds of head trauma will flatline a person too, but those usually lead to brain damage. At any rate, the goons presumed the engineer dead and went their way, leaving the stiff for the police. Instead, a dog walker found the engineer's body and called 911. When the engineer came to, a few days later, his first call was to us. He said he had evidence Dickie Hollars had sent goons to murder him. It took us twelve hours, a bottle of Magdalene, a Reuben Sandwich—Lyle—and a pack of smokes— me—to shoot holes through the engineer's so-called evidence. We ran with Plan B instead. Dickies's goons agreed to meet us at Standing Bear Lake for a "discussion." Lyle said if Dickie was there he was going to end him. I wished Lyle good luck and said we should better bring the engineer's money just in case. The engi- neer pulled a payday loan, which was a bad solution for squaring debt but not our problem since he owed us too. Loan sharks, I think, gave the engineer a heart attack a few months later, and the engineer never paid us. So but Dickie was at the lake, and I still don't think Lyle meant to go through with his threat, except one of the goons got hot about the engineer's debt appreciating. Words were exchanged, a shot was fired, and the smoke cleared. The engineer, in a wheelchair, went rolling into the night with his bag of cash. I knifed a goon in the throat. The other goon shot himself in the stomach—we still don't know how—and Lyle landed on top of Dickie, windpipe meet elbow. During all that, a mother nursing her baby in a house nearby called the police in response to the gunshot, and it was Mike Shotz who responded to the 10-49. We obeyed when the voice said "Hands up!" and Lyle's mouth started running freeway. It helped that Shotz was known as the least reasonable cop in Omaha, that he'd been moved off the downtown squad for his tendency to escalate tense encounters, that he was known for his vigilante appetite. He gaped at Dickie, dead in the grass, with a foot of sod hacked from the ground and asked how we'd managed to dig so much without a shovel. I indicated my knife, open on the ground where I hated to see it because that knife didn't deserve either what it had been used for or to be abandoned at my feet. Mikey got a shovel from his car and told us how it was going to be, and of course, no one ever heard from Dickie Hollars again, and we paid Mikey favors for a year until Lyle saved his life with a little thing called CPR. I've never been so thankful to a stray peanut shell floating in a cup of beer in my life, and now when I picture Mikey sprawled on the concourse at Rosenblatt Stadium, Lyle on hands and knees swiping the mouth and giving chest compressions, I can't help but visualize a halo over Lyle's head. Anyway, debts squared, we had a good thing with Mikey so long as we didn't bug him when he and his wife were on the fritz, which seemed to be most of the time.

He ran the license plates we gave him, but they belonged to a Janet Hamlin, Mercedes C-Class Sedan. She had no criminal background, no encounters with the police, no rap sheet. I crawled her social media profiles for a familiar face: found nothing.

Lyle dug a coin from his pocket and flipped it. "Janet Hamlin, huh?"

I snatched his coin and pocketed it. "Maybe our perp stole the license plates. We're looking for a Gold Suburban."

In the background Shotz's wife screamed his name. He cleared his throat. "Gotta go. Sorry I wasn't more help."

One dead end led to another, and we had time to burn before the confrontation at Christian Nobel. Lyle rubbed his eyes. "I need sleep."

I punched his shoulder. "Sleep now and by the time you wake up Marv'll be dead."

"Take it easy, Mike Tyson. Don't you think you're being a little dramatic?"

"How about I quit smoking if I'm wrong and you stayed up for no reason?"

He shoved half a cake donut down his throat. "Don't make promises you can't keep."

"I never do."

We drove back to Marva's place and parked a ways off, where Mrs. Stefevater couldn't see if she got the mind to snoop. One second-floor window shone in the DeLonghi house. Someone had as much trouble sleeping as I did. "Insomnia's a metaphor for guilt."

Lyle massacred a carrot. Flecks clung to the corners of his lips. "What are you guilty of?"

"You've been there for most of it."

"I don't have any problems sleeping." He peeled the lid from a yogurt cup and swiped a fingerful into his mouth. "Look, I'd be a moron not to point out there's something strange going on. Even if Ruskov called you with the lowdown, your knowledge of Marv's situation is eerie. But right now you're tottering over the edge. If you're so worried about her getting bumped tomorrow, why are we wasting time here, huh? If it's like you say, we might as well get some shut-eye, hit the streets rested tomorrow morning."

I almost consented. Now that I knew what to look for at Regency, we'd have the jump, but curiosity got me, and I told Lyle to wait in the car. "Rest your eyes. I'm going to see if I can get a look inside that window."

Lyle spat the shell of a sunflower seed into his palm. "That's the dumbest idea I've ever heard. You don't think they'll hear you climbing around on their roof, huh?"

I ignored him and eased out of the car. The night was cool enough to give me goosebumps, or it was my anticipation of trouble. I crept across the lawn and slipped behind a juniper shrub next to the stoop. A barrier of river rock encircled the foundation. It made for loud lurking. I slipped my shoes off. Around the side of the house, there was one drain spout and a vine trellis. I tested the drain spout, but it was flimsy in the tradition of new-build construction.

A six-foot post-and-slat fence separated the sideyard from the back. The gate was padlocked. Just as I hopped the fence, headlights illuminated the side of the house. I thought Lyle decided to leave without me, but irrational fears had a certain stench to them. More likely one of Marva's neighbors was arriving home, or Ransom had been out and was returning.

In either case, I'd cornered myself. If the car belonged to one of the neighbors, they'd notice Lyle's parked out front, and if the car belonged to Ransom, he'd question a rusted Oldsmobile parked on his curb. I ran toward the back of the yard and hid behind a maple tree. A moment later Marva's kitchen illuminated, which answered the question about who the headlights belonged to.

I was just devising a plan to flee by the yard backing up to Marva's when a winded grunt followed a loud thud. Someone laughed. "How's that feel, smart guy?"

Peeking around the tree, I considered the voice—almost familiar. A man stood over Lyle, who lay in the fetal position on Marva's porch. Time seemed irrelevant, because I couldn't make sense of the scene. How had Lyle so quickly been captured?

The man kicked Lyle in the face. I stifled a gasp. Not only had the blow come unexpectedly, but as the man had kicked Lyle, I recognized his violent shape. The tattoos climbing his neck. The gold, wire-framed glasses, the shaved head, the bony frame strapped by sinews of muscle. That explained who had pulled up to the house, and it suggested Laser had killed Marva on his way through. How had our being there changed the outcome so drastically?

Laser spoke to Lyle in a low tone. I strained to hear, but caught little: "finding out," and "cutting it close," and "sloppy work." Was he taunting my partner? Did he somehow know about us? Lyle lay fetal, sucking shallow rapid breaths. Laser spat on him and kicked his face a second time. I'd left my purse behind, but found my hand already wrapped around my knife. Armed, my tactical disadvantage still glared. If I delayed, I knew what Laser was capable of, but if I failed to overpower him—

I centered my nerves and focused on the moment.

If you're right in the main, you're wrong in the minutia. When Laser removed a long-barreled pistol from his waistband, I leapt forward.

He slammed the pistol butt on Lyle's mouth. Teeth skittered across the porch. "Stop!"

My body obeyed. Had he seen me? Porchlight illuminated my boots in the grass, but the rest of me still lingered in shadows. Laser rubbed his jaw like sympathy pains. "I didn't want her seeing this." He released the pistol's safety.

I chanced one more step, no time for more. Close enough for an accurate throw, I hurled my knife. It rotated a single time. The blade sunk to the hilt in the hollow of Laser's cheek. The pained expression on his face recalled the somewhat surprised stare of the old man from *American Gothic*. Laser fell hard, legs over head. His arms flung up, tossing the pistol as he tumbled off the porch and thumped into the shrubs.

The rest happened so fast. Someone pushed open the screen door. His baritone startled me, even though he managed only two words: "Who the—"

The pistol hit the porch railing, discharging a single shot before falling into the bushes beside Laser. The man in the doorway fell, a stray bullet through the center of his chest. Even as my feet pulled me across the lawn and up the porch steps, I knew it was too late.

15

MIKE SHOTZ TESTIFIED AGAINST ME IN COURT. HE told the jury I'd requested information pertaining to the DeLonghis. For his unknowing role in a triple-homicide, OPD revoked his badge, but found him innocent of criminal conspiracy. Still, the very-much-alive-Marva won a seven-million-dollar lawsuit against the city of Omaha when a judge ruled the police had misused their resources. I was sentenced to twenty-five years in prison. Larry Surlman, known by his coworkers and friends as Laser, was buried at Prospect Hill. Municipal funds paid for his plot.

I shared a cell with a woman named Betsy Davis, formerly a seventh-grade teacher. She'd molested her students. Thirteen-year-old boys know more than most people credit them, but consenting to sexual activity with a forty-year-old shouldn't fall in that category.

Betsy hung around the yard as often as she could, huddled in well-lit corners, keeping an eye on the inmates, because she heard the things said about her. At least one person knows how—though no one confessed—but one day someone hung her from the risers in the yard. A guard found her with her tongue lolling out and graffiti carved in her forehead: *CHIMO.*

My next cellmate was Annis Pim. We got on fine. She'd lost her temper when she found her husband lying with another woman. Some murders are reasonable, and Annis was released after a year.

Debbie Lenvil was my last cellmate, inmate 047468113. She heard voices. The voices told her she'd been framed: too bad no one else would listen. Debbie told me what the voices thought of me. I was a kind soul, a lesbian, the reincarnation of Queen Elizabeth II, had nice teeth and healthy ovaries. Some of these details may be accurate.

You might think a woman like Debbie belonged in a mental hospital, but she had an ability to converse with her voices. They kept Debbie safe. Mental hospitals were much more dangerous, they said, than state prisons.

Debbie and I played cribbage most nights after lights out. She'd spent three-months earnings at the commissary for the board and a deck of cards. Go Fish was her specialty, though. Debbie had defeated all the women in our cellblock at Go Fish more than we could count. Nobody agreed to play her after they'd lost a dozen times consecutively. I lost count of how many times she beat me, but I didn't mind because it made Debbie happy, and a happy cellmate is a valuable commodity. That and I appreciated Debbie's gifts.

As someone afflicted by the supernatural, having died and been reborn, not once but twice, I respected invisible powers. And Debbie's voices fascinated me. They never stirred Debbie to anger unless anger was the appropriate response. More importantly, they entertained her. She had a fierce wit. I never knew anyone who won an argument against her and her voices. She would be laboring a point and one of the other inmates would sound off on an opinion that seemed to have persuasive merit, and Debbie would get that distant look in her eyes for a moment, sometimes longer—whole hours or afternoons—before she'd come back with an obscure detail that toppled her opponent's attack.

Given I'm not Debbie, I can't say exactly how her voices worked, work being an inexact term for beings that shared a cranial cavity with a woman of unique talents, but so far as I can tell, they had no boundaries. Regarding Go Fish, I believe that was how Debbie always won. Her voices could peer at anything, past or present. Though they didn't always comment on what they saw. "Do you have a seven?" Debbie would ask, and the inmate would curse and contemplate lying before revealing the seven.

Somewhere in the fifth year I disclosed my own supernatural experiences to Debbie. Her voices were extremely interested in the exact physical sensation of bleeding to death. They wanted to know if dying of slit wrists was simply itchy or if a person got very cold as blood depleted from the veins and arteries. As I recalled, I told Debbie and her voices, bleeding out had itched, mostly, but the more I considered it, it was very cold at the end: cold but sensual. Debbie's voices argued that the bleeding wasn't the sensual part.

Debbie thought I still had an opportunity to relive my failed investigation. This was something she told me during my sixth year. I'd behaved myself out of four years already. Debbie was in for two life sentences and she wouldn't tell me why. "What makes you think the loop isn't closed?"

She had a habit of biting her cuticles, and as she gnawed on her middle finger, it began to bleed. "The pendulum swings on Marva DeLonghi."

Debbie said the universe had tripped head over heels for Marva. Its great life force had fallen in love with a woman, which happens all the time, but is rarely defied. So long as Marva lived, the thread of time continued. It's useless narrating the rest of the discussion as the conclusion has already been stated. To this day, the details still bother me, but given I'll never know the precise mechanisms that govern the loop, Debbie's theory—or rather, Debbie's voices' theory—is as good as any I've proposed.

That was how, during my seventh year, on a cloudy day, while eating lunch in the cafeteria, Debbie told me I'd have a visitor. In all my years on the inside, no one had come to see me. Debbie took my hand in hers. "You owe me." I found myself hugged. "Don't forget about me." She drew a line across her throat. "Make it quick, honey. The guards'll drop you fast."

Then a voice called over the intercom for Miss Luke Mia. My strength nearly failed. Debbie had that distant expression in her eyes. "Don't get confused by what you hear. Lyle Kuputchnik's death is not your fault, even if you can't save him."

A guard led me to a small room with bare concrete walls. There a nurse searched my cavities and pronounced me safe. Before the guard opened the door into the visitors' common he told me to keep my hands visible at all times. Any suspicious behavior could land me in the infirmary so I'd better move slowly. The on-duty officer in the visitors' room would use his weapon if pressed.

Marva sat along the back wall, beneath a barred window. Time had spared her legs: elegantly muscled, slim-ankled, safe from the sun, free of age spots or varicose veins. I approached and sat. She offered a cigarette.

I declined, pointing to the NO SMOKING sign. "To what do I owe the pleasure?"

She said she wasn't sure what possessed her to come—a dream perhaps, a subtle urging from something like a voice in her head. She wasn't sorry for what she'd done, but something told her she owed it to me to show herself. It was out of character, but even sleeping drugs couldn't repair the sleep she was losing.

I should've skipped the formalities and dispatched her

instantly, but after so many years, I deserved answers. "You know, I thought he killed you."

"Who?"

"*Who*? Larry Surlman. Laser. Who? You're something. The guy you told the jury your husband hired as your personal bodyguard." I eyed the pack of cigarettes between us and begged my tongue to stop panting. "Would've been nice to know you'd hired a bodyguard in addition to private detectives, don't you think?"

Marva laughed so loud the other prisoners and their visitors stopped to glare at her. "I guess I didn't expect the detectives I hired to follow me like a suspect. So sue me."

As I often do when my brain works hardest, I tugged at my earlobe. "You know Laser meant to kill you, right? Your so-called bodyguard. He meant to hack you into pieces during your appointment at Christian Noble."

"That would've been—regrettable." Marva mimicked me, tugging at her own earlobe. "But no. You know? The only thing I regret is that my husband's death chained him to me." She resented being known as "the wife of" but had no other choice. The media feasted on her court testimony that he'd been a sacrificial hero. According to Marva, Ransom had uncovered a plot against her life and hired a bodyguard to protect her. In that story, her bodyguard, Larry Surlman, had thwarted Lyle's attempt to force the door on the night of the incident, but was fatally wounded in the effort. I then had attempted to finish what Lyle began, murdering Ransom who stood between me and Marva. His choice to stand between me had cost him his life and bought her the time needed for police to arrive. Proof of Lyle's intentions was exposed by the police who'd found an envelope of cash on his person at the time of death, payment for his involvement. Learning the identity of the payor who had "hired" Lyle was dismissed in the scope of the trial, because that's what you get when you're represented by a public defender matched against an elite team of prosecutors.

My hands were fists. Marva knew full-well how Lyle had come by that envelope. "What would've been so wrong with admitting you hired us?" I nearly lost my composure, but for the flutter of a vision, Debbie urging me to be careful. "Because of you, my partner died. Don't you even care that people think he was a murderer?"

"It's not like I could've brought him back to life by setting the story straight."

But I could bring him back. "And you're just fine with me wasting away in prison?"

Marva agreed it hadn't been the ideal outcome, but public sympathies had given her a voice. She'd established a human rights foundation, two environmental research teams, and a host of city programs aimed at aiding the underprivileged. If she took time to "set the record straight" couldn't I imagine the impact that might have on all she built? Wasn't one mistake worth all the good she'd achieved? "Maybe it's hard for you to see how one life doesn't balance the scale when weighed against all the progress this tragedy had afforded our city, but I'm certain if you think it over, you'll agree." She dug in her purse and produced a copy of Time Magazine. The headline labeled her a champion of justice.

"Crooked justice."

"Don't be trite." Her eyes flashed the cruelty I knew she hid beneath her calm demeanor.

"You're a coward."

"I knew you'd loath the sight of me. That's why I stayed away. Maybe that's weakness, but you're not the judge of me."

I agreed on all accounts and told her so. The truth hovered between us, and I meant to have it. "One thing makes no sense to me. You know Lyle and I only wanted to help you, but you let us take the fall. To me, that points to one conclusion. You're protecting the person who *did* want you dead. Why? Who was Laser to you really? Were you in love? Is that all this is, another tired infidelity?"

Marva bit her lip. "Honestly?" I read it as a slight slip, proof I'd touched something real. Sometimes we see what we need to see, not what's right before us. "I wouldn't touch that Neanderthal with a ten-foot pole."

Pressure mounted behind my eyes. "Then why?"

She pocketed the pack of cigarettes. "What does it matter?"

"My partner died looking for answers." I laid my palms on the table. "It's the least you could do to see that I get those answers." Dying for any reason was foolish, but I ached for Lyle that he'd given his life for this egomaniac. She may have played at depth with all her just causes, but scratch the skin and all there was a woman who craved attention.

She flicked her wrist in dismissal. "If he couldn't protect himself, he deserved to die."

Until that moment, I'd managed to check my rage, but the thought of killing Marva, when she spoke of Lyle so flippantly, awoke me from a stupor of self-pity. Marva was wearing this smug grin on her lips. And she was going off on how she'd been stocking away money into an account for me when I was released from prison, and wouldn't that be nice to have a little nest egg. She said something stupid about telling my story, on my terms, offering to introduce me to some important reporter who'd give my version, in my words, because by then her image would only benefit from a little grit, some uncertainty.

It didn't matter at that moment whether Debbie's conjecture on how the loop worked was correct. The only question that pounced on my mind as hard as I pounced across the table onto Marva, who met my weight with her arms outstretched, was how long I had before the guard would stop me. With my hands around Marva's neck, I flashed, for the first time in years, on Lyle's face. I'd thought of him constantly, but never imagined the sharp angles of his cheeks or the cleft in his chin or the stony blue of his eyes.

I can't say whether I believed I had a chance to see him again, because seeing him mattered less than avenging him. Perhaps I *could* open the loop again. Maybe I'd see Lyle, watch his hollow chest roll in laughter, but maybe revenge was enough. I knew he didn't deserve to die for a heartless bitch like Marva. And yes, I know labeling a woman bitch contradicts my belief about women's inherent power, but I can't deny feelings—not now, not ever.

I buried my thumbs in her eye sockets as her chair tipped under my lunging weight. She cracked her skull on the concrete floor, which probably did her in, but I didn't stop. I crouched on her body and treated her to the Dickie Special. The sucking of the trachea collapsing evokes copper pipes shuddering with air bubbles.

They say rubber bullets reduce civilian casualties, and I'm sure it's true, but tell that to my skull, which cracked, splattering blood and brain on the table where an elderly woman sat with a young woman in prison for stealing plasma televisions. Lucky for them, they'd never remember the feeling of entrails staining their shirts.

In case you're wondering, the officer used his gun as a last resort. He'd followed protocol by discharging his Taser first. I can only assume I had help. Maybe some distant voices channeled determination into me. I don't know. What I do know is that as my limp body rolled off Marva's dead body, my eyes began to cloud and the last thing I saw was a surge of voltage pulsing from my hip where the Taser's hooks had burrowed in my flesh.

16

I LEANED AGAINST THE BRICK FAÇADE OUTSIDE OUR office, while drawing figures of infinity in the air with my favorite four-inch pocketknife. My thoughts were as stained as my shoes from wandering every dark alley in Omaha. Muffled voices spoke on the other side of the door. Anger subdued questions of fear and love as I burned my fist white and bloodless squeezing the hilt of my knife. I burst through the door, even as a swirl of doubt threw my sanity into question. "Why won't you stay dead?"

I closed the space between Marva and me in two loping steps, swung my arm back, and drove the knife through the soft flesh of her throat, burying the blade in her brain. A fat lip was the least of her worries. She coughed blood. Her knees locked. She fell. My knife didn't deserve such a filthy burial.

Lyle was pointing a ham and cheese hoagie at me. His jaw hung slack, horror stretched his eyelids. "What. The. Fuck."

So much blood leaked from Marva's wound that it surfed the carpet before soaking in. "It had to happen this way. I can explain."

Lyle scampered to his feet and side-stepped to our desk. His shoe squelched in the tide of blood. He aimed the sandwich at my chest like an accusing finger. His other hand fumbled on the desktop until it wrapped around the base of our brass accounting lamp. He dropped his sandwich and pointed the green glass lampshade at me.

I wanted to hug him. That was the strongest impulse. Hug and be hugged. "I can explain." But I couldn't, because I had no idea what had come over me. We'd been through so much. I wanted to ask him if he remembered Nelly hanging from his neck by a towel. It was so clear how he'd died. His eyes bulging from their sockets. Did he have a headache from Laser's axe? What about the pressure from a crushed skull? The image of Laser's boot brought bile to my lips. "You're alive."

His gaze lingered on the sandwich, lettuce spilled incidentally, shocked green, and mustard on the carpet. Blood soaked the nylon pile in an expanding ring. "You just—" He swallowed hard. "You —" He searched for words that wouldn't come.

Try explaining the inexplicable. "I had no other choice."

He waved the lamp at me. "Give me one good reason not to call the police, huh?"

The truth would never come through. "Because I saved your life."

He raised his free hand to his mouth and licked the fingertips. "You just killed a woman who came to us for help, and you're saying you saved my life?"

This was something I could speak to. "Marva DeLonghi is a rich, entitled narcissist who trades on other people's well-being for her own gain."

The look of puzzlement on his face gave me hope. "You know who she is?"

Try explaining past lives. "I know everything worth knowing about her, and I know she'd let you die without thought."

"That doesn't give you the right to kill her."

His words framed the situation nakedly. They accounted for so little. "No one matters to Marva but Marva. She's no good, and we don't need her money."

"So this isn't even about me, huh? Who are you to decide whose money is good enough for us? Since when has integrity mattered to you?"

I recalled sitting with Ruskov at Burke's. "No. Oh my god. You're completely missing it." I stepped over Marva's body and reached for Lyle's shoulder. He jerked away and stepped back. I hadn't counted on him fearing me. "Marva was receiving all those nasty text messages, and she wanted to play dumb, but I think she knew who they were from. Oh, god—" A revelation unfolded I hadn't even considered until—"She wanted her husband dead. That's what this is all about."

Lyle dug in his jacket pocket and came up with a banana. He peeled it with his teeth and bit down. Him eating was a great sign. But when he pointed the banana at me, I felt the balance shift. "I know you want me to ask questions. I know how you are. Questions give you the control. 'Why Ransom?' I don't care. 'What's Marva's political agenda?' None of my fucking business. I care that you committed murder."

I felt pathetic in the way a child feels pathetic when the only control she has is to bench herself in the final game of a YMCA basketball tournament because she's afraid to shoot and knows how many parents are counting on the team to win. *I'm a liability out there, coach.* "It was either you or her."

"You can paint a turd in gold flake, but that doesn't change what it is."

I think I knew, right then, I'd lost. Chalk it up to a good effort. I could explain, I was going to explain, but I knew how it would go. "Fine. You want to know how I know. I know because I've lived this day before. Three times already. This is the fourth. And every time, you die. You get raped, you get axed, your skull gets—"

Lyle lowered the lamp, let it fall at his feet on top of the sand-wich. A tense moment followed when I thought he believed me. "Great. So you're crazy. Too much bourbon. Drugs? I've wondered. The way you're out at all hours roaming the alleys. I didn't want to believe it." He buried his hand in his pocket and brought it back out holding his phone. "Mental hospitals aren't the worst. I don't think."

"Explain to me how I could know so much about Marva if I'm lying to you."

Lyle laughed an empty sounding laugh, one full of breath and humorless. "That's kind of how I imagine the clinically insane person might reason."

"I'm serious. How about this? What if I take you to the river docks? I can tell you who'll be there, and what they'll be doing, and then if you still don't believe me, we can go to the Walgreens by your house tomorrow and catch the Cereal Burglar."

Lyle unlocked his phone. "Fantastic." He hovered his finger over the dial icon. "And then we can place a bet on the Cubs game, huh? Because I'm sure you know the final score."

It hadn't occurred to me that I'd seen the future so much as that I was stuck in the past. "I never thought to look."

"Sorry if I'm not so sure, but maybe you're forgetting there's a dead body in the room and that doesn't exactly give me confidence that you're stable."

"I did this for you."

"You really seem to believe that."

"I do."

"I *have* always wanted to meet the Cereal Burglar. He's some-thing of a hero to me."

"She. Never mind. I know that. And we don't even have to—"

Lyle tapped his phone icon, punched three numbers on the screen and raised the phone to his ear. I moved to slap the phone out of his hand, but he pushed me. I fell onto the soaking bloody carpet. A nasally voice chirped something on the other end of his call. Lyle said he had a murder to report. I stood and flexed my hands into fists then stretched my fingers until the bones stung. You can't expect reason to prevail. I lunged for the office chair. Lifting it, I swung just as casually as unzipping a fly. One of the plastic caster wheels bounced off the side of Lyle's head. His body crumpled.

I slipped the phone from his hand and ended the call. Chainsaws revved between my ears. My lips and tongue were dry strips of old leather. I had a pair of handcuffs in the closet, buried beneath boxes of old case files.

Whatever I meant to do next hadn't come to me, but I knew I had to get Lyle to his car. We had to disappear before the police came and found a dead woman's body on our office floor. I couldn't find the cuffs, but behind a bottle of shiraz I found a roll of burlap twine. Before I tied Lyle, I contemplated the envelope in Marva's purse. *Taking her money was never the issue,* I thought, as if I needed to justify myself before Lyle.

Fingerprints didn't matter. Blood smeared my arms to the elbows as I dug through her bag. A minor problem. I slipped the cash into my back pocket then tied Lyle hand and foot. Only when I went to lift him did I realized how limp his body was. His eyelids hung open and his eyes stared coolly at the ceiling. His jaw sagged. I'd arrived on-scene at murder sites while a victim was still loose with primary flaccidity, but I'd never touched a corpse prior to rigor mortis setting in. It had to have been a perfect blow to the temple when I hit him with the chair—perfect being less than an ideal word since the result was the opposite of what I'd intended.

I shook Lyle's shoulders. His head lolled and his tongue flopped over his teeth. I've replayed it a thousand times in my head. Could I have said something differently? Maybe if I'd started over I could wait to kill Marva until she'd left our office. But I knew. Marva had to live.

My eyes drifted over the room, pausing on my knife hanging from Marva's throat. I wanted it with me when I left, but freeing it from her skull was harder than expected. Her head joggled like a puppet when I tugged the hilt. I braced my weight over her ear with one hand and pulled with the other. When the blade finally released, it gave with a sound like an apple splitting. I cleaned the metal on my pants and stared at my reflection in the chrome glimmer.

A knock at the door startled me. "Yes."

"Police. Open up."

I hoped it would be quick. I stood, ran bloody hands through my hair, and cleared my throat. A flare lit my mind, sparking questions into the dead night. *Suppose you're mentally unstable? Clinically insane? What if it's all hallucination? Or none of it?*

I twisted the knob, pulled the door open, and stepped back. The officer's face melted from curious to horrified. I lifted my knife to give him reasonable cause.

17

MY THOUGHTS WERE STAINED SHOES, WANDERING every dark alley in Omaha. I leaned against the brick façade outside our office, soaked in half-recollection, outlining figures of infinity in the air with my pocketknife. Two voices spoke in muffled tones beyond the wall: both love and fear. I flicked my knife closed, dropped it in my purse, and turned the knob. When I entered, the conversation paused.

Lyle pointed a ham and cheese hoagie at me. A smile formed around shreds of lettuce and a dribble of mustard. "Luke! We were just talking about you."

She had yellow hair. She wore high heel shoes. Lipstick was everywhere. "Marva, I'm Luke. You won't remember me, but we've met. Some people call me Little Cancer, and not just because I was born in July."

Her fat lip enhanced the seductive quality of her smile. "You weren't kidding." She looked at Lyle. "Your partner's a real charmer."

He took his time chewing a bite of sandwich. "She grows on you."

"Like—"

"A tumor," I interrupted. "You've said that before."

My cigarettes were in my jacket, but before I'd retrieved them Lyle said, "At least let me finish eating."

I slipped the hard pack of Sphere Menthol from my pocket and tapped the clamshell in my palm. "Sorry."

I lit up and tossed the pack on the desk next to the rent bill. "I bet I know what you're going to say." I studied Marva. "But I'll ask anyway. Does the name Larry Surlman mean anything to you?"

"The catfish philosopher? My husband's long-lost buddy? What's he have to do with anything?"

Sometimes a surprise can hit like strong drink. Other times you need a strong drink to catch your breath from a surprise like a left hook. "Say that again."

I returned with two tumblers of Magdalene bourbon neat, and one on the rocks. "I know you prefer wine, but we're out." I shed my jacket because it was hot, and because at some point I always discarded it. Lyle's body ran cold, and he always over-dressed, but I couldn't remember now why I'd been wearing a jacket on a muggy Omaha evening.

"Is this some kind of parlor trick?" Marva received her tumbler of bourbon and dispatched it with greed.

"I was wondering the same thing, huh? How do you two know each other?"

Marva tongued the rim of her glass and shrugged. "Never seen her in my life."

"Not true." I needed to process my shock on the express. "We met at a protest. Talked for hours about animal cruelty. You told me you were close to filing a suit against Jane Friedmanhoff at Christian Nobel Furs."

"Um—"

"Your husband's working on a drug patent for PharmTech.

THE 9 LIVES OF MARVA DELONGHI

Revolutionary sleep medication: Vivifica. You're always going out with him, and that's how you met Philipe Ruskov. Hot night. Box fans. Troughs of ice. Remember?"

"You weren't—"

"Don't worry. I know how it feels. You were sloppy drunk that night. Confessed a drinking problem. Wasn't it just last week you downed eight bottles of wine before passing out in bed? I think Ransom—that's your husband's name right?—he found you lying in your own puke."

Marva flinched like I'd struck her. "No."

"You don't have to be embarrassed."

Lyle sipped his drink. He walked toward the closet. "I think I remember where we might have a bottle of wine."

"You might be right." I snapped a glance at Marva. "Have a seat." I eyed the armchair behind her.

She obliged, the first time I'd seen her off balance. It almost made her tolerable.

When Lyle had uncapped the wine and brought Marva a glass, and after he'd refilled our tumblers with Magdalene we sat. I savored a mouthful of bourbon. Down on the street outside our office people walked arm in arm, hand in hand, stumbled, jogged, tripped, laughed, from bar to bar. For eight blocks from Radial Highway to 66th street, shops lined Maple. Most served liquor and beer; a few were restaurants; one served coffee and pastries, and several traded in clothing or shoes or both. Few of the bars lasted long under one ownership, and only The Waiting Room, where bands with names like Potassium Chainsaw and The Rubik's Cube Conundrum played, and Haney Shoes, owned by a man named Doug who hunted deer for sport, had outlived a decade.

Lyle crunched on a bag of wasabi peas, offering first Marva then me a handful. We both declined, opting instead to refill our drinks. I reckoned in silence with my failed attempts to save Marva's life, mourned my failed attempts to save Lyle's, and lit another cigarette. "I think you need to tell us everything you know about Mr. Surlman."

"You don't have enough wine. And my husband will be expecting me shortly."

"Maybe you're used to getting everything you want, but if you're interested in living through tomorrow, you need to quit acting like your problem is a case of dry mouth, put your drink down and tell us what we need to know."

Lyle crumbled the empty package formerly containing his peas. "Hey, Gestapo. Ever heard that honey catches more flies than shit?"

"I'm not the one calling Mrs. DeLonghi a fly."

"I didn't—"

"Fine. You want to piddle around, come find me when you're serious about preventing a murder." I stabbed my cigarette into the ashtray and stood to leave.

Lyle asked me to stay. Marva had kicked her glass and was mainlining from the bottle. "You want to know about Larry, you'd better get a pillow, because his story'll put you to sleep."

"I've got insomnia."

Marva looked at Lyle. He nodded. She said it was a little confusing in the first place, because she was sure Larry's name had been Reed something, and before I got all lippy with her again, she wanted me to know she hadn't really been into alcohol until lately. But anyway, Reed or Larry or whoever, her husband swore she remembered the name wrong, Larry had been at the University of Nebraska for law. It wasn't the most prestigious program, but he apparently had a fear of state lines. When he was a child his family went to Arizona and he got stung by a scorpion and spent a week in the hospital. "They don't have scorpions in Nebraska is kind of the punchline here." And so Larry got the idea he was safe as long as he didn't leave home. Still, he apparently always had to beat the trash out of his shoes before he laced up.

During his sophomore year he married a woman named Melina—"maybe they got divorced, I can't remember just now." They had a baby boy over Christmas, Junior year. Larry asked Ransom to be the boy's godfather, but six months later the baby died in his crib. Melina refused to leave her room for two months. She grew so thin her ribs clicked when she breathed. She refused any guests but Marva, which was how Marva met Ransom. By then, Larry—"I swear his name was Reed something"—had disappeared because he took the death of his baby so hard he couldn't stand to look at Melina. As the story went, Ransom had tried to keep in touch with his friend, but the guy wanted none of it. Then Ransom left for graduate studies in Louisiana where he interned for a scientist named Rinsce Shauerov.

There was maybe a letter somewhere, Ransom said, from the only correspondence he had had with Larry during those years, if he could only find it. Marva belched, lady-like, and it was apparent she'd finished her story.

I said I didn't see what was so boring about the story. If anything it was sad, but I turned to Lyle for support and saw he was snoring.

"Then you haven't seen him since college?"

"By the time I came around he was a fart in the wind. But like I said, I don't even think he was him. I mean, the more I think about it, I'm pretty sure the guy who married Melina was African American. I could swear his name wasn't Larry. I'm going to ask Ransom again."

"Why would your husband lie about a college friend?"

"Maybe he's embarrassed about befriending a deadbeat dock worker and wants to pretend the guy was at least a med school drop out."

"He doesn't strike me as the type who embarrasses easily."

"You clearly don't know him."

"The one I've—" I caught my tongue. "The one you've been telling me about, he sounds like an outgoing, altruistic, mixer."

"You're saying I'm lying to you."

Lyle's jaw worked over some feast in his dream as his leg twitched. I lit a fresh cigarette. "You're lying, yeah. I think the only thing you really feel comfortable doing is lying."

Marva peered into the bottom of her empty wine bottle. "Maybe I'm missing something, but I'm pretty sure you shouldn't call a prospective client a liar. Probably not good for business."

I laughed until I coughed. When I regained composure, Lyle had woken. I leaned forward. "If there was any way I could refuse your case, I'd give you the boot right now, but the truth is you're my responsibility in ways you couldn't begin to understand."

"What's that supposed to mean?"

"It means you wouldn't understand."

Marva aimed the empty bottle at my face. "In that case you better try being nice, because I can walk whenever I want."

"I know where you live."

Marva sucked her teeth. She clearly believed me, but couldn't explain it. "I'm not listed."

I related her general neighborhood. Her hands squeezed into fists. Lyle stood rubbing his eyes. "We wouldn't be detectives if we didn't have some tricks up our sleeves, huh?"

Marva's cheeks paled. Her eyes were slits. "This bitch doesn't have tricks up her sleeve. She's stalking me."

"Stalking you?" I thumped my chest. "I've got better things to do. At least I did before you came around. Now I'm stuck with you. But, hey, I've got an idea. How about you don't call anyone a bitch because it's demeaning, and the last thing any woman needs is another woman going around enforcing centuries of gender stereotypes."

"Blah, blah, big words." Lyle stood. "I need to take a leak."

For a moment, Marva and I stood on the same side of spite,

glaring at Lyle as he waddled to the bathroom. I cleared my throat when he'd closed the door. "What we both need to settle right now is that if we don't work together, neither of us gets what we want. You want to get to the bottom of some stranger danger, and I want to wake up tomorrow and the next day and the day after that. But if you don't cooperate, someone's going to hunt you down and murder you, and I can't let that happen."

It was Marva's turn to laugh, which she did, and I cringed at the sound. She had no humor. "You, I believe, are clinically insane. This is the last time I trust a stuffy old Russian." She rose. "Thanks for the wine."

She'd let herself out before Lyle flushed the toilet—which he did and then proceeded to run the sink for an eternity. He blew his nose, and by the time he'd opened the door I was sitting alone in the armchair where Marva had been.

He wiped his hands on his pants. "You chased her off, huh?"

"Guess so."

"That's all right. She'll come back." He dug in his jacket pocket and produced a manila envelope. "She gave this to me while you were getting our drinks."

Inside the envelope was a stack of bills. "Let me guess. Five grand."

"How'd you know?"

I hefted the envelope. The weight of money has always amazed me. A single bill is as insubstantial as air. Let it loose and it flutters away. But a duffle full of cash is heavier than a duffle full of firearms and ammunition.

18

LYLE WENT HOME TO SLEEP. I LINGERED ON VISIONS OF the street at night: first the drunk and jolly—those young twenty-somethings on dates or celebrating birthdays or promotions—the drunk and sloppy, who in their joy or sadness drink one too many drinks; the drunk and desperate who drank in sorrow, themselves abandoned by the night's victors, alone at a bar ordering another shot to puke in the curb—and worst, the drunk and destroyed, who needed alcohol for any reason until it overwhelmed and captured them.

I walked to Leo's Diner at first light and ordered a Fantasy Island. To the uninitiated, this is biscuits and gravy served over a bed of hashbrowns, topped with over-easy eggs, diced peppers, onions and ham. My eyes sagged with booze; my teeth ached. I paid and talked with Sandra, who had waited tables at Leo's since my childhood. She called everyone Hun, and though she'd never asked my name, she knew my life story.

Across the street I bought a pack of cigarettes from Big Bear Sinclair and chatted with Jessica. Her son had impregnated a girl and they were fighting over life and death. The father didn't want his daughter to ruin her life with a kid, but Jessica's son promised he'd take care of the kid, whatever it took. Jessica said she was kind of proud of her son's willingness to accept responsibility, but she wanted him to let the pregnancy go because raising kids complicated life.

My head felt like the cigarette butt I ground under heel in the parking lot. I had to talk myself through breathing. In several hours, Larry "Laser" Surlman would meet Marva at Christian Nobel Furs. I didn't want to be there. Instead, I texted Lyle and asked him to meet me at Walgreens in midtown. He lived within walking distance of that store in a renovated apartment building on 27th and Harney. I pulled up my rideshare app and contacted a driver. The man who picked me up claimed to know Warren Buffet. His car smelled like Juicy Fruit gum, which was as close to a connection as I could justify for a glorified taxi driver and the Oracle of Omaha. We all have dreams, I guess.

Lyle wasn't waiting for me, when I arrived. He hadn't texted back either. The witch in my brain, which I'd come to understand wasn't magic or even omniscient, told me Lyle was awake, so that led me to believe he was upset with me and pouting. When I brought him a snapshot of the Cereal Burglar unmasked, he might perk up.

I wandered the aisles of the store with an eye on the customers. A young couple stood hand-in-hand before the condom section, and I wondered at what young people did that they needed protection so early in the morning. An older man read the label on a bottle of antacids. After a few minutes the customers had paid and left, and I was beginning to feel like a vegan at the butcher when a slight young woman entered. She wore cropped hair, her eyes set far back in her face and carried a large leather purse over her shoulder.

It shouldn't have surprised me to find the Cereal Burglar small and sickly looking, but her size shocked me. I raised my cellphone camera and snapped a picture, then headed for the registers. The girl eyed me as we passed. Something like recognition flitted between us. Her eyes glowed clearest brown. She had full lips, healthy lips on a face otherwise gaunt. I guessed lupus. Maybe she was dying. The profile seemed logical. I bought a candy bar and waited outside.

Fifteen minutes later, when the girl exited the store with a box of tampons and no plastic sack to conceal her purchase, Lyle still hadn't texted back. I was faced with a choice to follow my gut or ignore what I knew. Something I'd done had tipped the girl off. Perhaps she'd seen me photograph her. Or maybe she only struck if no one made direct eye contact. She walked to the driver side door of a Ford Taurus with rust on the wheel wells.

At the last moment, when she'd opened the door and was about to fall into the driver seat, I called out. She glanced at me. There was fear in her eyes, but she composed herself quickly. I jogged toward her. "Don't think I'm weird, but I swear we know each other."

She turned her head toward the interstate onramp and watched cars drive by. I stopped at the bumper of her car. Maybe we'd met in school. Or did she shop at the downtown co-op? She looked back toward me and shook her head.

"I'm sure I know you from somewhere."

She shook her head vigorously and ducked into her car. I stepped up to the door and put my body between her and it so she couldn't escape. If you only have a moment to change the flow of events, you have to risk loss. "I have lupus. Maybe met at a medical clinic?"

The girl let her hand fall from the door handle. She looked at my face and squinted. A grimace danced on her lips.

I shrugged. "Yeah. Yeah, that's it. I think I saw you at one of the support groups."

She leaned into her car and came up with a notepad and pen.

Opening to a page in the middle of the notebook, she wrote three words in beautifully exact script: *Let me leave.*

"Can't you talk?"

She tapped the page with her pen. I stood my ground, digging into my pocket for my cigarettes. She flipped to a clean page and scribbled something new: *You shouldn't smoke.*

"Everyone tells me that."

She flipped back to the previous page and held it close to me. I shrugged and lit my cigarette. The smoke hit my lungs like a hug. "We need community. No one understands what we're going through."

The girl smiled and looked at my feet. She flipped to a new page and scribbled another note: *I need to get to work.*

"Where do you work? I don't imagine there's too many jobs for mutes."

I'm not mute.

"Then say something."

She crossed out the words on the top of the page and wrote beneath it: *No.*

We understood each other. "Your job pays poorly, right? Offers bum health insurance."

YES and NO...

"My partner's seen you at work. You know that?"

Do you actually have lupus?

"You do. And you're tired of living with it. Tired of all the meds. You're a control freak. I get that. Takes one to know one, yeah?"

The girl leaned back, lifted her legs, and kicked me in the stomach. I stumbled into the car behind me, lost my balance and landed on my ass. The girl's car door slammed with a whoosh of wind, and her engine fired. As I stood, she was reversing out of the parking space. I dusted off my jeans, produced my cellphone and snapped a shot of the girl in her car.

Later I'd see that the photo had come out blurry, the license plate a smudge of blue and white, nothing more. Its driver was indistinguishable from any pale person behind the wheel of a Ford in early morning light. But in that moment I felt alive. I knew something the police had failed to uncover for years. The Cereal Burglar was a young woman empty of malice, full of humor, smart. She was something for girls and women to admire. I knew her, even if she refused to acknowledge me.

My cigarette had rolled several feet away, but still lay smoldering in the parking lot. I retrieved it and smoked what was left. Then I called Lyle. When I got his voicemail, I hung up and tried again. I called nine times before he answered.

His voice was husky and clipped. "What?"

"I met the Cereal Burglar."

He punished me with a long silence before clearing his throat. "I don't believe you."

"Pick me up at the Walgreens. I'll prove it."

"Sure. Whatever, huh?"

Once in his car I couldn't get a word in edgewise. "You're going to tell me the Cereal Burglar's a lady, and we're going to go through this whole back and forth about how no one's taken her down because they're too busy looking for a dude. Been there, bought the shot glass, but I got news for you. Psychologists from the OPD have profiled these robberies and definitively characterized the approach as masculine in nature."

"How can a robbery be *masculine in nature*?"

Lyle bit into a tuna salad sandwich. "Read the reports, huh?"

"I don't care what the reports say. I met her, and she's a she."

"Look." He punctuated himself with a sip of cola from a can. "You win. You wanted me to drop what happened last night, and it worked. Don't push it."

"I'm not pushing, but I'll tell you another thing. If you can just trust me, we might be able to stop Marva's murder. We'll have to hurry."

He polished off his sandwich and licked his fingers. "Oh my god. What are you? Nostradamus reincarnated."

The idea appealed. Maybe all this time we'd given weight to certain people's words, those who seemed prophetic, but perhaps they'd all been like me, stuck in a loop. I thought of Jesus. How many followers would he have had in the age of Twitter? But no. I'm getting off topic. Get this. Some guy predicts his death. Wouldn't it make sense that he'd know so much if he'd lived it a dozen times? Maybe the universe had tasked him with finding a way to live through crucifixion—just for laughs. He'd've collected tips and tricks from a handful of failed attempts before he figured out the right people to pay off. Then, voila! on the final round a guard pretends to pierce the guy's side and another guard takes a bribe to pronounce Jesus dead. A few days later "the prophet" starts showing up at one party after another and a religion is born. Everyone wins. Except maybe two thousand years of duped Christians. I doubt it, but maybe.

"I'm Luke Mia, and whether you believe me or not, I know certain things. I know where Marva's going to be this morning, and I know who's meeting her there. I know his plans, and how he does what he does."

"So you're telling me someone's going to murder Marva at WheatFields this morning?"

"Yeah." I replayed his comment in my mind. "Wait. What?"

Lyle unwrapped a biscotti and bit into it. "Someone's going to murder Marva at WheatFields."

"You said this morning."

"I was getting ready to head out when you called. You say someone's going to meet her there and murder her."

"She's going to Christian Nobel."

"She didn't say anything about that to me."

I played a series of events through my mind. Maybe she ate breakfast with Lyle before her appointment at the furs retailer. But that couldn't be, because he'd never had an appointment to eat with her before. The only other alternative was that something about how we'd approached her the night before had sidetracked the morning. "Okay. Fine. But when we meet her I'm going to ask if she cancelled an appointment at Christian Nobel. You'll see. She—"

"We?"

"had that appointment—"

"You're not coming with." Lyle cracked a peanut shell, tossing the nuts in his mouth and discarding the remains on the floorboard. "I'm dropping you at your place. Marva doesn't want to see you again. She says you're crazy, and honestly, I'm starting to wonder."

"This is our case."

He balled the empty package, tossing it into the backseat. "It's *my* case."

I tucked a cigarette behind my ear like a threat. "You can't do this."

"She wants my help, and she's paying well." Lyle turned off onto Cumming. "I'll cover our office rent, and I can even spot you for your other bills, but you can't ruin this for me, huh? We both need the money, and I really need the money."

"We always need money." I felt empty and petty.

"And now we can have it if you don't screw this up." He pulled onto Maple and past our office, turning left on 61st Avenue. He parked out back of my apartment. "I'll call you later."

I contemplated violence. "Ask if she cancelled an appointment so she could have breakfast with you. She was supposed to be at Christian Nobel."

"Fine." He leaned across me to open my door. "I'll ask. What's it prove if she did?"

"That I know something."

Lyle rolled a blueberry between thumb and forefinger. He popped it in his mouth. "So you made some phone calls. Ruskov tipped you off. I don't know. I can't stand that creep."

"It's not like that." It wasn't worth arguing. "Whatever. Call me later."

19

I SLIPPED INTO A T-SHIRT AND JEANS, PINNED MY HAIR back, hid my eyes behind aviator sunglasses, and capped my head with a Cubs hat. Visa and Discover both declined before Lyft accepted my MasterCard. I was running out of credit.

The driver pulled to the curb. He lowered his window. "Luke?"

"You're looking at her."

"Morning, beautiful. Hop in."

Beautiful as a pet name is considered the equivalent of Handsome for guys, as in, Hey, Handsome, but it's different, because you'll see men of any appearance get the name tossed at them— say, at a bar, or a night club—but a woman who has physical blemishes never gets called Beautiful. "Don't call me that. Show some respect."

"Sorry." He emphasized the first syllable for ironic effect. "Didn't mean nothing by it."

"That's the problem. It's just engrained in you to belittle women by commenting on their physical appearance."

"Most chicks smile when I—"

"Don't say 'chicks' either. In fact, just don't talk." Most of the time, I would've argued for the fun of it, but my head hurt, and I felt desperately out of control already.

The driver stomped the gas. "Whatever you say, lady." He tailed vehicles down Dodge, wove through traffic without signaling, and nearly hit a student crossing the intersection by Memorial Park. I'd flipped his script; it was nice to see how a simple request for respect could make a chauvinist fool petulant. His glare at me in the rearview mirror brightened my mood.

He stopped near the front doors to WheatFields. I asked him to swing around back. He said he'd already ended the fare. Some revenge is trivial. I rated him at three stars, closed out with a one-dollar tip and checked the box for "good conversation."

Inside the restaurant, with the chatter of diners and the rush of serving staff, thought came as a luxury. The host quoted me a thirty-minute wait. I scanned the entry with its egg yolk wallpaper. Oak tables lined the walls, stacked with enough carryout pastry to feed a neighborhood. Tables full of buzzing diners littered the front of house.

I spotted Lyle, with his back to me, near the kitchen. He sat alone. I wondered if Marva had fled for her appointment at Christian Nobel. You might wish you weren't so petty as to revel in *I told you so*, but I don't know anyone who doesn't like to be right.

A moment later, though, Marva returned from the women's room and sat opposite Lyle. He looked lost without anything to snack on. His fingers explored a package of sugar. Little conversation passed between the two, and I wondered if I'd wasted my time tailing them since I wasn't going to get close enough to eavesdrop. Worse, I couldn't afford a second breakfast—I hadn't been able to afford the first much less two cab fares.

Just as I had resigned to leave, a face in the crowd caught my attention. A bald head and wire-frame glasses reflected the over-head light. The tattoos climbing his neck stood out against a back-drop of women in summer dresses and potbellied men. This man's presence defied the strings of pearls, the gold-plated wrist-watches, the Lacoste crocodile shirts, the calf skin boots and wedge sandals, the LV purses. Absent thought or plan, I pushed through the waiting area and wove between tables, until I stood before Laser.

I sat in the empty chair opposite him and tipped my hat. He glanced at me, sipping his coffee. "She thinks she can control me. That's her first mistake. I'm going to start with her fingers and finish with her toes. If you want to know what begging sounds like, stick around."

My pulse surged. The pads of my fingers numbed. The notion that Laser would recognize me hadn't occurred. Had he traveled through the loop with me all these times? "You know me?"

He buttered a slice of toast and spread jam with a knife. "Of you." He ate in silence. I waited because there was nothing else to do. When he finished he wiped his mouth with a cloth napkin. "Mrs. DeLonghi took a call from your partner last night. I ran a few searches on your agency. Cute operation. Boutique style private eyes. Intimate gig. Lots of lost pets I'm guessing."

A wave of relief washed over me. I was, at least, just another anonymous speed bump between Laser and his goal. The notion that someone else had fit inside my convoluted noose unsettled me. Knowing I was alone meant something, if barely. "Lost pets, milk carton kids, cheating spouses. Not enough to pay the bills."

"Tough to make an honest living these days."

"I imagine they don't pay much down at the docks."

Laser had been lifting his coffee mug toward his lips, but his arm paused. He graced me with eye contact. Life and longing lit the blues of his irises. "Enough to make ends meet, in fact, but I have other appetites."

I liked the idea that he hadn't expected me to know him. "Murder?"

"Meh." He set his mug down without drinking. "Murder's often a byproduct of my appetites, but I'm indifferent to it."

Small talk never suited me. "What's your problem with Marva DeLonghi, anyway?"

Laser relieved his face of the glasses, wiping the lenses with the tail of his shirt. "It's a 1099 sort of situation, if you catch my drift."

I thought I did: contract work, though I doubted he paid taxes on his earnings. Could've been referring to the police code for cardiac arrest—or both. "You're working for someone?"

Laser smiled. When the tendons in his neck tightened, the tattoos leapt into focus: an army of men and beasts scrambling out of hell. Flames licked at the heels of lions and goats and birds of prey and wolves drawn like naked women wielding scabbards. "I'll give it to you. You're good at what you do. People who know my extracurricular interests rarely live long enough to extract details. Anonymity tends to be a commodity in my trade." He replaced his spectacles and scraped his front tooth with the tip of his thumb-nail. "I hope you know your research has ensured your untimely death. I couldn't allow someone to go around knowing what I do. Bad for business."

I snatched the second piece of toast from his plate, shoving half in my mouth. "Since you're gonna kill me anyway, I guess nothing's stopping you from spilling what this's all about."

"Pride, sister. What else?"

He wore confidence like a second skin. I smiled. "Whose pride?"

"How do I know you're not wired?"

I have a deep wrinkle just off-center, left on my forehead, and it always shows when something angers me so I knew it showed then. "Don't insult me. I can handle myself."

Laser leaned back and smiled. He had a certain charm. I hated it. "Verbal testimony plays in any courtroom. You'd be a patsy not to use any advantage you could get."

Patsy is one more term on a long list that proves how sexist our society is, but with a guy like Laser, I didn't figure I needed to enlighten him. He chose his words with care. I unclasped the first button at my chest and showed him some skin. "No wire. You satisfied?"

Laser licked his butter knife. "Spread your ass cheeks, then we'll see."

The server picked that moment to stop at our table. She grimaced. "I can come back."

Laser fashioned a skeletal smile. He reached across the table and took her wrist between thumb and forefinger. His eyes traveled the length of her arm, up her neck and paused at her ear. "We were just talking business. I was telling this young lady I know a place where she could dance. Body like hers. Triple her income. Maybe you'd be interested?"

The server chuckled nervously. She turned from Laser's gaze and focused on me, asking if I'd had enough time to look over the menu. I said I wasn't eating. She scowled at me like a wine spill on carpet. "Maybe I'll have a Bloody Mary, though. Do you have Magdalene?"

"Magdalene?"

"Bourbon."

"Let me see." She turned back to Laser, who still held her wrist, gave a shy smile and shuffled away.

"Evolution is a scam." Laser drank from his refilled coffee cup. "Waiters are the proof. They aren't fit to survive."

"Interesting philosophy."

Laser waved his hand in dismissal. "And you're an insecure bitch without a father."

"I had a father."

"Who hated you, even the sight of you."

"I'm sure your family's so much better. They say psychopaths come from stable homes."

"I'm not a psychopath. Not a sociopath. The only path I adhere to is my own. I'm a well-adjusted man with goals and dreams, just like you."

He wanted me off balance and off-message. It was working. "I'm not a man."

"We're all men."

"You would say that."

"Hu*man*ity would say that."

"Look. As much as I love a robust dialogue on gender roles and sexual identity, maybe you wouldn't mind explaining what the deal is with all the text messages."

Laser eyed the server as she delivered my drink. They didn't have Magdalene, so she'd ordered Four Roses. I would've preferred a traditional vodka Bloody over off-brand whiskey, but any alcohol was fine, under the circumstances.

I sipped and wiped my lips with the back of my hand.

Laser drummed his fingers on the table. "As non sequiturs go, you've got me beat. Are you asking my thoughts on texting? I'm not a fan."

Perhaps in honor of Marva, or maybe because fear tickled at my tonsils, I inverted my glass and opened my throat. "For someone who doesn't like to text, you sure do enough of it. Marva should know."

Laser studied his coffee cup. "If I wasn't planning to kill you, I might care what confused notion—"

I interrupted. "We're going to find out who you work for whether you tell me or not so why don't you save me the—"

"Nothing can save you, peach. Don't go thinking just because I plan to kill you I'll get sloppy and spill my secrets."

I fished an ice cube from my cup and sucked it. "What'd be the harm? Or maybe you're not so sure of your skills after all."

Laser slipped into a smug grin as thin as lingerie. "Confidence has nothing to do with it. Maybe you've read Camus. He says the act of speaking dilutes the act of acting. You follow?"

I knew enough to know Camus rhymed with the sound a cow made, but I didn't correct his pronunciation. "I haven't come across that particular line in my readings."

"Actions speak louder than words, honey. Let's leave it at that." Laser checked his phone. "We don't have enough time for me to illuminate you. But if you're banking on my ego making me vulnerable, I'm sorry to waste your efforts."

Any time before I might've been thinking something exactly like what Laser outlined, but with queasy clarity I understood I was banking on dying. Not without pain or consequence, I'd seen how four deaths had granted me a distinct advantage over my situation. If the road to enlightenment is suffering, then death is the highway. And my blacktop stretched on perhaps forever. I imitated a buzzer. "Wrong. Sorry, try again."

"Everyone has a sense of humor until I get to work. By the time I'm wrapping your severed hands in wax paper you won't be laughing any more. And I admit, I love a dying woman's sincerity. It's so endearing."

I didn't doubt it. "Didn't you just say speaking dilutes action? Maybe you're trying to scare me. Won't work."

"Let's put it this way: I won't pretend our fifteen minutes in paradise here has shown me every facet of your admirable complexity, but I kind of like you, and I want to give you a chance to reconsider your approach. I've got a job to do, and nothing's going to stop me, which gives you a bit of a head start. If you're smart, and you seem like it, you'll use this time to hide. I'll find you. Can't leave loose threads. Some secrets have a way of coming back from the dead. But if you run now, you might live a bit longer. Perhaps that's worth something to you."

Did he know what he was saying? He certainly chose an odd turn of phrase, *coming back from the dead*, but I played it like a cucumber. "One way or another, you'll give me what I want, but it's a lot harder to remember details when someone's torturing you. Believe me I know."

Laser crossed his knife over the fork on his plate and pushed the dish toward the table's center. "Don't kid yourself. You have about as much chance of torturing me—"

"You misunderstand." I squinted, pursing my lips. "I don't doubt you'll come for me, and I'm counting on you being like every other egomaniac in the world. People have a way of running at the mouth when they're hurting other people. Didn't Camus say that too?" It felt good indirectly criticizing his pronunciation.

"Kudos to you." Laser mock-clapped. "I usually don't talk *this* much, but trust me. When we meet again, I won't say a word."

"Fair enough. Then what do you say we trade confessions, now?"

"I'm not Catholic."

"Fuck the pope."

"Right. You have daddy issues. That's resolved."

The bustle of the dining room hadn't quieted, but I'd slipped into a frame of mind so focused, a jazz band could've broken down the doors, and I would've been oblivious. "How do you think I knew who you were? Shoot. Marva hired us less than twelve hours ago. Thing is, though, I've spent years plagued by your actions. I've seen your work with an axe, and I've lain awake in a prison cell at night wondering how I could've stopped you. Whenever Marva DeLonghi dies, I die, and when I die I return to the moment she first came into my life, and from the moment she appeared, you're always close by."

Laser scratched his thumbnail along the table's wood grain. "You're insane, then."

"The repetition *is* driving me crazy. But take it or leave it. I know you work at the docks because I saw you there this morning, but not *this* morning. I saw you there this morning seven years ago. By that time, you'd already killed Marva, hacked her to pieces with the same axe you use to butcher catfish. You killed her at Christian Nobel Furs. There was so much blood and panic. You'd be surprised how vivid those images are for me all this time later.

"I missed you that first time, which of course I would because Marva gave Lyle and I no time to solve a problem that had been plaguing her for how long. By the time I met you that first go around you could act the injured party, but you also knew Lyle and I had gotten too close so you sent us to Nelly. Nelly, by the way is a psychopath for sure."

Laser picked at a hangnail. That he'd listened without interruption troubled me, because leave it to a contract killer to keep an open mind where a tamer story had alienated my closest friend. "Nelly is a psychopath and a nymphomaniac, and most probably a necrophiliac. That's what makes her so uniquely lovable."

"After she killed me I returned to the moment I first met Marva, like déjà vu, but the kind that makes your feet burn and your hair melt."

"I'm not familiar with that kind."

The server returned and motioned at my empty glass. I nodded. She found a bounce in her step as she retreated to the kitchen. Two bloodies, I guessed, was edging toward a proper tip.

"I'll spare you the rest of the details except to reiterate that your original plan was to kill Marva at Christian Nobel Furs, and that being here, right now, is a product of my having scared Marva away last night by telling her truths about herself she couldn't remember sharing with me. Now she's put all her money in Lyle's pocket and I'm chopped liver."

"Chopped liver and onions. We should've eaten at Petrow's." He licked his lips. "And their chocolate malts."

I cleared my throat, thanked the server for the Bloody, and drank. "So you believe me?"

Laser pushed his glasses up the bridge of his nose. "Why not? Though it's more likely your brand of psychosis results from high-velocity cosmic radiation, visions at the speed of light. Death is final. But since you're eager to test a theory, I'll be happy to help."

It's hard to explain, but the longer I sat with Laser, the more I liked him. He was the kind of guy who, if he wasn't married to an axe, might've made a decent romantic companion. "Then you have nothing to lose in telling me your story."

His lips twitched. "Too bad. I think you're interesting, more than causally so," like reading my mind, "but while I don't believe you've died and resurrected, I do fear the knowledge of the dead, and you already know too much to take with you to the grave."

My head buzzed because I could see the future like I'd just remembered one of my previous lives. Already my left hand had wrapped around my pocketknife. "At least tell me if it's true that Ransom DeLonghi hired you as a personal body guard for Marva."

He tented his hands on the table. "How about not." He smiled. "And the knife in your hand won't do you any good."

My smile faded. I lifted the blade and spun it business side toward him. It demanded attention. My other hand was free to roam. "I don't need this to kill you, but I appreciate your confidence." Drawing his attention briefly to my knife, I used my free hand to slip his cellphone into my lap.

Laser stood. He dug in his back pocket, removed a wallet, thumbed through it, and dropped a hundred dollar bill on the table. "Leave a tip. Keep the change. We'll settle up later."

Lyle and Marva had stood too. If I could get to them before

Laser did, maybe we could force a mistake. I grabbed Laser's wrist. "Why not do this the easy way?"

He jerked his arm free and turned his back to me. "That's what we are doing."

"Why would Ransom hire you?"

He spun, showing me a mouthful of teeth fixed in a scowl. "Don't waste your time asking yes or no questions. Ask yourself why Mrs. DeLonghi would trust me enough to chauffeur her in the first place."

20

FOR THE FIRST TIME IN MY LIFE, I WALKED AWAY FROM free money, leaving the Benjamin on the table. As I met the exit, my phone rang. The picture accompanying the ringtone was classic Putch: food-stained lips, happy eyes, all angles and chin. I shouldered the door and accepted the call. "How was breakfast?"

"I don't get all the hype about the food, huh? It's overpriced and tasteless."

I scanned the parking lot, but Laser had disappeared. "You would take that as a question about the food."

"What do you mean?"

"How's it going with Marva, dummy?"

"You were right." He drew a breath that translated through the receiver like torn paper. "She had had an appointment at Christian Nobel."

"You're headed there now?"

Lyle laughed. "She quit me, Lu. Don't you get it? You think I'd be talking to you if I was with her?"

I snapped my head side to side. A rush of heat washed my face. "You're not with her?"

"When I asked her about Christian Nobel she went quiet, and her lips did that angry-lady thing. Nah, bro. She knew why I asked and said she thought maybe me without you would be reasonable, but said she was wrong. She doesn't want to work with either of us. So, yeah. Thanks for nothing, huh?"

Nothing between the hunter and his prey. "Where is she?"

"Why do you care?"

My mistake grew arms and an axe. "Where is she?"

"Walking to her car. We just finished breakfast. She's—"

I spied him leaning against a concrete planter. "Look to your left."

He turned his head. I raised an arm. He hung up, and even from twenty feet away, his confusion was clear. We met in the middle.

I lit a cigarette and begged the smoke to calm me. A few people standing nearby scowled. Where's Audrey Hepburn when you need her? She could remind people of tobacco's elegance. "You told me where you were going, so don't pretend you didn't expect me to tail you."

Lyle wiped an apple on his sleeve and split it in half. "Maybe it doesn't mean anything to you, but I just lost the defining case of my career."

I ashed my cigarette with a flick. "We haven't lost anything yet, but if we don't hurry someone's going to take it from us."

Lyle spat a seed on the cement. "The sunflowers are resting. Time to wake up and smell the music."

Half of my best Tweets came direct from Lyle's mouth. "I'm not tracking, big guy."

"She's gone, baby, her and that weird-ass driver."

A gaggle of fifty-somethings with spiked hair and eyeliner shuffled past primping and preening. "Driver?"

"Big guy. Bald. Lot of tattoos."

Fire licked at the nape of my neck. "She's with him?"

THE 9 LIVES OF MARVA DELONGHI

A fleck of apple pulp clung to his lips. "Guy drives her every-where since the death threats. Shoot. Lady's practically got twenty-four-hour surveillance between, him us and whoever else."

I pinned the cigarette between my lips. "We've got to stop him."

Lyle turned and scanned the parking lot. "What for?"

"He's the killer." I snaked between aisles, head on a swivel. A man in a Trader Joe's button up smiled at me as he stepped out of his Geo Prism. He wore clean like an accessory. I shouldered past him. His nametag popped off his shirt and stuck in the fold of my purse. I handed it back. "Sorry, John."

Lyle sped to a jog. I loved him most in that moment for not asking questions. He raised a hand and pointed. "There!"

Inside a car, pulling up to the out-road, sat Marva. I broke into a run. Blood buzzed in my ears. I'd closed half the distance when she caught a break in traffic and turned. As the car angled around the median I caught a glimpse of Laser in the driver seat. How could she be so stupid? All my disdain for guns drained from me. I longed to pull a pistol and aim.

Lyle, meanwhile, had found a reserve of energy I didn't know he possessed and was sprinting toward the traffic light, moving faster than I'd believed him able. It appeared he intended to cut Marva's car off at the intersection. I wheeled hard and bolted.

You've probably heard someone say *scared to death* but you've likely never felt it. Fear, when it breaks a certain threshold opens on the future like sunlight bursting through cloud. You can see the outcome of your terrors and be powerless to prevent them. That's scared to death.

I was always faster on foot than Lyle, but he was too far ahead. A squeak of brakes preceded a woman's voice cursing at me. I'd loped in front of her car, as she circled for an open parking space. I bounded over the hood of another car and nearly sprawled yard-sale on the blacktop. My eyes watered and my mouth parched.

The sun beat down. My skin wept for the heat, beads of sweat running down my brows and shoulders. A wad of gum stuck to the heel of my left shoe. The pungent odor of crab apple and asphalt writhed in my nose. Try forgetting a single detail of your most hopeless moments.

Lyle leapt over the median as Marva's car closed on the same piece of road. Her car didn't even slow. In fact, the engine roared as it lurched forward. Lyle's body whipped forward, head slamming the hood, then slurped to the pavement as the tires thump-whumped over him.

"Oh my god!" a distant voice shouted.

A crowd converged on the scene. Someone said, "Did you see that?" Someone else asked if it was real. Another person said, "Get the license plate."

A group of twenty or more people closed on the spot where Lyle lay. It was suggested 911 be called. My body numbed. I fell to my knees at Lyle's side. His eyes dilated, staring into the sun. I thought he would blind himself. With a trembling hand, I shaded his view. You might expect you'd have something to say at a moment such as that, but I couldn't find words.

21

A POLICE OFFICER WITH A POCK-MARKED FACE AND chin beard followed the ambulance, escorting me to Methodist Hospital. He asked if I'd seen the accident. I said it wasn't an accident, and it should've been me who got run over. He said I was in shock. He asked why Lyle jumped into the middle of the road. I withheld comment. He dropped me at the curb of the emergency room and handed me a business card. "Call me when this guy pulls through, all right, hun?"

Perhaps doubt lingered in his eyes, or my imagination. "Sure."

I told the nurse at the front desk I was with the injured man who came on the last ambulance. Her left hand was missing the ring finger. "You family, sweetie?"

There's two kinds of people, those who use pet names and those I don't consider punching in the face. "He's like a brother to me. We're partners, best friends." I used the words "best friends."

Her eyes dropped to the counter as she fidgeted with one of her acrylic nails. "Rules prohibit nonrelatives from visiting ER patients." Her eyes came up to meet mine. "But I can see the man

meant a lot to you. I'll just have to fudge some of the paperwork."
She raised air-quotes around the word fudge, winking at me.

Nurses see death so much they grow immune. Or perhaps a wink is the precise balm for grief. "I need a smoke."

"Go on, dear. It'll be a while yet. These things always do."

"What if he— Um. What if before?"

"You go smoke, honey. Someone'll get you when it's time. You'll see him."

That's another thing about nurses. I know because I went through it all with my parents. A nurse had quoted me almost the same line with my mother, but I'd never seen my mother alive again after they rolled her body on a stretcher into the ER.

A half-pack of cigarettes later, a short man, heavily muscled, and deeply tanned, wearing white scrubs and white tennis shoes met me in the waiting room. He asked if I was Lyle's sister. I nodded. He said Lyle wasn't in any pain. The man handed me a tissue paper cap for my head, a matching paper gown, and white cloth overshoes with elastic mouths.

The corridor beyond the waiting room doors was miles long, bleached gray, with peeling wallpaper. Every footstep squeaked and crackled, echoing endlessly. The walls were lined with wood handrails. Outside most rooms was a white-sheeted mattress on a chrome stretcher. Some stretchers were occupied—patients connected to IV drips hanging from metal loops—but mostly those beds were empty. A man I passed had a kitchen knife buried in his neck. He reached out and said, "Holly." I shook my head, but tried to smile. My lips failed me, and tears were their replacement. The short man in white scrubs stopped at a door most of the way down the corridor and gestured for me to enter the room on his left. White light spilled from the doorway, illuminating the gray, speckled tile of the hall.

The room smelled of bleach, ammonia, and blood. Cornflower blue curtains hung on chrome rails mounted from the ceiling, dividing the space into several cubes. I searched for Lyle's characteristic body smell like proofed yeast, but he'd been washed clean, and unfamiliar. His head hung suspended just above the pillow in a little hammock and his arms were elevated with gauze and pulleys. Two nurses stood at a distance by a stainless steel sink. A heart monitor kept rhythm with Lyle's fading pulse. I drew close. His eyes were open and searching.

I touched his shoulder lightly. "Hey."

His eyes darted. My lips quivered. I leaned down and spoke apologies in his ear. His body radiated terrible heat, a fever raging. The part of me that knew I could have him back had fled. Each time I lost him was worse than the last, closer to some end I refused to imagine.

Lyle's mouth opened with a slight glottal click. His breath was loud, but the words hardly rose to a whisper. I leaned closer. A word that sounded like Marva. I tried to calm him by saying she didn't matter. We were too late. The image of his final moment rose in my mind. Marva hadn't even tried to stop it. She was the guilty one. In any incarnation, she'd let an innocent die to save herself. I hated her.

"Whatever she gets, she deserves."

"No," he rasped.

Tears stained my face. I started into an apology for failing to save him, but he closed his eyes and summoned one clear word: "Stop." Then his eyes closed and his chest relaxed.

I thought he'd died. The nurses, just within my periphery, turned as Lyle's heart monitor registered the effort he'd summoned to speak that one word.

The monitor resumed a steadier pace. Then a whispered word I lip-read as much as heard, "Closer." I brought my ear to his nose. His breath smelled of caramel and beer. "I think," a rattling breath, "you're more. Beautiful," two shallow breaths, "than her," and flat line.

Call it sentimental, but it's the goddamned truth. I stood upright, arched my back and sobbed. While one of the nurses attended to Lyle, the other comforted me—or that was her intent. She eased me by the arm out of the sterile room and back to the waiting area.

There followed hours of instructions, paperwork, police interviews, doctor interviews, statements, signatures, cigarettes, drinks, phone calls and exhaustion. A tall, round-bellied man in a long white coat with a walrus mustache and big clicking teeth brewed coffee and told me he was sorry for my loss. Those are the only words a suffering person can receive.

Some time later I woke in my own bed to the sound of Lyle's voice crying out in pain. I swam up out of a nightmare. Reality assembled itself in jags and fits. I groped for the lamp on my bedside drawer. Instead, I knocked a phone onto the floor. I rolled to the edge of my bed and reached for the phone. Confusion was replaced by fear was replaced by a sob. My phone would be in my purse, wherever that might be. I rose from bed and stood before my bedroom door. Tried to unlock the phone I'd stolen off Laser. It didn't like my fingerprint, and after a dozen tries, the phone informed me it would be locked for fifteen minutes.

I walked down the hallway to the kitchen. Two purses sat on the counter near the sink. How much of the night had I lost? And how had I gotten from the hospital to my room? I lit a cigarette and filled a pint glass with five fingers of Magdalene. Sitting at the table, I tried to reassemble the lost hours—from there to here. Instead, the nightmare that woke me, edged into consciousness. Lyle riding a cloud-white mare with muscle rippling along its hindquarters: piano strings beneath a coat of soft fur. A meadow and green grass, yellow flowers. Hawks riding thermals beneath a blue sky. I stood on a split rail fence, smiling, laughing. Lyle on a horse was the most unnatural sight. Then the horse banked, rose on two legs and charged. Lyle lost his balance. His spine arched, arms flailed, legs kicked. He plowed into the earth. I was laughing when the horse first startled, but when Lyle screamed in pain, I panicked. My hair whipped at my cheeks, as a strong gust kicked up. I meant to run, but my body refused. I could hardly descend the fence, fear in slow motion. And that's how I woke, knowing he'd died.

The glass of bourbon sat empty. Three cigarette butts rested in a tray in the center of the table. I dozed. The slurred voice of dreams echoed and what was possible in sleeping that waking wouldn't allow, the voice of my partner: *I think you're more beautiful than her.*

22

My surroundings confused me. In one world I returned to the front door of my office, fully dressed and ready to eviscerate. In another world, I fell asleep in strange places and woke to the comfort of my bed. If I'd had a choice, I'd take the latter.

The distant sound of dishes clanking startled me. Perhaps the foolishness of one recently waked, I called out. No one answered, but the apartment silenced. I beckoned again. Footsteps clacked down the hallway, growing louder. My jeans were folded at the foot of the bed. I reached for them but failed to find my knife in the pockets. The bedroom door eased open. A woman's head peeked in. She had soft wrinkles radiating from brown eyes. Her lips were pencil eraser pink and just as dry, her face clear as ivory soap. She wore her gray hair tightly curled, hugging her scalp. "How'd you sleep?" My face must've told enough. "You don't remember me. I'm Maddy. We met at the hospital. I work for the Lutheran Church. We volunteer spiritual counsel to the grieving. You were, naturally, quite distressed last night."

I buried my face in my hands, pulling the skin of my cheeks, until my fingers lost traction and my lips snapped back with a faint pop. The previous day. I clenched my jaw against swirling images of chaos. How much was true? I remembered Lyle's body in the hospital bed. What had he said to me? Why had I failed to say anything important? I sat up. "I'm sorry. Who are you?"

The woman smiled sadly. She stepped into my room and stood at the foot of the bed. "Maddy Engles. You came to the chapel last night. Father Benedics found you crying in your sleep." She tilted her head and sighed. "You really don't remember, darling?"

"Going to a chapel doesn't sound like something I'd do."

"We all behave unexpectedly in grief."

My experience of grief had shown me I became most myself at those times when others would later say I was out of my head. When the body took over and the mind shut down, I gravitated toward the most engrained self. Whole packs of cigarettes would go missing, drained quarts of Magdalene would march into the trash. The local bartenders would tell me I'd lost my temper and incited brawls. And until the police arrested me and revoked my driver's license, I'd often driven aimless miles to later wake in my turpentine-smelling car, on the shoulder of some state highway beside a cornfield. People fear their own shadow for a reason. And the argument that alcohol or rage abolishes inhibitions is merely a fancy way of proving the things we do in a fugue are those things we're constantly convincing ourselves not to do when we're sober.

The only explanation I could accept for having wandered into a chapel was that I meant to vandalize a sacred place in honor of what Lyle's dying had vandalized in me, but this seemed less than productive to mention to Maddy Engles. "How did we get here?"

"Sweetheart?"

Pet names piss me off, but I held my tongue, measuring my words: "How'd we get here?"

"You said you needed to die so you could take everything back.

You said if you died everything would return to the way it was."
She sneezed. "Now understand, when a person at a hospital hears
that kind of thing, they're obligated to report it, but the more
questions I asked, the more it seemed you weren't exactly
suicidal."

I seemed to recall a recent run-in with a police officer that
ended in my forcing him to shoot me center-mass. Though, in the
traditional sense, my moods would be considered compatible with
a desire to live. "I'm not."

"I didn't think so either, so I asked Father Benedics what we
should do. He told me if I would accompany you to your home
and ensure your safety he'd welcome that. We're not employed by
the hospital, so we don't have to follow *every* procedure, though I
suppose you shouldn't tell people I feel that way. I guess me and
the father just agreed maybe you needed to wrestle with the Lord,
and the fourth floor is no place for those kind of things."

Why every hospital's fourth floor is devoted to psych patients
is beyond me, but you'll find it's universally true: perhaps because
four stories is low enough to guarantee a majority of jumpers live,
but high enough to dissuade most from trying. Considering psych
wards often have bars on their windows, the option to jump is
largely moot.

My uncle Kennedy spent his last twenty years in and out of
psych wards. He contracted malaria on a trip to Panama, and
when he returned to Chicago, he believed he was part of a secret
operation tasked with assassinating the president. My father
would take midnight calls, waking the house with his yelling. He'd
storm about, throwing random artifacts into a suede duffle before
slamming the door and marching across the lawn to his car, parked
on the street. He'd disappear for days and return with a story of
how his brother had hitchhiked to D.C. or train hopped to
Miami. Over the course of a few months following one of these

episodes, we'd drive to Chicago frequently to visit Kennedy first on the fourth floor of one hospital or another, then at an open space treatment facility. Kennedy always smelled of baby powder. "I know what's what, now," he'd say, which became code for, "Just wait till they let me out of here."

I asked Maddy to step out of my room so I could dress. She closed the door behind her. I hunted for my knife to no effect. After I gave up, I slipped into cotton underwear, a green and black plaid button up with the sleeves rolled, navy blue jeggings, gray wool socks, and 1914 Dr. Martens boots. There are fifteen different ways to kill an enemy with Dr. Martens, but all of them involve bludgeoning.

Maddy had brewed coffee and scrambled eggs. I didn't argue her choice of breakfast, though eggs scrambled are the gag reflex's nemesis. The appropriate way to cook an egg is sunny side up. Just when the last of the white is firmed, you scrape the egg off the cast iron skillet and rest it on burnt buttered toast.

Maddy winced, wagging her head when I added a spritz of Magdalene to my coffee, but she refused comment. After I'd managed to stomach a bit of egg, I said, "I can't find my knife."

Maddy poured a second cup of coffee for herself. "When did you see it last?"

I covered my mouth and eased out a yawn. "I had it last night."

"I'll bet it's with security, at the hospital, then."

I nodded, staring at the plate of half-eaten eggs, unable to force myself into another bite.

Maddy sat in the chair opposite me at the kitchen table. She cleared her throat. "You came out of your room last night."

Was it a bad dream? Did I have Laser's cell phone? Had he lopped Marva limb from limb? I knew I couldn't dream the dead alive, coax Lyle back from death. I hoped Marva had suffered. If

she was dead, my countdown had started. I could picture a world
in which anvils fell from the sky to crush me if no other plans for
my death were in play. Some undiscovered disease might eat my
liver and thrust my wasted frame into a grave within days. My
stove might malfunction and burst into screaming flames, swallow
me in an explosion of gas and heat. An embolism might lodge in
my veins and drop me like a computer empty of charge.

A hand fell on my shoulder. I looked up, startled.

Maddy was staring at me. "Love? A penny for your thoughts.
I'm not a therapist by any means, but I am mindful of the Lord's
whisperings, and my spirit senses you need to unburden. I'm a
good listener, and I can't imagine how traumatic it must be to lose
a brother."

"He wasn't my brother."

"Pardon?"

"Lyle. He wasn't my brother. We were partners. I'm a private
detective and he worked with me. We were trying to prevent a
client...Never mind. I hate to ignore your kindness, but I need to
be alone."

"Oh, honey."

"I don't have time for tender moments. If your god's real, he's
got a piss-poor sense of humor, and I don't care for it."

Maddy's grip tightened on my shoulder. "You're in pain. You
don't know what you're saying."

I jerked my shoulder free, pushed past the nun, or whatever
she was, and marched to the mouth of the hallway. Spinning to
face her, I snarled. "You're a fraud."

She whimpered, raising her hand over her heart. Then,
mastering herself she offered a thin smile. "I can't imagine the hurt
you feel." She made to draw me into a hug, and I froze. All that
love and concern, the way it radiated off her, insulated her from
insult and injury, I envied it. There was no playacting in her. She
believed.

I believed her too, but I didn't want it. My limbs went stiff when her arms wrapped around me. I retreated into myself, closed my eyes and roused a dream of violence. When she released me, I fled to my room, closed and locked the door. With my back to its wood panel, I slid my body to the floor.

23

I CAN'T SAY HOW LONG I STARED AT THE SHADOWS OF clouds advancing over my bedroom walls, the shift of bright sun and tree limb dancing in the morning breeze. Sobriety, the clinical kind, fogged my body with various aches. I couldn't recall the last time my blood had run dry. Never envy the teetotaler. They live with the future in mind at all times: afraid of consequences, aware of others, envious, jealous, calculating. Alcohol numbs all of that, but I was sober.

Wondering if this was how a snared coyote felt moments before gnawing off its own leg, I rolled to my knees and stood on unsteady legs. I stumbled to my window and scanned the traffic on Maple. I told myself a meteor wasn't barreling down on me. I wondered what Lyle would do.

The phone on my bedside drawer vibrated. I went to it. The illuminated screen showed three missed calls from the same number. With my own phone, I dialed the digits from the caller on Laser's.

On the third ring, the line engaged. "Detective Mia, I assume."

You want me to tell you I felt a profound chill, or a surge of thrill, but recall, I was sober. I registered only mild curiosity. "Speaking. And who's this?"

"It's too late for introductions. She's already dead."

In sobriety, fear is three-dimensional. "I think now is the perfect time for introductions. Laser's obviously told you about our little chat, and so you know it isn't safe having me walking around. Imagine all the problems I'll cause when I start asking certain people questions."

"That's a little banal, don't you think?—" a spat of laughter— "You've spent the last day doing nothing but asking questions and see where it's gotten you."

Whoever this was, he had me pinned. "What do you say you eat a hot plate of cut-the-fucking-shit and get on with your business? Laser obviously told you his phone went missing and between the two of you, you were smart enough to realize (a) that's a problem, and (b) I was the likely culprit for its disappearance. If you weren't scared of what that meant for you, you wouldn't bother calling."

The speaker was a heavy breather, a prime candidate for a sinusectomy. "I rather think you've jumped to one too many conclusions. You know what they say about assumptions."

It's harder to fake a laugh than you'd expect, but I needed to show I wasn't vulnerable. "Yeah. They make an ass out of you and umption."

A sucking sound hissed from the receiver. "She's a clever one." If I had as much trouble pulling air through my nose as the speaker did, I'd likely panic and hyperventilate. "Unfortunately, clever won't keep you safe from us."

I slapped my palm on the side of my thigh. "Why don't I save you some time? We cut the cat and mouse routine. You tell me who you are, and we schedule a place to meet and talk. Straighten out all my false assumptions. Huh?" I felt like Lyle was in the room with me. Whoever this asshole was, I was going to punish him for his role in Lyle's death. "I may not know the why of your involvement, but I know you wouldn't've wasted your time trying to speak with me if I didn't pose a problem for you."

The nose-breather seemed to consider my proposal as a moment of speechlessness lingered. "I'm rather sorry to decline your invitation, as you do have quite the vim and vigor, but truth be told—how I love telling the truth—you've given me all I needed already. It's funny, you see? When Laser told me how quickly you latched onto him, I feared you might actually be a halfway decent detective, but it's clear you have no idea who I am, why I'm doing what I'm doing, or how it came to pass. You're no danger to me."

My temper seethed on a short tether. "I know more than you think."

"Don't bluff."

"So you won't mind if I give this phone number to the police?"

I thought he hesitated slightly. Perhaps an indication that he was more posture than confidence. "Feel free, but ask yourself, why is it always the ones we love the most?" The line disconnected. The rage in my confusion played like alcohol in my veins. I was half god, half lab rat. What was with his final cryptic line? Death nipped at my heels, but I felt no closer to an explanation. I stumbled dizzily into the kitchen for a tall drink, cursing under my breath.

Maddy sat at the table, still nursing coffee, head bowed over a small book lying flat and open somewhere in the middle.

I tapped the page her eyes lingered on. "You still want to help me, or did I blow it?" I sat in the chair opposite her. Laser would come for me, and when he did, I'd be prepared. "Because I need my knife, and I forgot it at the hospital. Will you drive me?"

She nodded, stood and shuffled out of the room.

I found her in the entryway, rifling through her purse. She

produced her phone, an old folding style, and typed a series of keys. While she listened to the ringing, she told me it was better to check with lost and found before spending the gas. I thought how rare it was to memorize phone numbers anymore. An idea struck me. After a day full of dead-ends a decent lead felt almost like hope. The only phone number I'd ever cared to memorize was Lyle's.

24

I LEANED AGAINST THE BRICK FAÇADE OUTSIDE OUR office, repeating a ten-digit phone number I couldn't quite place while drawing figures of infinity in the air with my favorite four-inch pocketknife. My thoughts were stained shoes, wandering every dark alley in Omaha. On the backside of the curtain there was a car crash and hot metal. The old woman named Maddy was driving. She bled from the mouth and eyes. Her teeth embedded in the steering wheel. Bone islands surfaced at her elbows where both arms had broken backwards. I felt I could've stood and walked away, but when I tried my legs didn't respond.

If you must die, hope you break your neck. Of all the pain myths, only a broken spine is fact. It's like ketamine. Lyle and I once snorted two lines of Special K and spent an afternoon on our office couch drooling while the pattern of sun traced a window-shaped line across our faces. You forget you have a body, or your body is the couch, and you're not hungry or thirsty, just very, very cottony.

You should know: The man who t-boned Maddy's car at the intersection of 78th and Dodge lacked malice. The minute Marva died, my life had started its inevitable circling of the drain. The end had been notarized with her last breath, and required only a careless driver and a red light.

I flicked my pocketknife closed, dropped it in my purse, pushed through the door where Lyle and Marva awaited me. "Sorry I'm late."

Lyle's mouth was buried in a half-eaten hoagie, tomato juice and mustard dripping from the corners of his lips. "Luke. We were just talking about you."

If for no other reason than that Maddy had helped me memorize a phone number, I hoped she'd glimpsed her heaven before the universe tugged her back into the drab service of the sick and dying. "All good things, I'm sure."

"Marva, here, came to me about a thing. We were just discussing some work, huh?"

Lyle's dying words pushed weakly at the back of my unconscious. "Fascinating. I hope she pays well. We could sure use the money."

I turned to Marva and introduced myself. She usually said something clever at that point, but maybe I'd perfected the casual entrance. First impressions are lasting, unless of course you don't remember them.

Nothing I'd done had resulted in her revealing unexpected details. Now, I thought, I would show her the mystery phone number. Hammer, meet nail. If my instincts were correct, she'd recognize it because whomever it belonged to was someone she cared for the most. Wasn't that how the mystery caller had put it?

I hadn't had time to think it all through, but I was about to find something out. Walking to the desk, I whistled a bar of Aretha Franklin's "Respect". Grabbing a pen, I scrawled the number on the back of our rent envelope and handed it to Marva. "My phone's dead. Mind calling Zio's for pizza?"

Her eyes fell on my writing. Her face squeezed into a rictus.

She burst from her seat, wrapping her hands around my throat. We toppled to the ground. I could've overpowered her—at least those first moments—but she was barking such nonsense.

Her hands were strong with fear. "This is none of your business!" Something in my throat popped. "You wouldn't. You couldn't."

Lyle sprung from his chair and tackled Marva. I rolled and gasped for air. Marva squirmed out of Lyle's grip. I crawled to my purse and freed the knife from its belly. Flicking the blade open, I meant to defend another attack, but Marva was a whirlwind of rage.

She kicked my hand. The knife skittered away. Lyle lunged for it, but Marva rose a leg and kicked his back, sending him headfirst into the wall.

I pushed to my knees as Marva seized my knife. She slashed the blade in an arch. I raised my hands to block the blow. The blade severed my pinkie. It curled on the carpet like a worm. My body flooded with numbed shock. Marva drew the knife back, and thrust, burying the blade between my ribs. I gasped.

Lyle rose groggily to his feet. Marva drove the knife into my ribs again. I coughed blood. My vision wavered like an aquatic landscape. Lyle staggered toward Marva. He grabbed a handful of her hair. She whipped around just as he slung her head. Her arm wheeled, the blade of my knife sliced across his neck. Blood shot in thick gushes. He gurgled.

Marva's body catapulted headlong. Her eye struck the corner of our desk, and her head stuck fast. Her body slumped, but she was lodged half upright, with her ankles crossed. Pulsing waves of light and dark constricted my view. I shivered. A sucking sound whistled from my chest. Lyle lay facedown on the carpet. My thoughts grew sluggish, clinging to the only words that mattered. *I think you're more beautiful than her.*

25

I leaned against the brick façade outside our office, drawing figures of infinity in the air with my favorite four-inch pocketknife. My thoughts were as stained as my shoes from wandering every dark alley in Omaha. A struggle for breath prompted me to trade my knife for the compact in my purse. Twin bruises flanked my throat. Inside my chest, a vacuum roared. I imagined a world tired of giving new chances. Perhaps the loop had its limits. I didn't want to find out.

Dropping my compact into my purse, I mussed my hair and rubbed stars into my eyes. I palmed my knife, and burst into the office to find Lyle licking mustard and mayonnaise from his fingertips. Marva's jaw hung slack. I aimed my knife in her direction. Her eyes travelled from my face to the blade in my hand. I recited the phone number clattering around my brain, speaking each digit with finality.

Her jaw locked and the bulge of muscle at its hinge formed a perfect marble. A low growl rose from her throat, perhaps a word I failed to understand.

I shot a glance at Lyle. "There's wine in the closet. For Marva.

Pour me a Magdalene, double neat. Don't argue." I returned my eyes to Marva who'd stood when I'd shifted my gaze. She heaved air in shallow gasps, her fists tight knots. "You're wondering how I have your husband's phone number." Lyle hadn't moved. I gestured with my hand: "Go!"

Lyle advanced one step, tentatively. "What's happening here?"

"Why don't you ask her? She's the one married to a man who wants her dead, and yet nothing we do can get her to admit his role in it all." I drilled into her with my eyes, the knife still aimed. "And don't try to make this about how I got his number. It doesn't matter."

She hadn't moved: neither toward me or away. Her lower lip quivered. Her eyes were beautiful and bright, full of hurt. I saw Lyle seeing her, and a wave of jealously washed over me. She was magnificent. Long muscled legs. Strong tan arms. All curves and soft angles. The exact replica of everything a woman wants to be.

"I got news for you, Marv. I'm not the enemy. I think you might believe I am right now. I know you wanted to strangle me when you heard those numbers, but here's the deal: everyone in this room ends up dead unless we save you, so you need to talk."

Lyle stepped between Marva and I. "What are you going on about, huh?" He palmed a handful of sunflower seeds, glancing at them in his cupped hand before tossing his head back and slapping them home.

I spun my knife over the ball of my thumb, and righted it, blade pointed at Marva's eye. "Go ahead. Tell him. Your husband's the one who's been sending you all those text messages."

Her shoulders had been stiff, her spine arched. By increments, then, her body relaxed. A slow smile replaced her burning-eyed expression. She even managed something similar to a laugh. "Tell him what, honey? That you're crazy. My husband doesn't want me dead." She pointed at my knife. "You're the one threatening people with a weapon here."

I struggled to translate her tone. The arm holding my knife relaxed. I let it fall to my side. She couldn't be trusted so I tossed a lie in the pond to see how it splashed. "I've already spoken to Ransom. He's working with a man named Laser, or should I call him Larry? Larry Surlman."

Marva made pouty eyes, large and round, doughy. She blew kissy lips. I couldn't've found solid ground if I was standing on a mountaintop, her response so surprised me. "That's not my husband's phone number," she said, "but I *am* intrigued that you think you solved my case before we ever met. How does this work?" She looked toward Lyle. "Did you text her my name the minute we met. I'm actually really curious. Or is this some kind of Penn and Teller routine? A magician never reveals his secrets."

Lyle crammed half a bean and cheese burrito in his mouth. "Are we still wanting drinks?"

Marva waved a hand of dismissal at him. "Whatever, honey. Can you just get scarce?"

I marched past Lyle and stood toe to toe with Marva. Her chest rose as her shoulders rolled back. I'd never noticed how tall she was. "Don't talk to Lyle that way."

Lyle wiped a smear of grease on his jeans. "Oo! Cat fight."

"Shut up." I closed my knife with one hand, and raised it hinge side out in Marva's face. "This man—" I tapped the knife on her cheek—"this man is the kind of man who will give everything he's got. Maybe you're used to the kind of men who strut around schmoozing with rich, pampered pricks and maybe men like your husband need sleeping pills because they're too coward to face the dark, but Lyle won't back down, even at the gates of hell. He cares. I doubt you know what that's like, but I know who you are, and I know you'll let a person like Lyle give everything he's got and you won't feel grateful." I was deep inside myself, mad as a hot cast iron pan, spittle leaping off my tongue as I drilled into Marva with a hate six deaths deep. She didn't deserve help, not by me, but we were stuck with her, and something told me she knew it.

She examined her fingernails, sighing theatrically. "Are you done yet?"

Heat rose from my face like fire breaking. "Am *I* done? Am I done! I'd give anything to be done, but you won't let me. I don't know what kind of masochistic incantation you uttered, but I couldn't be done if I wanted to. So we're going to go with the next best thing."

I pressed the hinge of the knife into the hollow of Marva's shoulder, and with my free hand I gripped the curve between her neck and clavicle and shoved her backward until she fell into the armchair opposite my desk. Her face revealed nothing, not surprise or anxiety. She'd steeled herself against my attack, though I'd managed to stop her from the mad frenzy of my last wasted life.

I leaned in to scream at her, to burst her eardrums, to make sound bleed from her eyes and nose, but Lyle took me by the elbow and pulled me back. "Slow down, slugger. I'll get us drinks, huh? Take a breath. Chill."

"Go fuck a wood chipper, asshole."

"Hey, that's more like it." He winked. "You were starting to scare me with all that good man talk."

I leered. "And I meant every word."

"May I cherish each one forever."

He left us there, silent, locked in a stare-down. Thuds and clanking echoed from the kitchenette. My lungs wept. I dug in my purse and retrieved the cigarettes. With the first kiss of nicotine a revelation bowled me over. Such a simple plan. Marva loved to drink, so get her drunk. Get her drunk and grill her. The sight of the phone number had driven her to murder once. We just needed to loosen her tongue.

Lyle returned with two high balls of bourbon and an empty wine stem. He distributed the drinks before plodding to the closet. He seemed almost ghostly, as if I couldn't soak in his living. I can't explain why, but that moment with Marva and Lyle was when I accepted nothing I could do would save him. I knew if I ever succeeded in saving Marva, it would cost me Lyle, a trade I wasn't sure I could tolerate.

26

MARVA SAID SHE DIDN'T WANT TO DIRTY OUR DISHES SO she drank from the bottle. I plied her with Magdalene once she'd dispatched the wine. Whatever it took to get her mouth running. Lyle wanted to pace her drink for drink, but I wouldn't let him. Nonetheless, by midnight we were five, unless I closed one eye. Just before 2AM, Lyle offered to run across the street for more booze. No one argued.

Liquor softened the atmosphere. We laughed at everything. My purpose faded under the shroud of normalcy. Marva told a story from her youth about butchering a chicken at her aunt's farm in Vermont: steel killing cone, sharp knife. Lyle told of his dog Ted, the black Daniff who carried children piggy-back. I never had pets, and children terrify me so I told stories constructed from the residue of strange dreams: One where I curled in a ball and rolled down a grassy slope, another where I knew I could fly but had to hide my powers lest I gain fame and attention.

We took turns serenading the toilet as the night deepened. There were a few drunk Tweets, several bouts of dancing—thanks to Hall and Oates "Sara Smile"—and one or two upset stomachs. Nothing more liquor couldn't exploit.

Marva met her match in a box of Franzia, much of which she spilled on the floor in an attempt to transfer it into the empty bottle she'd already drank from. She finished her task and promptly passed out with the dawn. Lyle and I had clung to consciousness by heat and fire: cigarettes for me and wasabi peas for him. The sun greeted us on the tail end of a hard drunk. I suggested Leo's for carry out. Lyle said he needed salt in the worst way.

I slipped my boots on, half laced, and snuck out the door. Sandra was chatting with an apple-faced customer at the counter. I asked her to throw in a bottle of Crazy Gringa. She said the sauce would melt my face off, and I said that was what I needed.

Marva snored while Lyle and I shoveled biscuits and gravy down our throats. I marked the occasion with a tweet: *Salt, spice, and generous portions of wheat flower with ibuprofen on top is the approved treatment for any excess of alcohol. #LiesWeTellOurselves*

At ten, as Lyle and I were tossing cards into my upturned Cubs hat—he had me beat three to one—Marva surged out of dead sleep, blurting, "I'm late!

Lyle smiled, calm as if he'd missed the demon springing from the armchair. "For what?"

"An appointment at Christian Nobel," I said. Marva cocked her head and squinted at me. She'd already outlived herself.

She leapt to her feet and stumbled toward the bathroom. Vomiting sounds were muffled by the door.

Lyle unwrapped a box of raisins. "Nature's candy."

His sweet tooth mystified me. I ambled toward Marva's purse and snagged the car keys from its side pocket. Lyle asked what I was doing. I told him to trust me. Shrugging, he agreed.

Marva emerged from the bathroom with some semblance of composure. Her hair would pass for messy-chic and her face for post-breakup sassy. The eyeliner, mascara, and eyeshadow had all blended into a soil-colored smear that lengthened her already cat-eyed face to its full predatory potential. She shouldered her purse and dug through its belly.

I winked at Lyle. My timing lacked sobriety. Marva's glare wiped the smile off my face. "Give me my keys."

"What keys?" I slipped them from my pocket and jangled them before her nose.

She swiped at them. "I have an appointment."

I tossed the ring to Lyle. He caught the keys and laughed. "This is kinky!"

Marva turned and slapped his cheek. The keys fell to the carpet. I dove for them. Marva fell on me. We wrestled on the ground. Lyle watched from the corner, cradling his cheek with his hand. It's unfamiliar, fighting with intent *not* to harm. And Marva had different plans. She buried her elbow in the hollow beneath my shoulder and breastbone. I yelped. Lyle jumped on top of us when Marva pinned me to the carpet. He poked at her ribs and squeezed her thigh. She fell back in a fit of involuntary laughter. He tickled under her arms and beneath her chin. Her arms flailed, and her feet kicked. She laughed, but tears peeled from the corners of her eyes, painting the makeup beyond its extreme boundaries.

"Stop it! Stop it! I'm going to pee. Stop it!"

If you've never seen a grown man tickle a grown woman, you haven't lived. It's an image of Lyle I'll never forget, and if you should ever meet me and find yourself inclined to romance me—unlikely, for so many reasons, I know—understand I *want* to be tickled.

Marva didn't. She ended Lyle's intervention with a bite to his forearm. Blood creased from tooth marks and ran around his wrist and palm. He kneed her in the stomach and her jaw released. An unfamiliar expression crept over Lyle's face. His eyes dulled, the blues shading toward gray. He stabbed at the keys next to her on the carpet, sprung to his feet and stomped to the bathroom. He dropped them in the toilet, unzipped and urinated. "Go on to your stupid appointment, huh?"

Marva wiped the blood from her teeth and chin. Her breathing came in shallow pants. She stood, wobbling, drunkenness still lapping at the borders of her adrenaline flood. With the handle of our plunger, she fished her keys from the toilet bowl.

Lyle had walked to the window and was staring out on the sparse morning traffic. The blood on his arm congealed in a deep ochre. He seized a half-eaten Reuben from the desk.

Marva dropped her keys from the plunger handle into the sink basin. She cranked the knobs, water swirling and shushing down the drain. Soap and a towel.

I met her at the front door. "Before you do this, understand that if we get separated, you're on your own."

She reached past my hip for the doorknob. "That's my plan."

I slipped the phone from my purse and offered it to her. "Do me a favor, then. Call the number."

She brushed my arm aside. "What's the point?"

Had I seen a glint of fear? "Humor me."

Her hand, on the doorknob, stilled. We met eyes. "What'll it prove?"

My lives were all jumbled in hangover and grease. I couldn't remember discussing one element of her case for all the alcohol we'd consumed, but the details had been there, hiding behind every embellished story we'd told. "You said this number didn't belong to your husband. So. Prove it."

She dialed without me reciting a digit. Of course she did. She pressed the speaker button and raised the phone to eyelevel between us. The office was silent save for the trill of the outgoing call.

Halfway through the fifth ring, the line engaged. Breathing.

My face felt cold and my palms crawled with sweat. "Hello? Ransom?" Marva's eyes narrowed. "Ransom, can you hear me?"

An anger-edged voice spoke in clipped tones. "Sorry. Wrong number."

"Ransom?" I felt unsure. "I'm with your wife. We know what you've done."

My memory flashed on the night Laser had caught Lyle and I spying. Ransom had been in the doorway. He'd only spoken a couple words, but I remembered his unearthly baritone. This voice didn't approach that depth, and I couldn't think why I hadn't remembered before. "You have the wrong number."

"You're not Ransom?"

The speaker cleared his throat. "Sorry, Detective Mia. You have the wrong man, and the fact that you've called me bodes poorly for your future. The minute she gave you this number—"

Marva snapped the phone from my ear and disengaged the line. Her eyes were blurred by tears. She refused to blink.

Lyle had turned his back to the window. He stared at Marva. "You know who that was."

"No. I—"

"Don't lie!" His lips drew back in a caged snarl. "What are you hiding?"

"And why pay us if you won't let us work your case?"

"I don't want to die."

Lyle puffed out his chest. "It sure doesn't look that way. Who are you protecting?"

Marva tried to open the door, but I kicked it shut. Lyle lurched, grabbing Marva by the elbow. She blinked and the tears that had hung in her eyes plunged to the carpet. Lyle ground his jaw. Marva sniffed. Lyle and I exchanged a glance. Marva pushed between us and ran for the window. She tried to shove the frame open, but the latch was locked.

Lyle caught her by the wrists and spun her. "Who are we dealing with?" He so rarely spoke sternly.

Marva whimpered. "It doesn't matter."

I lunged around Lyle, but he caught my wrist and pushed me back. I found my knife, opened, and aimed at her. "Why don't you save me the trouble and slap yourself."

Lyle splayed a palm above my chest and fixed Marva with a stare. "You're setting us up. Why hire us if you don't want answers?"

Marva looked from Lyle to me, and back again. Her chest stuttered with after-cry. She wiped her eyes. Her shoulders slumped.

27

THE OFFICE HAD GROWN STUFFY AS LYLE MOWED through his third bag of caramel corn. I'd reached that rare threshold where cigarettes felt like cat litter in my throat, and coffee was on the burner. Marva could've played the lead in some new TV drama about sexy zombies.

Maybe I was too threadbare to feel impatient, but as Marva recounted her story, I listened with only slight impatience for the details to coalesce. The narrative featured volunteerism with PETA and Urban Abbey and the Appleseed Project. There were too many causes to count. She said she'd been a faithful attendee at every open city council meeting, went prepared with questions and motions. I couldn't get enough coffee.

Her husband gladly funded her causes because all he wanted was her happiness. "Like I could ever be happy with a man whose greatest achievement is putting people to sleep."

I scratched my elbow. "So you'd say your relationship with Ransom is rocky."

She laughed, crossing her legs and resting her head on the back of the chair. "Not like you think. He wouldn't kill me if I asked him to. Our relationship is suffocatingly smooth. He puts money in the bank. I spend it on worthy causes. He takes me to fancy fundraisers. I insult his guests."

"That doesn't bother him, huh?"

I mimed a gun with my fingers and thumb. "It bothers him. He might've been punch drunk for those beautiful legs, once, but something's put him over the edge."

"I've always had more than legs going for me. Even if no one else realizes it."

"You sure know how to get a rise out of people." I shifted in my chair. "And at some point you finally pushed your dear, sweet husband just a little too far, didn't you? But I'm still a little lost on the specifics so how about you tell us whose number we just called so we can make a tidy bow of this case and never see each other again."

Marva rubbed her temples and sighed. "It was clear you didn't like me from the moment I walked in this office."

"Was it the knife that gave me away?"

"I'm good at gauging those kind of things." She told a story about how she'd come to a point several months ago where no one would speak to her. She'd demanded action from people who claimed to want justice, but those people ended up being nothing more than big mouths.

It got so bad at one point that she turned to the church, attended a Sunday service at Urban Abbey, even liked what was going on there. It looked like genuine outreach until she got to know the owner. That person got tangled up in pronouns, "Demanded people used *they* instead of *her*, because 'they' didn't identify as male or female. I tried to go along, but one day I laughed at *them* and they said mockery wasn't welcome in their community. I asked for a vote, but they said no."

I picked cotton pills from the office chair and closed my eyes. "What's this got to do with your situation?"

"I don't know. Maybe it helped me realize no one was going to do a damn thing about the problems of the world."

Lyle unwrapped a candy bar. "But you would, huh?"

"A couple days after I left Urban Abbey, I saw an article in the paper about a new condominium development going up by TD Ameritrade. Of all the stupid things to protest, I don't now why I went after those guys, but I couldn't handle it. There was a lake on the property that was scheduled for draining and fill-in. The lake served as one of the landing points for the Sandhill Crane migration, only one east of Grand Island. Couple thousand birds each spring and fall. The previous tenants, some insurance company, were moving west to a new campus and the landowner wanted more money for the property. I got a lawyer, detailed my claim and had him file a motion to block the development."

My eyes were heavy. "That when the trouble started?"

"Not right away. It was a couple weeks later when a temporary hold was filed because of my motion."

Lyle sliced a piece of sharp cheddar and folded it into his mouth. "You know who threatened you, don't you?"

"Someone's definitely trying to scare me into withdrawing my injunction."

I took a wild stab at a half-formed conjecture. "How deep would we have to dig to find out how much money the condo developer donated to PharmTech?"

"You don't know what you're talking about."

I sprung from my chair and pounded my fist on the desk. "You're lying. We know what's happening. And I think—"

"We do?" Lyle shrugged.

"Leave it." I turned back to Marva. "Why won't you take the threats to the police? What do you gain by coming to us?"

Marva leapt from her chair, followed by Lyle. It seemed we were on the threshold of another scuffle. "Who do you think you are, you broke-ass bitch? Nobody in this city trusts you to solve a kindergarten puzzle, and you think you can flip a coin and solve all my problems? Sorry to break the news, but you're a waste of oxygen."

Lyle tossed a handful of cashew pieces in his mouth. "Is that why you hired us? You thought we'd come up with nothing, and that's what you want, huh?"

"Maybe you and Ruskov have something going. He sent you to us. What's his game?"

"Ruskov! Ruskov? The only reason you think Ruskov is worth piss in a toilet is because you're that stupid. He's a fraud. Ever wonder why every government agency works with him? If that doesn't prove how worthless he is. And when he came to me with his sympathy and those weasel eyes I knew whatever he thought was best was a sure crock of shit. Ruskov!"

Lyle unwrapped a sucker. "What's Phil got to do with this?"

I ignored him. "Then you don't think someone's trying to kill you?" It finally settled on me that trying to coax anything from her was wasted time. If I wanted answers, they had to come from else- where. "Those tears you cried earlier were just an act?"

"So I cry when I'm hungover. Big deal. And sure. Someone's trying to kill me. I know who's behind it, but they won't succeed. The whole thing's blown so far out of proportion. When the media finds out someone made an attempt on my life."

"It was all a hoax, huh?"

"A hoax? No. Publicity. This all would've been fine if it hand't been for—"

28

OUR OFFICE DOOR EXPLODED OFF ITS HINGES, CRASHING into the desk. Laser stood framed in the jamb. He aimed a hatchet and buried it in Marva's chest. With revelations still on her tongue, she fell. Lyle's mouth hung open, his cheeks stretched tight. I thought to dive behind the armchair, but my legs wouldn't listen.

Laser produced a cylindrical canister from his trenchcoat pocket, pulled a pin and tossed it at our feet. It bounced, spun, and sighed blue-gray smoke. Lyle leapt laying his body over the canister. When I later understood his sacrifice, it only hurt me more.

Laughter echoed distantly, but by then, I'd lost interest in Laser. Lyle sprung to hands and knees. He pawed at his face and fell sideways. Fumes licked from the canister, curling into the air. When the pungent odor hit my nose, my legs understood the danger, but my brain was slow to accept its fate.

My knees buckled as chemical gas burrowed into my pores, attacking my nervous system. I wanted to cut it out. My mouth burned copper-tasting acid. Laser retreated, speaking words I failed to interpret. I reached for my knife.

From there, all intention and will dissolved. Both Lyle and I writhed on the floor. He batted and scratched at his chest. I lost my mind, slicing my body to bleed the pain. The smoke hit my eyes and blinded me. It snaked down my throat and sliced my lungs more efficiently than any blade. Violent coughing wracked our bodies. My stomach clenched, and I vomited. All my muscles tensed. The last moment put a fine point on my pain, drawing into a silent focused scream.

29

My shoes were stained from Omaha's dark alleys. I leaned against the brick façade outside our office, gasping for air while drawing figures of infinity on my face, bleeding burning memories from my skin, with my favorite four-inch pocketknife. Blood dripped off the hilt. Life was growing tired of me. Feelings on this matter are never mutual.

I groped for the door and stumbled into the office. My ears rang. Tears carved molten channels down my cheeks. Lyle dropped the sandwich in his hand. Sliced tomato, shaved ham, and shredded lettuce spilled on the carpet. The mustard stained bread lay face up.

"Lu? What in the—"

I sunk to my knees. "Water."

There was a scramble of feet, a series of clipped expletives, and a clamor of metallic shuffling. Then Lyle was at my side with one hand on my shoulder and the other hovering before my face with a glass outstretched.

I managed to focus my strength and reach for the cup. The liquid seared my tongue and throat, focusing the gaping gulf inside me. I emptied the glass and asked for more. My voice, so raspy, belonged to someone almost dead. My gut wretched and I vomited bile.

A form eclipsed the overhead light. My eyes followed the long, smooth legs, up the skirt, over the tapered waist. The face that looked down on me was neither surprised nor sorrowed. She wore a black eye like Van Gogh's *Starry Night*.

30

A SHARP PULSING TONE COAXED ME FROM A DREAM. THE sound of rushing water, and a hazy image of a broad river cascading over rocks in a mountain forest full of grass and mossy rock was replaced by the sharp, sterile surroundings of a white-walled hospital room. The bed where I woke was narrow with white plastic railings on either side. Something was clipped to my left index finger. My right wrist was handcuffed to the bed railing.

The pulsing tone that had roused me repeated at intervals of about a second: the strength of my heart as depicted on a square black screen with a rolling green graphic of peaks and valleys. A large window looked out over pale blue sky smeared in orange and salmon, the slight marbling of wispy clouds burnt by the fire of dawn. I lay alone. My face itched. I reached to scratch it with my left hand and the heart monitor on my finger detached. A penetrating whine, deeper than the pulse, droned monotonously. Bandages crisscrossed my cheeks and forehead.

As I explored the itching beneath my eyes, two men in green scrubs pressed into the room. We exchanged glances. Each of the men relaxed when he looked into my eyes.

"I'm thirsty."

The taller of the two men approached. "You have a nurse call button, you know?" He took my free hand and reattached the heart monitor to my finger.

I asked what hospital I was at and how I had come. He said Methodist. The other man, shorter and stalky, said, "Mr. Kupchinink brought you."

Slowly, something resembling a linear narrative arranged itself before me. "It's Kuputchnik." Scorching pain and self-mutilation. "Is he here?"

Shorty said he didn't know.

"Can you check?"

No response.

"Why the handcuffs?"

Tall Boy said I was on seventy-two hour observation. He looked warily at Shorty. Perhaps they shared a telepathic connection, because after the silent consultation with his coworker, Shorty told me a doctor would see me soon, and Tall Boy nodded. I asked for a glass of water to which Tall Boy said he would see what he could do.

The two worked to tidy my bed. Tall Boy asked if I wanted the curtains drawn. I didn't. Shorty showed me the remote for the bed, how to raise and lower the head and foot, and explained the television. They left.

I sat in the stillness, counting the repeating tan swirl pattern on a small burgundy armchair by the window. After I'd satisfied myself that there were ninety-six swirls on the chair's back, I closed my eyes and focused my mind on questions no one could answer: Why were hospital beds so uncomfortable? Was Marva still alive? Did Lyle think me crazy? Where was my glass of water? When could I smoke? How would I pay my medical bill? What was that smell? Who inserted my catheter?

At some point a subtle knock startled me. "Come in." But the knocking wasn't for me.

Some time later a round-bodied man with a face like a pecan and black hair, tightly curled stepped into my room. He adjusted his bifocals. "I'm Doctor Christopher."

I remote inclined the head of my bed. "I'm not a criminal."

His smile was full of judgment, the sort that men in power express toward vulnerable women. "How else would you explain the bloody knife in your purse and the cuts on your face?"

"I had a rough night."

"That's an understatement." He cleared his throat and tugged at the white lapel of his jacket. "I'm told you're a detective so I don't have to explain to *you* why precision matters." He used the word explain like he could hardly contain the urge. "Maybe you can start by telling me who gave you the ammonia vapors. Because that person is going to be in a lot of trouble."

"I don't follow."

He slipped a click-top pen from his jacket pocket. "I'm not sure I do either." Click-click. "There's more ways to commit suicide than sports drink flavors, which is saying something. And you choose ammonia vapors." Click-click. "You must really hate yourself."

"Hate myself?"

"Come now, dear. It's one thing to regret a suicide attempt, but another entirely to pretend you didn't do it."

"Someone attacked me."

"Yes. That's clear." Click-click. "And that *someone* was yourself."

I could feel an expert analysis coming on. "It most certainly wasn't."

"While I'd love to believe you, the lab reports are explicit. You sustained chemical burns across your body, and throughout your circulatory system about twenty-hours prior to the lacerations on your face." Click-click, "And the only fingerprints on the knife found in *your* purse, coated in *your* blood, belong to *you*."

"I'm dying to know what an educated man like you thinks. Don't spare the least detail."

He adjusted the stethoscope around his neck. "I'm sensing hostility and sarcasm."

"I'm just waiting for you to enlighten my feeble mind, doc."

"It's simple." Click-click. "Someone gave you access to ammonia gas, but your suicide attempt failed because the vapors were dispensed in a room with circulated air so instead of asphyxiating, you woke with chemical burns, temporary blindness and searing pain. Then—"

"I what?" I interrupted. "Drove myself to my own office, cut my face and stumbled in on a conversation between my partner and Marva DeLonghi."

Dr. Christopher lowered the hand holding his pen. His face was a bruised peach. "It's true the cuts were administered hours after the gas burns." He examined the pen as if it held some cipher he couldn't decode. "However, it's also true that you administered the cuts."

"I'm not arguing the cuts." I jerked my hand and the heart monitor slipped off. The flatline tone wailed.

Dr. Christopher waddled to my bedside and reattached the monitor.

"Is this really necessary?"

He refused comment.

"I cut my face, but I didn't gas myself. That's absurd and you know it."

"What other possible annotation could you offer to suit the evidence?" Click-click.

"Put the pen away!"

Dr. Christopher smacked his lips. He slipped the pen into his coat pocket, and smiled slightly. "You *are* energetic for a suicide risk." He tap-tapped his front teeth with the edge of his fingernail. "But we see all kinds here."

"What I don't get is that you know what I do for a living, but it never occurred to you my situation might've resulted from an encounter with someone who didn't like being investigated."

He flipped through pages on the clipboard. "You cut your own face, but someone else gassed you?"

"That's correct."

Tap-tap. "You cut your own face with a hunting knife."

"A pocketknife. After Laser lobbed a gas..." I trailed off because I couldn't explain my dying.

"Are you investigating any farmers?"

I squinted, boring into him with confusion. "Not that I know of. Why?"

"Ammonia gasses are used in farming." Tap-tap. "About the only place."

"How about fishing?"

"State laws prohibit its use within one mile of public waterways."

"You know a lot about farming."

Tap-tap. "My father."

"I want to see my partner."

"No visitors."

"It's a professional concern."

"Does he have a phone?"

"Who doesn't?"

Dr. Christopher walked around my bedside and grabbed the phone console. "You may call him." He asked for the number and dialed, handing me the receiver. "After I see your MRI we can discuss your treatment plan further. I'll be back soon."

Lyle answered on the second ring. "Detective Kuputchnik speaking."

His voice was never so sweet. "It's Luke. Listen. You need to get me out of this place. Like yesterday."

A sound like plastic foil tearing preceded his answer. "How you feeling, Lu?"

"My face itches like hell, and I have to deal with Dr. Mansplain who thinks I tried to commit suicide, and I'm handcuffed to a hospital bed. How do you think I'm feeling?"

"You know how close you came to dying?"

"Close only counts in hand grenades and horseshoes."

"Dancing. Hand grenades and dancing, like my granddaddy used to say."

Life had the upper hand on me—or was it death?—because Lyle couldn't understand the textures of what I had to say: "I'd save your ass if the situation was reversed."

The telephone mic seemed enthralled in every texture of his chewing. "I never pinned you as the suicidal type."

"Christ! These hospital people sure have a song and dance. You actually think I tried to kill myself?"

"You scared the shit out of me last night. Not to mention you ran off the best chance of a paying client we've had in six months. Has it crossed your mind I might be a little upset with you, huh?"

"I—"

"Don't get me wrong. I'm glad you're okay, but honestly."

"Marva DeLonghi's probably already dead. She had an appointment at Christian Nobel."

"How'd you—"

Dr. Christopher appeared in the doorway. "No planning dramatic escapes now."

"I'm a prisoner here." I hung up.

"I hope I didn't deceive you into thinking that was a private conversation, but you need to understand your partner is as worried about your safety as we are."

I turned my head and closed my eyes. Betrayal tastes like

iodine. It dries the tongue and numbs the fingers. I didn't open my eyes until the sound of footsteps retreating silenced.

For what seemed hours, I lay alone in bed, flirting with sleep but never consenting. The heart monitor beeped away. Occasional chatter echoed in the hallway. Hushed conversations floated past my door. It felt like a basic violation of my rights to keep me from smoking. Every nerve in my body wept for want of nicotine. And a strong drink would've suited me just fine.

It's impossible to know how long it was before Dr. Christopher returned. When he did, he loomed over me. His clipboard was tucked beneath one arm, and the click-top pen hung, taunting me, from his coat pocket. "I'm guessing you won't be surprised when I tell you what turned up from last night's MRI readings."

"Illuminate me." I pushed a laugh through my nose.

"Bullet shrapnel." He tongued the corner of his mustache. "You've tried to take your life before. Now I understand why you used gas. Not too many people fail with a shot to the head, let alone two. And all I'm left wondering is what else our body scans will turn up. The bruises on your neck already suggest manual asphyxiation."

I held my breath. All the aches and pains hadn't been simple memories. I lifted my free arm and stared at the soft pale flesh. Maybe I was imagining it, but the faintest trail of a scar running from wrist to elbow glowed in the fluorescent lighting.

"Here I thought you'd overcomplicated a death wish. Now I'm thinking your body is incredibly resilient and you're weary of failure."

I wondered if all doctors were condescending, or if I simply happened to have that kind of luck. "There's a perfectly unreasonable explanation for this—"

"Freudian slip, I'm sure, but you said *un*reasonable."

"I meant unreasonable. You're too busy congratulating yourself on pinpointing my motives, but since you're so busy telling me how it is, I think I'll take a turn. It's probably my last chance. I doubt if I can make it through another time."

Dr. Christopher set his clipboard at the foot of my bed. "Is that regret I hear?"

"I want to live. I really do."

"So you understand the paradox of your mental illness?"

I turned my focus to the IV line hanging from my arm and pictured wrapping it around the doctor's neck. "Nothing against mental illness. Just isn't me." If he tried to enlighten me one more time, I wouldn't be responsible for my actions. "I'm stuck in a loop of some kind where I'm responsible for a woman's life, and every time I fail to save her, it's fatal to Lyle and me. There's no margin for error, either. Once I meet her, I have until a little after ten the next morning to save her. I can't tell you why, but she waited to the last moment to seek help. It's like she wanted this to happen.

"What I can't understand is that I did save her once, but Lyle died, and I wound up in jail." I glanced at the doctor to see if he wore a mocking smile, but his face was nothing if not curious. "I served the better part of a decade behind bars before Marva visited. She came to gloat over all that happened, but I got Lyle back when I leapt over the table and strangled her. That was the second time a cop shot me in the head. I've been raped, shot, hacked to pieces, stabbed, choked, paralyzed, gassed, and I'm probably missing something. It gets tough, keeping track. She dies, we die, but the funny thing is, I'm positive if we saved her, but died trying, we'd stay dead. I know it's true for Lyle, and I'm afraid the whole thing is setup so he *has* to die."

"You really care about your partner." Dr. Christopher clicked his pen and scratched a note on his chart.

I dismissed his comment with a wave of my hand. "It's some cruel kind of tradeoff I can't seem to beat. At first I thought I had as much time as I wanted to puzzle it out. It only hurt a little the first few times I came back. Some stiffness, like I slept in an awkward pose, but I'd materialize right back at my office door, knife in hand and Lyle talking to Marva." A flicker of memory, something critical, pinballed across my unconscious. "All this time I thought I was supposed to learn how to get Marva talking, when the key was to realize she stood in my way."

I swallowed a bullet of emotion, because something else occurred: "I said the only way out was to save Marva, but I bet there's another way. I bet at some point my body won't have enough gas to pull me through the loop. Then it's game over for everyone. And what would I care then? Maybe that's been the point of this exercise from the beginning."

Dr. Christopher, who'd been reviewing the chart, glanced up. "It's interesting you chose the verbiage 'game over.' Would you say you're a fan of video games? The reason I ask is that I had a patient not long ago, a teenage boy whose only pleasure was a game called *Halo*, and he attempted to take his own life with a hand grenade. It surfaced that his grandfather stored mementoes from his tour in the Vietnam War that the boy knew of."

And just like that I knew he'd only listened long enough to refine his own impressions. "I can't remember the last time I played a video game."

"I see." His face slackened into the scowl of a disappointed child. "Too bad. It would be a fascinating case study to examine the impact of video games on the human brain through the lens of suicide."

"Look. Like it or not, I'm not suicidal. Though I am dying for a cigarette."

Dr. Christopher smirked. "Over sixty-percent of schizo-phrenics identify as smokers."

I wondered what it would feel like to be a man, so confident, so certain, so deaf to any conflicting rationale. "You think I'm suffering a schizophrenic delusion?"

"If you don't play video games, what other explanation is left?"

"You're telling me the truth isn't an option?"

"I'm sorry, dear. You must be tired. And I have other patients. You need rest."

"When can I see Lyle?"

"And plan your grand escape?" He shook his head. "I'm sorry—"

"Then humor me."

"How's that?"

"Go to the KETV website, or call the OPD and ask about Marva DeLonghi. If you find she was murdered this morning around ten outside Christian Nobel Furs at Regency Mall maybe you'll reevaluate your views. Because if what I'm saying is true, there's no other way I could know the future than that I've seen it."

Dr. Christopher looked at his watch. "It's not ten yet."

"Then there's still time. Send the police."

"That would be irresponsible of me." He lifted the pen in his hand, and clicked it twice before slipping into his jacket pocket.

31

Hours after Dr. Christopher left me, a woman rolled a knock down pan rack to the door of my room. Her face startled me, but I couldn't quite place her. A nurse whispered in the woman's ear before removing a tray and bringing it to me. The nurse rolled a pneumatic table over my bed and set the tray on its wood veneer. On the tray sat a burgundy cloche, a cardboard container of skim milk, and a plastic spoon. Knives and forks, the nurse said, were prohibited for watch patients. I managed to stomach a few bites of the limpid broth and mushy vegetables, but starvation seemed an appealing alternative.

The woman rolled the pan rack away, but the nurse stayed. He told me I should stop attempting to dial out on the bedside phone. The receptionist was growing tired of disconnecting my in-network calls. Without the passcode to call out, my efforts were pointless, and somewhat time-consuming for the hospital staff. If I ever wanted to begin my rehabilitation, I needed to demonstrate behaviors of a functioning participant in treatment.

I didn't want to participate in anything. It didn't matter since Marva would already be dead, and since she was dead, I wouldn't be far behind. Did my body have enough to pull through one more time? If it did, I knew what I would do.

Regarding the answer, you might scoff. Certainly, I view the events of that second night at the hospital with incredulity. My death and salvation came at the hands of a friend.

During the afternoon, I was moved to a single-patient, locked room with a barred window, metal cot, and aluminum toilet. The vinyl mattress had no bedding, and my door lacked a knob. Sometime after dark the woman with the pan rack arrived with dinner. She came alone, and in the cold glow of fluorescent light, I immediately placed her. The Cereal Burglar bringing me dinner. Imagine. She worked in food service. Perhaps that says something about people, what we're drawn to, how the things we gravitate toward shape us. A young woman with lupus whose insurance is decent, but who still pays too much in medical bills to afford a living makes a hobby of robbing convenience outlets.

She floated to the foot of my bed, movements assured, carrying the tray with the cloche and the cup of canned fruit. "When you graduate to Level 2 you can eat in the commons with the other patients." There was no judgment in her. Her voice had the mellow tone in it that could rock a person to sleep, the soul of someone who knew loneliness and pain, at ease, with the faintest jagged edges, a real radio voice, a midnight DJ. "Take your time, but I have to stay with you until your done."

I sipped from the cup of soup. "I wasn't sure you could speak."

She crossed her arms and probed me with her eyes. I'm probably reading too much into that first moment, because there was no way she expected a lunatic in a hospital bed, confined to a locked room, a woman with bandages on her face and subdued bruises on her neck to know anything damning about her, but nonetheless, I thought a flash of fear colored her cheekbones.

If not, I set it there with my next comment. "The way I see it, you have two choices. Either you help me out of here or I tell the doctor I've met you at Walgreens."

Slowly, she shifted her weight to her left leg and jutted her hip to the side.

I drank the heavy syrup from the fruit cup. "Maybe you'd like to consider your options over a bowl of Cookie Crisp. Take your time. I think you'll agree, I don't really need to be here." The carton of milk tore when I opened it. "Write me a note with your answer, if you'd prefer. Finding the right words in real time can be challenging."

She closed her eyes and raised her chin to the ceiling.

Milk dribbled down my chin. "If you're banking on no one believing me when I tell them what I know, you're probably smart. I'm just a crazy lady with absurd notions and far-fetched stories. But then, I'm guessing if anybody looked too hard into what I tell them, they'd find you on a few surveillance videos at some interesting locations. Maybe you won't mind being a fugitive, having to start over in Canada. You've got a hell of a talent for going unnoticed."

She covered her face with one hand, bowed her head, and froze. I admired her self-discipline. It didn't surprise me. You don't come to be the most revered robber of a generation without poise and self-control. She'd hit dozens of stores, collected thousands—more?—in cash, fooled every police officer, detective, and state trooper who'd pursued her and managed all that while working in a hospital where psychologists daily evaluated social strictures.

I pushed the tray toward her, my meager appetite satisfied. "Thanks for dinner."

She collected my tray and left, but I knew she'd return with more than just my next meal.

32

THE FOLLOWING MORNING A PARADE OF NURSES AND
doctors marched through of my room. Dr. Christopher talked
about me like I was absent, deaf, or dead. He used five-dollar
words as if he owned a million-dollar dictionary. "Her body is
inimitable in the annals of medicine. See here, evidence of
multiple fatal wounds, none which managed to slay her. We find
no remediation for shattered lumbar vertebrae, no treatment for
bullet shrapnel in her temporal or sphenoid bones though an
MRI indicated at least two bullets penetrating the cranium. She
sustained heavy scarring in her lungs from ammonia inhalation,
and though utilization of all four limbs can be demonstrated,
internal scarring and bone fragmentation suggest dual, femoral
amputation. No less curious are the bruises on her throat. The
depth of two inches subdermal would indicate tracheal trauma
commensurate with manual strangulation within the past forty-
eight hours, yet the presence of ammonia vapors contradicts those
findings, appearing nearly at parallel chronology." Dr. Christopher glowed as he approached his hypothesis. "Her ability to heal
suggests experimental medicine. Given the absence of procedural

documentation, all tests support some form of undocumented regenerative therapy.

"Of course, what we expect to find is that this woman has been treated under an alias, which when we ascertain could establish medical chronicity, but until then we must operate with the scholarship at hand. Considering only the evidence, her traumas raise false positives from multiple suicide attempts. The images of Miss Mia's body indicate unique cellular pathways, a most fascinating discontinuity, a new branch in lymphatic evolution. Additionally it provides primary avenues for inquest and interrogation regarding mental health and its relative impact on human survival."

Periodically a nurse—accompanied by several orderlies who appeared eager to wrestle should I attempt escape—would transfer me into a wheelchair and roll me into a bright room where technicians in lead-lined vests microwaved my body. Who knew you could empathize with a corndog?

On the third day, they moved me to a two-patient room with open access. Everything in the room was affixed to the walls or floors by metal brackets and heavy screws, but otherwise freer than my previous accommodations. The second bed in my room lay empty.

Daily, nurses administered medicated oxygen to rehabilitate my lungs. An ENT spent hours with me, producing a post-treatment care regimen. Toward the end of the first week, an OR doctor took me to the first floor, put me under and removed the shrapnel from my skull. When I was returned to my room, the headache throbbing behind my eyes felt like punishment for every foolish decision I'd ever failed to make.

Following a week of minor surgeries, and respiration therapy I felt stronger than I had in years—whatever that meant in the context. Dr. Christopher said my vitality was also likely a symptom of sobriety, noting my liver and kidneys showed acute damage from alcoholism. I didn't plan to quit drinking, if the choice was mine, and if I would've smelled smoke on anyone's jacket I might've licked the fabric while clawing at the pockets for a cigarette.

Midway through the second week, Dr. Christopher appeared in my room after hours. He tended to appear on his final rounds between 5:00 and 6:00 PM, but somewhere around the tenth day he dropped in after dinner. By then I'd graduated to Level 2 and ate with my peers, who all smelled as crazy as they acted. I'd just returned from dinner, wondering if I'd misidentified the Cereal Burglar when Dr. Christopher's form filled the jamb of my room. His arrival startled me out of deep thought. Facing the door, I sat on the floor in the corner.

He stood there, looking down on me. "I need to tell you something, but you've been thriving in your treatment, and I worry."

I already knew: "Lyle's dead?"

"He's in a coma. But Marva DeLonghi—"

"Does that mean you don't think I'm crazy?"

"Crazy is never the word I would've used."

"Do you believe my story?"

"No." Dr. Christopher scratched his chin. "I don't believe the properties of linear time function any differently for you. I don't believe you've ever died, but I *can* acknowledge you knew something important." His ear, scratch-scratch. "I erred in dismissing your warnings on the basis that you suffered from psychosis."

"You still think I'm psychotic?"

"Not exactly, but—"

"If you're working your way up to an apology, I don't care. Lyle's as good as dead. Marva *is* dead." I wanted to say, I won't be far behind, but I didn't need to distract Dr. Christopher so I scratched his ego. "Tell me how it happened."

"Someone attacked and murdered Mrs. DeLonghi at Regency,

just as you said." Scratch-scratch, his forehead. "Mr. Kuptucheek was wounded defending her."

"Kuputchnik." I corrected him absentmindedly. "Defending her?"

Dr. Christopher adjusted his eyeglasses and scratched his upper lip. "The police failed to detain the suspect, but they're conducting a city-wide search as we speak."

Of course. "How?"

He said an ongoing investigation was underway. Eyewitnesses at the mall described a tall, tattooed man assaulting Marva DeLonghi. He carried a heavy axe. The owner of Christian Nobel Furs said Lyle had spotted the attacker moments before the man entered the store. A brief scuffle ended when Lyle was knocked unconscious by the dull end of the axe. The attacker then confronted Marva. After murdering her, he fled. Lyle sustained brain damage. He would never recover beyond a vegetative state.

"The police," Dr. Christopher scratched his chest, "I don't know how to say this," scratch-scratch, "have opened a homicide investigation. They've requested an interrogation regarding your prior knowledge of Marva's situation."

Fragments from a lifetime of dreaming pulsed through my mind. There wasn't enough air in the world to fill my lungs. "I had nothing to do with any of this." But I wasn't sure. Try mapping a reliable alibi from the psychedelic soup of my life the past days—try even finding language to explain what a day looks like when death and resurrection feature prominently in the time-line. "What can I tell them, that I haven't already said?"

Dr. Christopher scratched his hand. "They think you might have involvement with the man they're hunting."

If I didn't find a way out fast, I was going to be starring in primetime manhunt, framed as an accomplice, and kept on round-the-clock surveillance. "I'm a victim in all of this. Why can't anyone see that?"

Dr. Christopher stood quietly, eyes fixed on the wall. "You'll forgive me—" Scratch-scratch—"if I doubt your claim. The victim paradigm is common of many mental illnesses, but the truth is, you knew the location and approximate time of a gruesome murder."

"*You'll* forgive *me* if I don't buy the scientific method mumbo jumbo. There's a perfectly good explanation for everything that's happened. I mean, do you really think my partner would've been trying to prevent a murder I had a part in planning? Does that make any sense? I've already told you what *does* make sense, but you refuse to believe because it doesn't fit your predetermined understanding of the world." I scanned the room for a pack of cigarettes I knew wasn't there. "So do your worst, because it's clear you haven't listened to a word I've said."

Dr. Christopher turned his head and fixed me with his eyes for a long time, scratching his elbow. Finally, he stood. "I'm sorry." He left the regret open ended.

It turns out we can't prevent much. I don't want to wax philosophical, but it took a great deal of failure for me to resolve myself of blame. I watched Lyle die so many times, and every time I thought I could stop it. But he had to die. It was written in the script. Don't ask me who writes the script. I don't know that answer, but I know there are dramatic rises, and climactic falls, endless falling. If events derail, if the story goes off script, life can erase a page and start fresh: start from the moment before we enter our office, return our belongings and our loved ones, but never deliver our dearest hopes.

33

THAT SAME NIGHT, AFTER SHIFT-CHANGE, THE CEREAL
Burglar appeared in my doorway. The backlighting obscured the
figure, but I glimpsed a golden glow off the tips of her hair. I asked
for the lights to be turned off so I could sleep.

"They say you think you're a cat."

I closed my eyes. "You've got me confused with someone else."

"You think you have nine lives."

"Oh." I probed the darkness behind my eyelids for something,
for nothing. "Ten. Twenty. Eight. I'm not sure. Too many. Not
enough."

"Must be nice."

I smiled. "Torture, in fact."

There was warmth and familiarity to this young woman that
left me regretting my failures. She hovered just inside my room like
a vulture haloed in light. She drifted to my bedside, bent low and
pressed her lips to my cheek. I let her kiss linger.

Her hand trembled like butterfly wings, landing on my breastbone. "If you die, you'll come back?" The warmth of her fingers

flowed into me. She left a vial of fluid on my chest. "Help yourself."

I thought, *She doesn't believe me*, but chose to keep her skepticism a silent secret. Raising the vial to the light, I peered through the yellow liquid. It distorted the ceiling tiles. "What is it?"

She threaded her fingers and stepped back. "Vivifica. Twelve thousand miligrams."

Fitting. Fated? "Will it hurt?"

"Everyone from the clinical trials loves it."

I uncapped the vial, considered whether I'd embraced death one too many times, and drank. A bitter taste like rose petals and orange pith coated my tongue. My mouth watered, and my jaw clenched. "Since you think I'm insane, you won't mind telling me your name."

She took the empty vial from my hand, the lid from my pillow and tucked both into the pockets of her scrub pants. "I'm not hiding anything." She pointed at a tag clipped to her jacket: SUSAN. "Just, no one's ever really looking."

For a detective, I sure lacked basic skills of observation. What else did I miss for failing to look? "Susan's a good name." I smiled. My body felt like butter softening over a flame. "My partner's one of your biggest fans. He's the one who saw you first."

She gripped my hand more firmly. "Does he know who I am?"

I jerked my hand free. "I do, and that's all that matters."

She stomped her foot. "Does *he* know who I am?"

"He's in a coma." My eyes fluttered heavily. "And he won't recover."

A burst of stillness. Susan's eyes shone. I didn't have long to ponder what I witnessed there, but it was enough to recognize the birth of a murderer, the knowledge blooming on her face that she'd gone through with it.

Amazing how quickly the drug acted. I could hardly find my

voice. "Oh." Breath trickled down my nose and throat. "What," warm breath like honey, "what—" the closing curtain dimming my light, finally, "what—"

34

THE DARK ALLEYS I ROAMED WERE CORRIDORS OF SLEEP.
I emerged from a labyrinth of torpor with the soles of my shoes
soiled. The night hugged me, whispering vespers in my ears. I
drew figures of infinity with my favorite four-inch pocketknife.

Lyle and Marva spoke in muffled tones on the other side of the
office door. I knocked. Silence. After a prolonged moment, Lyle
answered. He held a half-eaten, ham and cheese hoagie in his left
hand. "You have a key, huh?"

I rubbed sleep from my eyes. "I couldn't find it."

"The door wasn't locked."

I slid past him and into the dimly lit room. Marva stood at the
back of the office by the window. Her lips were swollen and her
eye blacked. My arms and legs throbbed with fatigue. *Get it right*, I
thought. "Sorry to interrupt. I wasn't expecting company."

"My partner." Lyle looked at me. "Everything okay?"

"I'm dead tired."

"Luke, this is Marva DeLonghi. Marva, Luke."

I traced the contours of my teeth with the tip of my tongue.
"Let me guess. Your husband's acting a little strange lately but you

221

refuse to believe the obvious so you want us to find proof that it's really someone else who's threatening to kill you."

Marva crossed her arms, shrinking into herself. "My husband's a good man."

Lyle stepped up to me and guided me to a chair with his hand on the small of my back. "You look like you need to sit."

"I need a cigarette."

Lyle helped me into the armchair. He dug inside my purse, produced my pack of Sphere Menthol, tapped one out, handed it to me, replaced the pack and traded it for my lighter.

I wanted to scream: *Don't complicate things!* But I received the flame with gratitude and swallowed back a sob. Through a veil of smoke I examined Marva: to have legs like those. "Lyle?"

"What's up?"

"I think you're crazy."

Through a mouthful of bread and meat and mustard he said, "There a mirror in here?"

"She's gorgeous."

Marva tilted her head, squinting at me.

Lyle looked at her, then at me. "Whatever you took, you might want to sleep it off, huh?"

I winked at Lyle, his choice of phrase, but it was a private irony. He looked away, like he knew, unconsciously, that he'd been peering in from the outside of an inside joke.

Someone had painted Marva in the warmest tones: caramel and gold and tangerine. She reflected the light in our office like a saint on a canvas in a cathedral. How at ease she was. She would be equally at home in a French palace or a dumpster. "You think I'm prettier than *her*?"

Lyle cocked his head, staring at me sideways. "Did you get hit in the head, huh?"

Marva laughed.

I smoked my cigarette and looked out the window, into the

night, examining the situation, the setting, the humidity, this woman, this man. "We'll talk later."

Marva rose. "Have at it. I should be going."

I stood. My legs wobbled. "Please don't."

"My husband will worry."

I doubted it. "How'd you two meet?"

"My husband and I?"

I brushed a lock of hair off my face, tucking it behind my ear. "You and Lyle."

"Mutual acquaintance."

Lyle sucked mayonnaise off his thumb. "Who's that?"

"Mr. Ruskov."

He finished the last of his sandwich. "You know Phil?"

Marva moved toward the door. "He was at a fundraiser my husband hosted."

I didn't want the details. "Must be pretty serious if he put you in touch with us."

"Well you're not wrong that someone wants me dead."

I studied my cigarette. "That's pretty serious."

Lyle opened a package of candied pecans. "Someone's been sending her threatening text messages."

"Are they the ones who roughed you up?"

"I ran into a door."

I mimed punching my cheek. "That door wear brass knuckles?"

Lyle crumpled the empty wrapper and tossed it toward the trashcan. He missed. "Women are all beautiful in their own ways, but I don't—"

"Drop it." I exhaled a spine of smoke. Life was renewing itself in my veins. As I walked to the kitchenette to pour drinks, I said, "Who wants to get drunk?"

When I turned to bring back the drinks, I came face to face with Marva. "Why are you doing this?"

"Doing what?"

"Trying to make yourself jealous. So I'm pretty? There's more to a woman than her face." She took one of the drinks from my hand, lifted it to her nose and inhaled. "I'm not really a fan of hard liquor." She poured it down her throat, wincing.

"Me either." Bourbon was easy. "We have wine in the closet."

"Would you mind?"

"Not at all."

But when I moved to get it she put her hand on my chest and held me in place. "Lyle doesn't know."

"Know what?"

"That you love him."

I sipped my Magdalene. "Do I?"

"It's obvious."

"Yesterday I didn't." I stared into the empty highball. "Today. Well. It doesn't matter." I took her by the elbow and guided her hand off my chest. "But since we're having this impromptu heart to heart, tell me, why now? I mean, you didn't start getting threats yesterday, but you ignored them till the last moment."

"What do you know?"

"You're like me. Yesterday you weren't desperate. Today you are. I want to know why, but I'm guessing you're not going to tell."

Marva tugged at a lock of her hair. She opened her mouth with an answer ready, but Lyle appeared in the kitchenette. "Don't forget about me, huh?" He looked from me to Marva and back again. "I'm parched."

I handed him his glass. "You don't know the meaning of parched."

He sipped. "Very thirsty."

"She means you've never been *very* thirsty."

"Have too."

I nudged his shoulder. "When?"

224

He, shrugged, swirled the rocks and drank. "Right now."

I threaded past Marva and Lyle and made for the closet. Somewhere beyond the windows *they* waited. If we didn't go to them, they would come to us. I dug beneath the filing case and retrieved the bottle of red.

Lyle walked behind me, a refreshed glass of bourbon swirling in his hand. "I didn't know we had that."

"Can't remember why."

Marva sauntered past me. She took a seat in the armchair nearest the door. The back of her head was as beautiful as the rest of her. "You two have a real comfort with each other."

Lyle sucked a lemon wedge. "It's all the drugs and alcohol."

I frowned at him. "More than that."

He belched. "Who are you, and what did you do with Luke, huh?"

I tore the foil seal from the bottle with my teeth. "Yeah. You're right." I spat the foil on the ground. "Go fuck a cement truck."

"You're a real trip yourself, honey."

Marva turned her body halfway on the armchair. "What's your story?"

I wanted our history private. "Don't recall."

Lyle raised his glass, opened his mouth then paused there like the statue of liberty. "You know? I don't remember either." He lowered his arm and stared into his lap. If I could guess, I'd say he was replaying our first meeting in his head, but I preferred our run in at Lauritzen Gardens, before we partnered up, when we were investigating a lost child from a milk carton. "She probably bought me a drink at some hole in the wall bar."

"I don't buy people drinks," I unscrewed the wine cap. "You probably stole my beer."

"Sounds more like it."

Marva pushed a lock of hair behind her ear. "I can come back later."

I held the wine bottle out to her. "There *is* no later."

She received the bottle like a smoking gun and sighted me over its mouth. "You take pleasure in being the cryptic type?"

"Not usually." I returned to the kitchenette and rummaged in the cupboard for a jelly glass. We owned goblets, but they didn't fit the mood.

Marva took the glass from me and helped herself. She offered the bottle around. Lyle declined. I lit a cigarette and shook my head.

The tense silence that followed described the whole of my regrets to perfection. A slight humidity colored the air. The overhead light flickered with the age of night. Even light bulbs grow tired. Muted traffic sounds assailed the window facing the street. I couldn't stand the quiet.

Lyle had bought a record player with our earnings from a previous case. Our collection included Michael Jackson's *Thriller*, Johnny Cash's *Greatest Hits*, Pearl Jam *Ten*, and *Lady Sings the Blues* by Diana Ross. Don't ask about the latter. A drunken barter, I think.

I made my selection and set the needle to vinyl. The first two songs went good with bourbon. Lyle rolled cheese curds in salami. Marva finished her wine. Then the third song opened with its upbeat synth and simple drum track. A young Michael Jackson who had more in common with Stevie Wonder sang about a woman who walked into his dreams.

It would be hard to imagine a simpler tune, more obvious rhymes, but then the song breaks the fourth wall: Michael and Paul debate about who the girl belongs to, as if she's property to be owned. I can't help but love the futility of their argument. It's what gives the song such charm. You can almost imagine the context between the lines, these two men watching from a distance as the girl leaves them both for another, because she belongs to herself.

We listened through the whole album, without saying much. When we reached the end of side one, Lyle refreshed our drinks. Meanwhile he worked his way through a bag of chocolate covered raisins, one of dried apple slices, and a canister of macadamia nuts. I opened Twitter on my phone and browsed the same posts I'd seen night after night. The thing about Twitter is that it never changes. If I had lived nine lives, Twitter was like an infinite replay of itself: vain attempts at wit and humor flooded with pictures of women in spare costumes and photo filters that left the subject vaguely familiar behind cat ears or big black alien eyes. What never made sense to me, and still doesn't, is that I never clicked on links inside of Twitter. The accounts that tried to promote learning and education, profiles that @ mentioned the New York Times or CNN, I scrolled past them in annoyance, because I knew Twitter wasn't meant for thinking. It was the purest outlet for anonymous emotion.

As "The Lady in My Life" closed, Marva stood and brushed wrinkles out of her blouse. "This was fun." She pulled a manila envelope from her purse and dropped it on the seat cushion where she'd been sitting. "I'm going to go now. Please save my life."

She laughed at herself and seemed to want us to as well, but Lyle and I were both sunk in thought. I rose from my chair and walked Marva to the door. She stepped into the hallway, and as she began walking away, I touched her elbow. "How are we supposed to help when you haven't given us anything to help you with?"

Not bothering to turn back, she shrugged, rounded the corner down the stairs and descended. Watching her go, I knew what I'd failed to accept before. She wanted to die. She wanted to die, always until the moment when death came. She'd hired us because her hidden desires understood what nine lives had taught me very well, most people don't get a choice.

35

LYLE NEEDED NO CONVINCING WHEN I TOLD HIM WE had to visit 20's Showgirl. He microwaved a bag of popcorn, snagged his keys from the hook by the door, slipped my Cubs hat over his head, and asked how he looked.

Out on the street, young women and men laughed, bouncing down the sidewalk like bowling balls on bumper lanes. Lights flashed and pulsed over doorways leading to bars. Inside one of those bars, my truest ambitions were drowning in bourbon and singing karaoke.

Lyle opened his car door. "You thinking about a new line of work?"

I opened mine and sat in the bucket seat. "Maybe. I've always wanted to be a Benedictine Nun, but I think nuns have to believe in god."

He was counting the cash from Marva's envelope and punctuating awed sighs with handfuls of popcorn. "I believe in god." His chin and cheeks were two days unshaven. The skin washed out beneath the greedy lamps of midnight. "I also believe there's like five grand in this envelope." His breath smelled like a movie theater. "You don't have the body of a stripper."

"You mean a dancer?"

"Your tits aren't big enough." He fanned the cash. "But you do have a nice ass."

I shimmied my shoulders. "The first guy who tried to slip a fiver in my underwear would get his nose sliced off. I don't think I'm cut out for a brass pole."

He started the engine and pulled onto Maple with a jolt. "So no firefighting?"

"Could I have a Dalmatian?"

"Did you hear me? That broad gave us five thou."

"She probably feels guilty."

"Guilty for what?"

"You didn't answer *my* question."

He licked salt and imitation-butter from his fingers. "Which one?"

"Can I have a Dalmatian?"

"Why not."

"Okay. Sign me up, but I'm not running into any burning buildings to save some damn cat. I've saved enough cats for ten lifetimes."

Lyle unwrapped a granola bar. "I'd go to ump school."

"Like for umpires?"

"Yeah."

"Really?"

"What could be better than going to a hundred sixty-two baseball games a year?"

"I don't think it's that easy to get to the majors."

"Sure, but I'm young. And I'd love to eject Bryce Harper just once. He's such a slimy bastard with that oiled hair and that blonde beard. God I hate him."

"He'd be retired before you got there."

"Also, he's a millionaire how many times over, and he won't get that nasty skin-tag, mole-thingy removed from beneath his eye. Gag me with a spoon!"

"Listen to you. I thought I trained you better. You can't judge someone based on their looks."

We stopped at the light on 72nd. "I can, and I do."

I lit a cigarette, cranked the window, rested my hand on the lip of the roof and sent my smoke skyward. "If you had to do it again, would you get into this business?"

"You mean like detective shit, or things with Marv?"

"Yes."

"Probably." Lyle popped a peppermint candy. "You?"

If I got into sleuthing to help people, a decade and change had beat that notion out of me, which meant the only allure was knowing the truth about things hidden. "I'm not sure. Sometimes it feels like an ego trip."

"Which part? The never having money or the always looking like an idiot to anybody who hires us?"

I smoked. "Always looking like idiots until we don't."

"Then they're pissed at what we show them." He fumbled at the seal of a bag of potato chips. "For all her going on about getting killed any day, Marv sure didn't seem too worried about giving us a scoop."

"And we didn't push."

He shoved a handful of chips into his mouth. "When has pushing ever worked?"

I shrugged. "Labor."

"For who? I don't think babies seem to appreciate all that pushing."

"Doesn't mean they don't need it."

He licked grease off his fingers and crumpled the empty bag. "So what the hell? We treated her to a bottle of wine and a little mood music."

I wondered how well he'd paid attention. "She mentioned the guy who hangs out at the 20's club."

"When was that?"

Lyle kept up better than I credited him for. "In the kitchen."

"Oh really." He dug in his jeans pocket and came up with a package of Life Savers. "It looked more to me like you were sizing each other up."

It had felt like a standoff, like Marva knew I had the jump on her, but I can't explain why, and I knew she didn't know what I knew. "She told me she'd seen a big man like a figure out of a Grant Wood painting except with tattoos all the way up his neck. Said she'd caught the guy following her a few times."

"I'm calling bullshit?"

"Honest."

Lyle peeled a dill pickle in a bag and drank the juice. "And how'd she know he hung out at a strip joint, huh?"

"Topless club, actually." I flicked my cigarette butt out the window as 20's came into view across the intersection at Dodge. "Tails go both ways."

"You're lying. I'm not sure why."

"Wait and see. He'll be here." My ears tingled, that final caution your body signals when you've deadened all other feeling by force of will.

Lyle parked closest to the U.S. Bank across the side street. There were men and women loitering out front of the club smoking and speaking in raised tones of drunkenness and arousal. I can't explain why I'd had to die so many times to accept 20's was where we *had* to go. It seemed like years—it *had* been years—since I'd stepped inside this hole. Time had not dulled my apprehension, but it had beaten the inquisitiveness out of me. Until I had the right people in the same room, nothing else mattered. It didn't matter what Omaha Magazine wrote about Marva. I didn't care if she'd pissed off every activist in the city. And if Ruskov wanted answers about Marva's mystery, he might just have to find someone who gave a shit. No more aiming for the root, I had a clear-cut approach that called for plenty of violence, which suited me just fine.

We were at the door when I stopped and took Lyle's elbow. I leaned close. "When you see him you're going to get excited, but I need you to stay cool. No matter what happens, all you need to do is keep your eye out for an ambush."

"An ambush?"

"Let me finish. Keep your eye out for anyone paying too much attention to us, and when I say it's time to go, we go." I pinched his elbow. "Understand?"

"You're starting to creep me out."

"When I say we go, we go."

He finished the last of his pickle and shrugged. "Things never go according to plan."

36

THE OVERHEAD TRACK WAS "HUNGRY EYES," ERIC Carmen belting his undisguised appreciation of the female form, and the dancer on stage was already topless. Referring to breasts as melons makes sense considering plastic surgery. Though I don't understand why men find melons stimulating. The dancer swayed her breasts in pendulous rhythm, hypnotizing the onlookers. Lyle's head swiveled back and forth, up and down as she gyrated and oozed on the pole. The air in the club was humid with the panting of sixty men and a handful of women.

Laser sat at the bar, his back to the action, drinking beer from a pint glass. I bumped Lyle with my elbow. He grunted. I bumped him harder. He bit into a peach and turned his head reluctantly. I aimed my eyes at our man.

Lyle said, "Son of a bitch," loud enough for a nearby table of two to look at us. I elbowed him again. "Right. Cool as Ranch Doritos."

I took the only open table in the place and reminded Lyle of his job. "Keep your tongue in your mouth."

He grunted.

I went to the bar and squeezed into the gap between Laser and a woman whose black hair obscured her face—something familiar about the cruelty of her posture. She was reclined with her back leaning against the bar top. When I pushed between the two, I interrupted a conversation. The woman said, "You better get going. He's expecting you."

I hadn't prepared myself to see the woman who'd first introduced me to death, and my heart pounded. "Some show."

Laser didn't bother to look at me when he replied. "Too many distractions."

I caressed the bar top. "Oh, yeah. Lights and lasers."

He saw me then. The air thickened. He knew me. It was like seeing myself through his eyes. From the first time we'd met, so long ago, down on the docks, when he was covered in fish guts and sweat, he'd had the jump on me. "Hi."

"Don't waste your time." He made fists of his hands, smiled. "I'm taken."

I dug in my purse and fished out the knife, teasing a glance of the hilt. "A girl can dream, can't she?"

"I prefer handcuffs and whips." He pushed his gold, wireframe glasses up. "You know what I mean?"

"Oh, Nelly."

"She's clever." Laser jerked his thumb at me.

Nelly laughed and pressed her shoulder to mine.

They had me like a sardine in a can. "We've met somewhere. Maybe the docks. I buy catfish for the Grey Plume."

"No." He finished his beer. "I know that chick. Catherine. She's a bitch."

I shot a glance at Lyle who was lost in sexual fantasy, then at Nelly. She had a length of twine twisted around each fist and held slack in her lap. "They need to get some air circulating in this place, maybe—"

"Should've said you were a cop. We don't mess with cops."

"I'm a cop."

Nelly laughed, low and seductive. "Too late now."

I asked a throw-away question to buy myself thinking time: "What do you want with Marva, anyway?"

Laser scratched his brow. "She's not my problem."

Nelly put her lips to my ear. "I'm gonna like you." She nibbled my earlobe.

I swung my arm back and elbowed her mouth. She said something that sounded like "fluff-gunper" and fell on her ass. A few nearby drunks stood in a panic and backed, staring.

Laser jumped off his barstool. "Nel?"

I stood, turning. Blood dripped onto Nelly's half-exposed breasts. Her vacant eyes caught the light. She reached for her face. I kicked her. "She doesn't stop with whips, does she?"

Laser's head swiveled toward me slow and full of intent. "You're going to wish you didn't make that mistake."

The top of my head came to the middle of his chest. My eyes scaled the tower of his torso until our eyes met. "The only mistake I regret is not coming here sooner." I raised my fists.

Laser cracked a grin. "Nelly always says she likes it rough, but you took it too far."

"Gee. I'm really sorry."

"You will be. I'm going to rip your tongue out and shove it up your ass."

"Can I order a drink first?"

"You think—"

Just then Laser's gaze went distant as his eyes turned milky. Something heavy and round had thudded off the crown of his shaved head and ricocheted off his shoulder. When he fell, Lyle was standing behind him. I shrugged like, *What the fuck?* and showed him my jaw agape. "You had one job."

Everyone around us had parted to form a distant circle of onlookers. Lyle yelled over the music, which still blared, though the melonous dancer no longer danced. "The dude was fondling a blade behind his back."

Lyle hadn't lost track of me, and it occurred that maybe he did find me beautiful. What did it matter? Beauty is only a function of gender roles. But it mattered. "Take his feet."

Lyle looked from Laser's felled body to Nelly, moaning with her hand cupped over her mouth, then me. "Do what?"

I knelt and hooked my arms beneath the giant's shoulders. "His feet."

Lyle squatted, scooped up the feet and stood. An assassin's dead weight is greater than the sum of his parts.

We hobbled a few steps before someone bellowed over the music to ask what we thought we were doing. I yelled back: "Saving a life."

"The police have been called," the voice shouted back. It was the bartender. "Bruce! Don't let them go anywhere."

Lyle grunted. "What are we doing?"

Bruce. The name rang familiar. "Going."

At the door we met Bruce. Once, he had watched us die. He and Nelly had forced us into the club's basement where Bruce had hidden in shadows as Nelly raped and murdered us. He was the rare sort of hulking figure who could blend into his surroundings when he checked IDs at the entrance or he could command all attention when he stood between you and where you wanted to be.

As we made to carry Laser away, a bear paw of a hand squeezed my shoulder until the tendons popped and my knees gave. Lyle dropped Laser's feet and the shift in weight pulled me forward. Bruce kept hold of my shoulder and was pulled forward, off balance. Lyle stepped up and shot the butt of his palm into the bridge of Bruce's nose. The big man in his Hawaiian shirt stumbled back, but he was the greater mass, and though his nose bled he seemed undisturbed.

People were gathering behind Lyle, seeming to gain courage from Bruce's resistance. I groped for the knife in my purse. Just as I freed it from a tangle of clutter, Bruce strode past, cocking his arm. I flicked the knife open and thrust.

The blade slipped through the denim of Bruce's jeans and anchored in flesh, stuck between chords of muscle. He hopped and crashed to the floor with a yelp. That's the last I saw of my knife.

Lyle feinted right to avoid Bruce's falling momentum.

"Hurry." I panted.

Laser's breath seemed to be gaining speed. He was rousing from the blow to his head. If he woke before we made the car, we were beat. If the police arrived before we left, we were beat.

I don't know how we managed to escape both fates. We passed through that horny crowd of smokers and made the car unchallenged, and when Laser's body was stuffed into the back seat, I struck his head with a blow for good measure. "Hope there's no brain damage."

Lyle fished his keys from his pocket. "That place had lousy music."

I sat in the passenger seat. "You didn't seem to mind the entertainment."

Lyle fired the ignition. "The pole dancer? She was okay." He pulled out of the parking lot and turned onto Dodge. "I slept with that broad when she waited tables at Denny's. That was before her boob job. She never had any imagination."

37

I COULDN'T RECALL MARVA'S EXACT ADDRESS. WE TOOK
plenty of wrong turns. Between last minute "Left! Here!"s and
"Right! Here!"s Lyle pulled what details he could from me. I
wanted to tell him the truth: killed eight times, dead ends,
betrayal, an unsolvable mystery, logic and detection when violence
and a knife were always the answer, but I couldn't afford Lyle
questioning my sanity so I lied, telling him Marva had tipped me
off about Laser, said at the bar Laser had mentioned something
about a guy who lived in Grove Park or some such place. When
Lyle asked why I didn't look the place up on my phone I tried, but
nothing came up. "Look, I know it's out west. I'll recognize it
when I see it. There was a lot of adrenaline, you know?"

Lyle nodded. He shelled pistachios and took orders. We
crossed back and forth on the numbered streets between Dodge
and Center until we arrived at the outskirts of West O and a
glowing lamp hanging over a brick and wood sign sparked a
memory. I pointed. "There."

"Yeah, I can see how you'd confuse Oak Park with Prairie
Heights."

THE 9 LIVES OF MARVA DELONGHI

"Go fuck a blast furnace."

"Maybe next time."

He turned into the subdivision, and from there I knew my way. When I saw the house I imagined Ransom DeLonghi. His face half obscured in the shadows, that deep unnatural voice. How had I failed to understand that moment? I'd chosen to believe Marva when she labeled him a victim, perhaps not an intentional victim but certainly not in collaboration with Laser.

We parked on the curb out front of the house and I told Lyle to follow me. "Keep an eye out." I struck a blow to Laser's temple, though he didn't seem to be coming around anytime soon. He deserved so much pain.

When I began to pull him from the car Lyle balked. "Where are we, anyway?"

"Don't worry about it."

He crossed his arms like a child ready to tantrum. "Don't worry? We're parked in some fancy suburb and you're making to pull an unconscious body out of the back of my car. Give me a reason not to worry, huh?"

"It's the middle of the night."

He chuckled nervously. "Rich old ladies see things."

Like Mrs. Stefevater, I thought. Was Lyle accumulating unconscious memories from previous lives? How much did the loop affect him and others? "We don't have other options."

He shook his head and squeezed his eyes shut. "I'm not doing this. You've gone insane."

"No. I'm finally thinking clear."

I wrestled with Laser's dead weight until his body plopped to the concrete walk. His head bounced on the curb. I hoped he felt it in his dreams. Lyle helped me carry Laser up the wooden stairs to the front porch, all the while mumbling something about prison food. We positioned Laser so his face was in full light under the porch lamp. At some point we'd cracked the right lens of his glasses. I told Lyle to crouch behind the stairs where his form was in shadow.

When he was in position, I hammered my fist on the door three times and crouched on the knob side out of view of any windows. A long moment passed before the clack and click of a deadbolt. First the maple door, then the storm door came open. Ransom's voice was even deeper than I remembered. "Larry?" He stooped. I jumped on his back and boxed his ears until they bled. He'd fallen long before the blood did, and Lyle had had to pull me from the man's body.

38

LYLE EXPECTED RED AND BLUE TO FLOOD THE LIVING room any moment. The bartender at 20's Showgirl had called the police. When they found we'd vacated 20's, they'd run Lyle's plates, flip our office, our homes, and broadcast an APB with our vehicle information and crude descriptions of our appearances. The search would be a lot quicker if anyone in Ransom's neighborhood reported a man and a woman lugging a dead body. When the police found us there was a good chance they'd shoot first and ask questions later.

I stripped the unconscious men to their underwear, cutting the white and yellow striped pajamas off Ransom, and the mammoth jeans and t-shirt off Laser. I contemplated using a strip of the duct tape I'd found to silence Lyle's blabbering, but I needed the whole roll to fasten Laser and Ransom, back to back, in two kitchen chairs.

A motion sensor light in Ransom's driveway kicked on while we were taping the two men's chests. My heart hammered. A cat darted through the illuminated path, chasing some bald and bloodied possum.

Lyle had said, "At least not their heads," when I tore and stuck the last strip of tape, but I liked the panic of it. Whoever woke first would try to move and find himself immobilized at each extremity: the intimate sensation of full body paralysis.

Lyle plastered me with questions. Whose house were we at? Why the violence? Why the tape? Did I know what prison was going to be like? I had answers for everything, but provided none. It would all make sense when our ringmaster roused.

After a time, Lyle relented, though he said if he'd known earlier where the night would take us, he'd sure as hell not've driven me to a strip club.

I glared at him. "Topless."

"Haven't you ever heard the stories about prison gruel?"

I jerked my thumb toward the kitchen. "I'm sure there's plenty of good stuff in there. You raiding the cabinets will be the least of the cops' concern."

Lyle pillaged the pantry and refrigerator because only culinary concerns could reliably calm his nerves. Though I couldn't show it, I was afraid too.

He found a loaf of ciabatta in the cupboard over the dishwasher, a jar of pickled jalapeños in the fridge, something that looked like meatballs in a plastic container, pasta sauce, parmesan, cheddar, hearts of romaine, red and green peppers and fresh cherry tomatoes, from which he built two cold sandwiches that described all the best parts of our shared life.

We ate to fill every starved appetite. I thrust a bite deep into my mouth, moaning with disregard. My tongue directed newly composed symphonies written for yearning and discovery. The spice from the pepper and the sweetness of the pork sent a quiver from my throat to my toes, which curled with delight. Subtle balances of moisture, the firmness of vegetables, the silky finish of red sauce dribbling from my lips, lit every pleasure sensor in my brain. I trembled at the saltiness of the fine-crumbled parmesan.

Spent and satisfied, I lit a cigarette, exhaling luxurious velvet to dance along the lofted ceilings. Lyle's grunts of delight were the finest companion. A man who loves food will always have in common with women a love for food.

Some time later a throaty protest sounded from the living room. Lyle stood, pushed in his chair, wiped his palms together, and went toward the echo of human suffering. I followed.

Ransom had woken. His eyes locked on Lyle. "Pardon me?" he said, in a tone that suggested he was the only person alive who could endure the line at a DMV. He smacked his lips and blinked in rapid succession. "What's happening here?"

I finger-waved. "Hello, Ransom."

Lyle belched. "As in 'Ransom DeLonghi?'"

Ransom's eyes roved between us. "Who are you?"

Lyle sucked grease and marinara off his fingertips. An odd expression played in his eyes. Perhaps regret. "Lu?"

"We're here to ask you some questions about your college roommate, Larry."

Ransom closed his eyes. He was so still in his bondage, so silent I thought he'd returned to sleep, but then he sighed. "I told him that story would come back to haunt me."

Lyle circled the room and knelt in a corner. His face contorted into a pensive grimace. He ducked his head between his knees and rocked slightly from side to side as if nauseated.

Ransom's deep voice cracked. "I can explain."

I swatted the air. "Don't waste your breath."

"Cut me loose. I'll tell you everything. This was never supposed—"

I backhanded his jaw. "Shut up. I know who 'Larry'—" I raised air quotes—"is, and I know what you're planning, but it's over, and you'll be spending the rest of your life washing dishes on D Block."

39

WHEN I RETURNED WITH THE KITCHEN KNIFE, RANSOM whimpered. "There's been a misunderstanding here. Please. If you want money, name your price."

Lyle lifted his head from the hollow formed by his knees and arms, resting his chin on the intersection of his forearms.

Ransom construed the gesture as interest. "What is it you want? Anything. Name it."

I poked his shoulder. "What I want, you can't give me." I couldn't look long at Lyle. "I want to see my partner tomorrow. I never want to hear the name Marva DeLonghi again. I want my lives back."

Ransom animated. His expression shifted from relief to concern. Still he managed to find a sliver of conviction. "Yes. Yes. You can have that. Let me go, and I'll never utter a word about any of this."

Lyle began to stand, but I halted his progress. "It's too late for that." He slumped to the floor. "But you can tell me why you want your wife dead so badly. At least tell me that so when I'm lying in some damp, lumpy prison bunk I can comfort myself, knowing I understand something about this stupid case."

"You're mistaken." Ransom legs rippled with some failed effort to adjust his posture. "I've never wanted my wife dead. I love her so much."

Lyle sprung to his feet. "That's enough—"

I pivoted and swung the knife toward him. "Don't."

He revealed a new expression, one perhaps familiar to any woman who'd ever refused him a kiss. I could imagine his hurt, but there wasn't time to explain what he didn't know.

I spun the knife in my hand and raised it over my head, doubling my grip on the handle. "This is pointless." My chest tightened. I missed my pocketknife. Overhead light glinted off the metal blade. "Explain why you hired Laser right now, or we're done."

Lyle lurched, grabbing my elbow. "You aren't the only one who pays for this."

I'd seen Lyle die every worst death. "Tell me something I don't know." He was as good as dead no matter what I did. Except I had this crazy notion like a fist on my lungs that if I just did what I did, just do it, just end Ransom's life, maybe, maybe, maybe, Lyle could live. Maybe. Violent heat radiated from my chest. Lyle's grip was stronger than I imagined: to feel him want something with conviction. I wondered what that want would feel like if it focused on me.

Ransom seemed to sense an opportunity. "Listen to your friend."

Lyle's fingers relaxed. He was nodding. With a swift motion, I jerked my hand free, swung my arm and caught Laser in the temple with the butt of the chef's knife. The transfer of energy whipped Ransom's head to the side, and he groaned. "You think I won't do this, but you're wrong. You have no idea how desperate I am."

Lyle retreated. He raised his hands like a man cited by a gun. "That's it. I won't be part of this." His voice was full of calm, a poise I didn't know he possessed. "We have a perfectly reasonable solution in front of us, and you won't take it."

Because I can't bear to see you die again. Because I don't know if I can survive another death. Because I'm tired, and short of killing this pathetic little man, nothing has kept Marva alive, and not even that has saved you. I raised the knife once more. "We both know what happens if I do this, but unless you start talking I don't see another way to stop Marva's dying."

Ransom swallowed a heavy lump. His lips barely parted: "You can't stop her."

The colors in the room dulled. Cool forced air gushed from the floor vents. "What do you mean 'stop *her*'?"

If Ransom had been able, he would've hung his head. "My wife is sick. She's very sick, but she won't listen to me. She needs professional help, help I can't give her. I've begged her to see a doctor, but instead she's out there trying to get herself killed."

Lyle raised his hands and grabbed the side of his head like palming a basketball. He stumbled two steps backward. "Can someone please wake me up?"

I lowered the knife and repositioned it beneath the hollow of Ransom's left eye. It formed a dimple in his cheek. The twitch of his muscles travelled up the blade, tiny vibrations on a guitar string.

"Miss." He winced. "You're hurting me."

A pinprick of blood raised around the tip of the blade. This notion that Marva wanted to die stirred me. "Why would she be trying to get herself killed?" A new avenue opened before me. "Or is that your way of justifying bad behavior, saying you're just trying to give her what she wants?" Men were always blaming women for their own violence. Every battered spouse could tell the story of an abusive husband who pleaded with her after an outburst, Why do you make me do these things?

Chemical stress began to show on Ransom's face. His breath came labored. Sweat shone on his brow and upper lip. He closed his eyes. "Several months ago, she..." I waited for more, but he seemed stuck.

His next words had the power to end his life. If he said she'd done such and such and was asking for trouble. But that also didn't seem like Ransom. "You better be careful."

"I came home from the lab one night to find her all made up. She was wearing my favorite dress and earrings. Her makeup was just like I liked it, and she'd painted her toenails, which she never does anymore. I thought I was the luckiest man alive. She's so beautiful." Ransom swallowed. His eyes darted around the room, searching for something they couldn't locate, sharp darting glances. "She'd made reservations at the Flatiron Café. We were finishing our first bottle of wine when she said she needed to tell me something. I guess it proves how weak I am that I felt afraid when she said that, but I always told her she could tell me anything."

Ransom's body must've exerted some great effort because the chair he sat in creaked and moaned. He smacked his lips and said he was thirsty. Neither Lyle nor I spoke or moved. Ransom drew a heavy breath and held it, his cheeks inflated. "She said someone wanted her dead. She said she hadn't wanted to involve me, but she was scared." He exhaled his lungsful in a forceful jet. "I'm ashamed to say I laughed. I laughed because we'd danced around the subject a thousand times, and it was always the same. She'd relate some story about how someone had sent a threatening message to her after one of her protests, and I'd try to encourage her because threats were proof her work mattered, and then she'd cry, and the craziest thing was, the craziest thing was, she said it wasn't the

threat that upset her, but that there weren't more of them."
Ransom swallowed a great gulp of air. "I probably shouldn't be
telling you these things, but maybe it will help you understand.
Every time a threat came, she redoubled her efforts, but the threats
were never enough until they were too much, and that's what the
dinner was all about, so I asked her what she wanted me to do
about it, and she got really insane, I mean, just insane, yelling at me
in front of all the diners and the wait staff, saying it was my job to
protect her, and wasn't I hearing her? She was in danger. And then
she threw a glass of water in my face and stormed off."

Lyle sunk to his knees.

I walked to where he knelt and rested my hand on his
shoulder.

"I feel sick."

"Why?"

"Cause everything's wrong. Cause we shouldn't be here."

"Where should we be?"

He shrugged. "Crawling some dark alley. Roughing up dope-
dealing kids. Drawing a bead on the usual suspects. You don't just
hop in the car and drive here and torture some woman's husband,
and what are we even doing?"

I massaged my temples. "You're upset."

"This is wrong. What we're doing. We shouldn't be here. I
thought we were trying to save Marva."

"You don't know what I know." I laughed. "Maybe someday
I'll tell you more, but let's just say I've got a jump on you where
Marva's concerned. No luck involved. Actually, I take that back.
There's been a lot of bad luck."

"Wait. Who are you? If you're trying to save my wife..."
Ransom trailed off.

I mussed Lyle's hair like a mother calming a son, spun and
posted my hands on my hips. "Your story's charming, but it
sounds like a lie."

Ransom sighed. "I swear—"

"Don't—" I interrupted him—"lie."

"I'm not."

"You're almost convincing. In fact, I believe everything you said right up to the point where you claim your wife asked for your help. Unless we're speaking in euphemisms. What she really wanted that night must've been something that pissed you off bad enough to want her dead. And now you need to justify your choices by blaming the outcome on her. Don't get me wrong, your wife has all the charm of a rusted nail, and I can even appreciate your frustrations, but that doesn't change the facts."

"No."

"You hired Laser to give you a clean start."

Ransom's face contorted into a rictus of agony. "I don't know what you think you know, but you're gravely mistaken."

I shot a glance at Lyle, who seemed to be slumping toward sleep, or something worse. I drew the knife toward my face and stared at my reflection in its dull gleam. Positioning it broad side for Ransom I said, "Do you see that?"

His eyes searched, and when they settled I knew he knew. "Yeah, you see him, now, don't you. You didn't expect this. But since you're not willing to tell the truth, we'll wait. Laser'll wake up soon enough, and when he does, I'm sure he'll be perfectly civil. We'll just clear up this whole misunderstanding and everybody can make up and hug it out." I turned to Lyle. "Sound good to you?"

Lyle shrugged. I'd never seen him so dead-eyed. "It's your dream."

Ransom let off a weak chuckle that swelled into a stuttering giggle. "What's he doing here? Wait. What's happening?"

"So you admit you know him?"

Ransom moaned. "Of course I know him. Like you said, I hired him."

I tapped the butt of the knife in the cup of my palm. "You mean you hired your old college pal, right? Now we're getting somewhere. Glad you feel like talking."

"College? I don't think so. Christ! This is Larry. He's one of Magnus's security guards. I hired him to protect my wife." A flash of anger played on Ransom's face, the first time I'd seen that emotion from him, and much less fitting than I'd expected. "Guess you get what you pay for. Lot of good he's done." Ransom blinked. His jaw worked silently. "Where is she anyway?"

The name Magnus faintly tolled a bell of recollection, but I wasn't about to sacrifice the momentum of our situation so I ignored it. "Well, if that's your story, I guess you won't mind if we get on our way. I'm sure when Larry wakes you'll have plenty to talk about."

Turning, I beckoned Lyle to follow. He shuffled a few steps toward the door. Ransom asked us to wait. I asked him why. His voice trembled. "You said someone wants her dead?"

"Don't play stupid with us, Mr. DeLonghi. You might have everyone else fooled, but I see through you. *You* want your wife dead. And I've seen enough of this guy—" I gestured with my chin at Laser—"to know he's got an appetite for murder. So I'll just leave you two alone and hope, for your sake, that when he comes to he's got fraternal feelings for you. Otherwise you might not enjoy his temperament." I reached for the door and opened it, extending my palm for Lyle to go first. When he was out, I looked over my shoulder. "I wish I could tell you dying only hurts until you're dead, but experience tells me different."

40

WE HARDLY MADE THE PORCH BEFORE RANSOM'S yelling halted Lyle. I grabbed his elbow and tugged, but he wouldn't budge. He'd deteriorated so far he wasn't even snacking. I didn't understand my own play. "Look. You heard what he said. Don't let his pitiful little act confuse you. It's guys like him who are at the center of everything that's wrong with this world. Too cowardly to handle their own problems. He's the kind of guy who thinks he can bury his shit by throwing sawdust on it." Except, it didn't feel right to me either. "We'll call The Shotz and sort everything out from here, but in the meantime we need to get scarce." My thinking went something like this:

It wasn't about answers anymore. So what if my story had holes? With Ransom and Laser detained and morning a few hours from dawning, the killer would be in custody, and no one would be there to kill Marva. Once the police arrived Laser and Ransom would begin the panicked motions of trying to save themselves, which would take care of the confession needed to ensure no one was released to pose a new threat to Marva. In the meantime, the police were still searching for us and until the whole story emerged considered us a primary threat.

I wasn't quite that linear. My only thoughts were on getting Lyle far from danger. I couldn't shake the sense that so long as a sliver of doubt surrounded Marva, fate would murder Lyle, and at some point his life had become my priority. I tugged his hand, but he pulled back.

Hardly louder than a whisper, he said, "If this is Ransom's house, where's Marva?"

His question was so innocently pointed. I didn't want to care about the answer, but one distinct possibility arose. Since I knew we'd followed Marva to her home on this very night in a previous incarnation, I knew something we'd done had changed her destination. But why? Perhaps something we'd said altered her priorities, which bothered me even to consider, because maybe somehow Laser had already gotten to her, and we were too late. This outcome seemed unlikely until you considered he seemed always to have the jump on us. I'd been ready to leave some fates to chance, considering the main trials overcome, but Marva's absence left too much unspoken. It felt wrong. It was wrong. Why hadn't I seen it?

Maybe if I could rule out the worse of two options there was still hope. I plowed back into the house crossing my arms over my chest. Ransom was yelling Larry's name.

"Here. Let me help you." I marched past the two men, taped to their chairs, into the kitchen and to the cabinets. I flung doors wide until I found the glasses, selected the largest offering, filled it with water, returned to the living room and splashed the contents onto Laser's face. If I'd expected him to come triumphantly to, I'd miscalculated the sleep of head trauma. Resorting to Hollywood tactics, I slapped his cheeks, pinched his ears, twisted his nose and knocked on his forehead. His eyes twitched with faint signs of registering the disruption, but he slept on. Then I yelled, "Hey,

Laser!" and like a television powered on, his eyes illuminated. They absorbed the surroundings before settling on me.

I shrugged off a moment of panic where I saw the mistake I'd fallen into. Turning I expected to find Lyle at my back. I wanted the comfort of his presence to center me, but he wasn't there. My ears rang. I pressed on anyway.

Laser seemed remarkably calm when I told him he was going to jail. "Your friend Ransom tells me he hired you to protect his wife, but we all know that's bullshit, because what would he have to protect her from? He hired you to kill her. I already know everything. I even know you were planning to kill her tomorrow morning at Regency."

How he found the will to smile I can't say, but his grin set me reeling. "She's a cunning lass." He worked his jaw. "My head hurts." He smacked his tongue. "May I have a drink?"

Ransom, meanwhile, all heavy breath and snorting, was a racehorse crossing the finish line. "Tell her, Larry. Tell her everything."

"You know," Laser licked his lips. "I like the name Laser better. It's of my own choosing. I've never understood why parents get to name children. It's such a possessive tradition, as if naming me, they could really own me. Maybe that's why I turned to murder."

Ransom fell silent.

If my given name was Larry, maybe I'd've turned to a life of murder too. "Where's Marva?"

Creaking sounds issued from the chairs and the duct tape began to shimmer beneath the overhead light, its fibers tensing and crimping. Ransom's eyes bulged, and as they did, I understood Laser was using his considerable strength to master his bondage.

Adrenaline flooded my body. I slapped Laser across the face, knowing he'd repay me tenfold if he escaped. "Where's Marva? Don't act like you don't know." When he failed to answer, and as the chairs continued to creak and Ransom began to gag, face shading toward purple, I wound my fist back and delivered a punch to Laser's kidney. Even the strongest person is vulnerable to the sour vacuuming pain of a kidney punch. As Laser absorbed the blow, his struggle to break free eased, and Ransom gasped for air. "Where's Marva?" I asked again and punctuated the question with a second blow to Laser's kidney.

Laser flexed his hands, first splaying the fingers then forming fists. "Really, your guess is as good as mine." He winced. "But if I had to take a stab, I'd say she's gone to prepare for her death. Or maybe she's begging for her life. Neither would surprise me."

What he said should've been enough. Marva was alive. I'd learned enough about Laser to know he didn't lie, that if he'd killed her, he couldn't not gloat. I could've escaped then, called Shotz and fled with Lyle. There might've been a happy ending had I let it be, but I'd committed myself to answers. "Who would she beg for her life if—"

"One moment," Laser said, talking over me, "I think you're clearly brilliant. It's not just anyone who could take *me* by surprise. The next, I realize you're merely lucky. I can't pretend to know how you found me, but it's clear you have no idea what I am."

This notion of luck people had. "Do you deny you planned to kill her?"

Ransom, who had, until then, remained silent said, "Larry?"

"Try again." Laser tapped his toe. "Not past tense. Present tense. I *plan* to kill her."

Ransom made gagging sounds. "No."

"So we've confirmed intent." I circled the captives. "What's the motive?"

Ransom's breathing gained volume. "No."

"Motive? Opportunity. What else? Someone paid me to make

a spectacle of Marva, and I enjoy violence. Does there need to be more?"

Coy games didn't tempt me. "It's too late to protect anyone. Ransom paid you. Admit it."

"Oh, you're absolutely right." Laser's voice gained strength. "Ransom pays very well. At the suggestion of his dear friend Magnus, Ransom hired me as a bodyguard—"

Tears shuttled down Ransom's cheeks. "I told you!"

"Shut it." Laser clicked his teeth. "A rather brilliant gesture, I say, since Magnus hired me to *kill* her. Imagine my delight. One minute I'm speaking to Omaha's most powerful citizen and thinking how fun it would be to torture him. The next he's offering money to dust a young woman, but he says there's a catch. Well I like catches so I agree." Laser flexed his fists. "Though I'll let you in on a little secret: I would've done it for free. But if life's taught me anything, it's taught me you should never overestimate a person's intelligence. Never leave money on the table. And plus, Magnus wanted drama, which isn't really my style. So he paid me for intrigue and clues and near misses. With friends like Magnus, you know."

Drool collected at the corners of Ransom's mouth, a telltale sign his body was preparing to vomit. "I don't believe you."

Laser chuckled. "It's always hard to believe what fools people can be." He strained his eyes far left to pinpoint me. "First Magnus has to plant the idea of protection in Ransom's mind. Then, when Ransom bites, it's a hush-hush operation because the Mrs. is deeply offended by the notion that she'd need a bodyguard. I only wish I could've seen that part. Broken china and enraged screams, am I right?"

Ransom blubbered. Through sobs he said he'd only just suggested the bodyguard and Marva had lost her temper.

"So he took my advice and pretended we were old chums. It's

hard for me to keep straight. Triple-double agent or something of the sort."

The scene was pointless. Laser had the kind of ego that could monologue for days, but I had a short temper and a nicotine Jones —latter feeding the former. "As much as I love Philosophy 101, I think I get the shape of things, though I can't pretend to understand why it had to be so complicated. Hasn't anyone ever heard of arsenic?"

Laser chuckled. "You and me both. We're the same, really."

I rolled my eyes. Psychopaths always want to identify with others, not because they care about justifying their actions, but because they fail to fathom motives different than their own.

"Since I hate to bore you, I guess you'll be on your way. You clearly think I'm no longer a threat. And as has been plainly revealed, your real problem is with Magnus Adderpaine."

"Okay?" I cracked my knuckles. "Since you're aching to tell all, be my guest."

"There's really not much to tell. You know of him, I imagine."

I drifted toward Laser, crouching so we were eye to eye. "Every man I've ever met gets off on explaining things to women so go ahead. Illuminate me."

Laser bellowed laughter. "You don't know Magnus Adderpaine?"

"Should I?"

Laser eyes rolled, large and exaggerated. "He's only the richest man in Omaha."

"I might be a little slow on the uptake, but I know Warren Buffett is the rich—"

"I'm talking power." Laser interrupted. "The only wealth worth having."

"How could I have been so stupid?" Ransom seemed to have mastered his sobbing as if some key had slipped all the tumblers in his brain. It unfolded that Marva and Magnus had collaborated on

THE 9 LIVES OF MARVA DELONGHI

several environmental panels. They'd grown close, and the Adder-paines and DeLonghis regularly met. Then Magnus invested in a land development project slated to drain a pond in Old Mill, but not just any pond, one that was the only landing spot east of Grand Island for migrating sand cranes. Marva opposed Magnus, and their friendship disintegrated. "I should've known he was behind this somehow."

Laser took great pleasure in the details, highjacking the story and pausing to laugh frequently. Marva, he said, resorted to legal measures, filing a motion to stay Magnus's development. Since she couldn't be persuaded by reason, Magnus decided he'd scare her into submission, but a woman once afraid, usually evolved into a terror. "Enter yours truly, and yes, Magnus made it so much more complicated than needed with all the threats, but the gist is, if we make it look like Marva dies defending her cause, the outpouring of community support will strike our opponents dumb. They'll be so desperate for a manifestation of their outrage that they'll need a symbol like Magnus's development. No one will be able to see the situation for what it is: simple, expeditious murder." Conspiracies would abound, and if Marva hadn't withdrawn her protest against the Old Mill development by then—"which by the way it looked like she wouldn't"—Magnus could simply operate in the background free of scrutiny, burying the injunction in legal paperwork. Without Marva alive to carry the torch and Ransom grieved, "Well, you get it, but the sad thing is—if you call it sad—the plans will change, because Ransom can't be allowed to live with all he's heard."

Ransom again had devolved into blubbering. "None of this makes any sense. What's my wife ever done to deserve such treatment?"

"Cut the shit!" Laser worked his fists. "Don't pretend you regret any of this. You want that bitch dead as badly as the rest of us."

Ransom pushed off with his feet, rocking the chairs danger-ously. "How could you—"

"You can't act like I haven't listened. How many times did you tell me you wished her dead? Just once, in those words, but you meant it. How many times did we meet out front of your house and you'd complain that she was on the war path again? We were doing you a favor."

I opened my mouth, but my thoughts scattered when the phone in my pocket vibrated: Mike Shotz's name on the caller ID.

"Luke?"

"Mikey."

"Hey! There's not much time."

"Why are you—"

"We know where you are, and we're coming."

"God am I glad to hear from—"

"Listen. We can't talk. There's an all points out on you, and a half dozen squad cars—"

"Good. Hurry. I've got a surprise—"

"If you're there when we arrive—"

"This one's going to make you famous!"

"Are you hearing me, Luke?"

"I know how things might look."

"Where's Lyle? You two need to get out of there."

Abstractly, I'd clung to Lyle but forgot he wasn't in the house. "You tried calling him?"

"He's not answering. You need to go."

I pulled the phone back, staring at Laser. "You hear that, fuck-face? The cops are coming. Looks like you won't be killing anyone this morning."

Laser smiled. "Hurry along."

Mikey chirped something in the receiver I failed to hear. I smashed the phone to my ear "How long do we have?"

"The first squad car's already in the neighborhood."

I didn't die eight times to end up handcuffed. Bells clanged in my head. I backed toward the door, shouted, "Thanks," into the phone, hung up, and told Laser and Ransom "Sit tight."

Laser grunted. "Wait."

To my regret, I hesitated.

"Don't you want to know where you can find Magnus?"

I should've fled. Instead, I took down the address and crammed my phone in my pocket, then sprinted out the door for an encounter with every bad choice I'd ever made.

41

I PUNCHED LYLE'S SHOULDER AND YELLED AT HIM TO drive. He sat, limp, in the driver seat. I told him to go. He keyed the ignition, engaged the transmission, and pulled away from the curb, but at such a leisurely pace I feared I'd missed some head injury. He had no sense of urgency. I slapped his cheek because it was a good day for hitting men. He rubbed where I had struck him and steered with his knee. I slapped him again. "Now is not the time for whatever this is, a crisis of conscience, or some shit."

He would've driven into someone's lawn at the end of the block where the road curved to the left if I hadn't taken the wheel and cranked the tires. I thumped him on the temple and begged him to come to. In my periphery the familiar shape of a police cruiser emerged, and just as Lyle's car slipped behind the houses of the adjacent block, the cruiser stopped in front of Ransom's house.

It wouldn't take them long to realize their targets had fled. Moreover, they'd have all exits to his subdivision blocked already.

I placed my palm over Lyle's eyes. His innate response braked the car with a jolt. I shifted it into park, flung open my door, jumped out, hopped over the hood, swung his door open and pulled him into the street. He was hardly anything more than awake. I forced him into the backseat and laid him out.

Since my DUI, I hadn't driven, but it's a skill easily recalled. Toward the end of the block, I set my eyes on a bike trail between two houses. It appeared wide enough to fit a car, and I took it. The path wound down to a wide trail running along West Papillion Creek. A pair of cyclists some way distant, stopped their bikes, and tented their hands over their eyes to stare at the car bumping toward them.

At an overpass, I guided the car through the grassy berm and up onto a numbered road. A car sped past, its driver laying on the horn. I pulled onto the road, then across traffic. Without time to plan, I acted on instinct. Luck suddenly seemed imperative. I hoped it would favor me. I punched the address Laser had related to me into my phone's GPS and thumbed *GO*. From 156th, it was a straight shot, ten miles north, to Bennington. At the intersection of Peterson Dr. and Pacific Street, three police cruisers shot past, lights flashing, sirens blaring.

I took a moment to light a cigarette, and smoking adjusted the rearview mirror to sight Lyle, who lay catatonic in the back. "What's the matter, Putch?"

He showed no sign of hearing me. I pulled onto Pacific and sped past Mama's Pizza. A foolish thought came to me. Maybe he'd been slotted to die at Ransom's house. Perhaps I'd outsmarted fate. How easy that would've been.

Passing over Dodge, I stomped the gas and coaxed the car to sixty miles-per-hour. The sun colored the land in tangerine light. A rippling of clouds to the west were pink and carmine. The first hints of morning commuter traffic flowed toward town.

I wondered what awaited me at Magnus's house. Would he be

a man of spare emotion, weathered, cynical, nerves as calm as chamomile, or would he possess the energy of a star? He'd managed to evade me through so many lifetimes only to emerge at the center of this absurd drama. Marva's life, and Lyle's, rested in his grip. I didn't know whether I meant to persuade him to abandon his plot or to end his threat by shoving him violently into a grave.

At the four-way stop on State and 156th, a rustling from the backseat drew my attention. Lyle mumbled something unintelligible. I squeezed my eyes shut. "I can't understand you."

A car horn honked. The driver behind me was eager to move. I let off the brake, but hesitated on the gas. Lyle mumbled something else. It wasn't language.

On Bennington Road, I hung left. With the window lowered and birdsong in the air, with cigarette smoke rippling in the wind, with my mind full of worries and unshaped fear, I spoke my thoughts: "I don't know where you've gone, Putch, but I need you. Maybe it seems strange, but I'm doing this for you. I don't care about Marva, not Marva or her money, not her safety or solving her case. What I care about is *you*. You told me once you thought I was beautiful, and I know you don't remember, but the truth is, I liked it. I think you're beautiful too."

I'd hoped my words would stir him. If they did, his response was too deep, too hidden, for me to receive.

The house on the hill with its terra cotta roof materialized near the turnoff for N. 173rd. I engaged the blinker and slowed. It was my last chance to hide. If I wanted, I could pull the car to the curb, flip a U-turn, aim instead for northern parts and flee consequence. But I knew how fickle fate would be. Maybe Laser wouldn't author her death, but so long as there was a chance, I had no choice. We might survive the day, but soon enough a sleeping driver would drift across lanes of traffic and total our car, flinging Lyle and me onto the road, breaking our skulls and requiring our lives. Or we would stop at a diner for lunch and our food would be spoiled with e. coli. Any such damn thing.

I guided the car to the driveway of Magnus's home and parked on the steep incline, killing the engine. Let the engine be the last thing I killed.

42

A SLENDER WOMAN, SKIN OVER BONES, SHARP JAWLINE and a severe nose between close-set eyes answered the door. Her neutral expression said nothing, as if she would wait indefinitely for me to announce my purpose. She wore a cashmere throw over a cotton blouse, cream-colored slacks and house slippers with a pink-rose print pattern. Her hair was yanked fiercely into a bun. A delicate leather lanyard around her neck held reading glasses. In her left hand a rolled copy of a thin magazine hung.

"Is Magnus home?" Even as I asked, I glanced back to see if Lyle had stirred.

The woman cleared her throat. "May I notify him who requires his audience?"

I processed her words through the filter of wealth and cultural remove. "Detective Luke E. Mia. Some people call me Little Cancer, and not because I was born in July."

She turned, gliding over the tile foyer, leaving me where I stood with the door ajar. I looked toward Lyle's car. I projected a plea for him to awake, but while life may not obey the boundaries we expect, telepathy wasn't my gift.

The shape of a prolonged wait surrounded me. I considered that the woman had dismissed me, left me to conclude myself unwelcome, that it was my job to close the door and depart, but if that was her purpose, she'd failed to recognize my desperation. My only question was whether to await her return or let myself into the home. I clenched my jaw and stood firm.

Some moments later a robust form appeared at the end of the hallway connecting some distant room to the foyer. It ambled toward me. "You must be Detective Mia. Mrs. DeLonghi told me to expect you, and my wife says you have no manners."

I'd heard his voice before. My heart thumped double-fast. "Manners? Who has time?" When had I heard that voice? "I'm determined."

"Ah." He offered his hand. "The curse of youth."

Why is it always the ones we love the most? "Have we spoken before?"

He stepped aside, ushering me in. "You'll have to forgive me. I have so many fans."

I glanced once more at the car, willing Lyle to rouse, and slipped past Magnus. "I'm not one of them."

Magnus closed the door behind me and extended his arm, palm upturned toward the room adjacent the foyer. It was a carpeted space: short, beige shag. Antique sofas and armchairs surrounded a glass-top coffee table with magazines fanned on its surface. In the corner stood a grand piano, something of luxury married to something of the waiting room. "Have a seat. Tea?"

When did I not need a drink? "Bourbon." He'd answered when I dialed the unknown number using Laser's phone.

"Bit early, but why not."

He returned carrying two china teacups and a ceramic pot on a tray. "The wife wouldn't like to see me with a nip at this hour." He winked.

I accepted the cup and sipped: caramel on walnut with a burn like silk set aflame. Magnus placed the tray on the coffee table and sat opposite me. He lifted his teacup, inhaled. "I knew a private detective once." He drank.

"Call off Laser. Tell him you won't pay. Tell him you've changed your mind."

He bared his teeth against the liquor's burn. "Interesting."

His calm hardened my nerves. "Name your price," I said, knowing I couldn't pay. "I'll see you're compensated."

"Mrs. DeLonghi already tried this." He paused to retrieve a handkerchief from his sport coat with which he dabbed the corners of his lips. "But if I share one thing in common with Laser, it's that I can't be bought. Surely you must know Laser cares not for money."

I meant to say something sharp, but my throat wouldn't open, and I had to force it with a slug of bourbon. It was looking like the kind of morning for a bludgeoning. I scanned the room for something small and heavy and decided on an iron sculpture of a lion. "When's the last time you saw Marva?"

He chuckled. "I like you. No small talk. All business."

Start with a metaphorical bludgeoning of words and work my way up to a physical manifestation. "Larry Surlman is in police custody."

Magnus removed his glasses. "Is that so?" The lines in his forehead rose and receded. "Did you see it with your own eyes? If so, I thank you. He was more ornery than anticipated."

"I wouldn't get too excited." My voice lacked conviction. "The police are going to be asking him questions, and I wouldn't doubt your name will surface."

"That seems—" Magnus examined his teacup, thumbing the contours of its mouth—"unlikely."

"Did I forget to mention Ransom knows everything? We had a good old-fashioned interrogation at his place. Funny what you can accomplish with a roll of duct tape and a knife. Or didn't you think it was a little strange, me showing up at your doorstep?"

Magnus clapped lightly, like a fan at a golf tournament responding to a two-foot putt for par. "You're every bit as charming as I'd hoped." He smoothed the lapel of his robe and smiled, leaving a breath of silence to unsettle me. "But perhaps you're victim to your own fatal flaws of assumption. I imagine after years working the same boring cases, you grow somewhat numb to the possibilities of something truly different. Or perhaps you know you're not the only person dear Mrs. DeLonghi engaged." He leaned back, delight animating his face.

Magnus's wife appeared at the doorway between the receiving room and the dining room. He raised a hand to her. "Darling, a skosh of business to attend to. A moment please."

She nodded, retreating, though her posture suggested she might stand just out of sight, eavesdropping. Magnus replaced the teacup on the serving tray and reclined in his chair. When he spoke next, he did so barely above a whisper, confirming my suspicion that his wife remained nearby. "You look surprised. I can't blame you. In one way, you have us all dead to rights. All the actors have taken the stage. You've sussed out the main plot points. And congratulations, by the way. Marva didn't think you had it in you. She told me so herself, just last night when we spoke." He raised his hand, letting it linger for a moment. "Though, for all that, you may find it more difficult than you expect to connect me with these happenings."

"Money can't shield you from the law." I spoke loudly for eavesdropping ears.

Magnus wagged his finger. "Are you so sure? I still remember the morning I approached him." He examined the fingernails of his left hand. "He told me he had several unique gifts, among them, brutality and invisibility. You can imagine I struggled to believe him. In fact, I nearly wrote him off, that is, until he provided evidence of his exploits. I assure you, if he doesn't want the police to detain him—" Magnus cut his thought short with a slug of bourbon. "But I'll not bore you with details. I'm more interested in my own conscience. Why did I demand he accept a million dollars for a job I clearly knew he'd perform for free? Was it absolution? I'm usually not the guilty type." He rubbed his palms together and deliberately placed them on his knees. "Perhaps his appetite for debauchery disgusted me. He said once that if a woman wasn't willing to fuck him, he was willing to kill her. But I digress. He couldn't see the benefit of our stage play with Marva. I confess, it took a great deal for me to keep him focused." He slipped an envelope from the pocket of his robe and extended it to me.

Chaotic details buzzed about my head like flies on a cut of rotten meat. I finished my bourbon and considered the warmth in my throat. "What's this?" I received the envelope.

Magnus offered what may have passed for a smile if he were in the company of weasels and jackals. "Marva asked that I give you this." He removed his glasses, examined the lenses, wiped them on his jacket tails and replaced them. "You just missed her. She's headed to Regency now for her grand denouncement."

I opened the envelope and peered at a stack of bills, much like the envelope Marva had given me so many times before. My hands were leaden, my arms heavy. I thumbed the cash. The envelope suggested a finality I couldn't accept. I raised my eyes to Magnus and spoke for all to hear. "I don't know what this is supposed to mean, but I do know the police were closing in on Marva's front door when I left there, and if I were you, I'd be a little more than passing scared Laser won't escape this time. No matter what messes he's squirmed out of before. They had the neighborhood surrounded." I picked a hangnail. "You might want to call your lawyer now, is what I'm saying."

"Ah." He raised his eyebrows, and tented his hands before his

THE 9 LIVES OF MARVA DELONGHI

face. "So Laser was *not* in police custody, as you said. On what legs do you stand to threaten me when you yourself escaped police custody?"

His calm unbalanced me. "You've spent too long getting exactly what you want, you pompous prick."

"Darling, dear?" Magnus cleared his throat. "I know you're listening. I can feel your ears burning. Make yourself useful and bring us hors d'oeuvres, would you?"

I leaned forward, tossed the envelope on the coffee table and rested my elbows on my knees. "You know what I think? I think this money was for you, and I think it was meant as an insult. I think Marva came to tell you the game was up. I think you cheated on some agreement with her and she got wise to you. Did it hurt your feelings that she hired detectives? Did you even know she hired us? Maybe she came last night to give you one last chance, and you were upset because involving us—" I arched my thumb at my chest for emphasis—"meant you were in danger of being exposed. Maybe you thought you had Marva right where you wanted her."

Magnus shifted in his seat. He closed his eyes for a long moment. "No one has ever *had* Marva. She's never given herself to anyone, not her husband, not the People for the Ethical Treatment of Animals, no one. But I will have her death, because death is something to be taken by force." He crossed his left leg over his right, opening the gap in his robe to briefly reveal the pallid hair of his inner-thigh. "As for being exposed, I'm afraid you credit yourself too much. I assure you, when the time comes, Ransom will look as guilty as you thought he was, and who will listen to him then? As for you, I have a sworn statement from Marva that she hired you to investigate her husband on suspicion that he was plotting her demise. It's only a contingency of course, an emergency eject so to speak, because framing him would deliver a death knell to the whole purpose of Marva's plan for posthumous glory. I dare say the choice is yours."

The room began to spin. Waves like heat radiating off pavement shimmered before me. My shoulders felt heavy, and my lungs were impossibly small. "You're lying."

Magnus produced a second envelope from his robe. From it he removed a sheet of paper, which he handed me. The text was simple, penned in black, and in spirit, exactly as Magnus had described. "As I said, Marva told me to expect you, but you can't comprehend how or why, and I can't blame you. I almost can't believe it myself, though again, who will take your word against mine even if you try to escape this predicament?"

"What if she has a witness to corroborate her story?"

Reality, so dangerously spinning, crashed with the weight of an anchor. I turned, startled. Lyle strode into the room, erect, pink-faced, mischief in his eyes. I imagined wrapping him in a hug. The chair beneath me dissolved, and I floated free of gravity.

"Pardon me?" Magnus rose. "You must be the partner."

"Starving, actually. I heard hors d'oeuvres?"

My heart fluttered. "What happened to you?"

Lyle ignored me.

Magnus tightened his robe belt. "Charmed."

Darling-Dear emerged carrying a tray of meats and cheeses. She placed the tray on the coffee table, nodded and backed out of the room.

I bit my lip. "You were catatonic."

"Have a seat." Magnus indicated a chair. "Before you grow too adulated. Understand, Marva's letter implicates you both. Marva hired MK Detective Agency to investigate her husband. She transferred to me power of attorney should any misfortune befall her. I've seen the papers. When she is murdered, I rather think you'll find it impossible to present a convincing case that I had anything to do with her misfortune. Especially when I execute her will without benefit to myself, and when I christen the development in Old Mill as Marva DeLonghi Park, in her memory. But really, you have no idea how lonely I've felt these past months. This constant choreography of such ridiculous plots, speeding cars and empty elevator shafts, all the while entertaining that brute, Laser. What kind of name is that anyway? Imagine having to scheme and plan with such a fool. I'll tell you, since Marva began these misadventures, I've sent more text messages than I had the rest of my life combined."

I peered into the bottom of my empty teacup. Magnus refilled it from the pot. I thanked him and drank. Darling-Dear reappeared carrying a tray with small plates full of bite-sized toasts, olives, sliced fruit and cut vegetables. She set the plate next to the meat and cheese and asked Lyle if he thirsted.

He looked at the teapot. "I guess."

When she left for a teacup, I whispered that it wasn't tea we were drinking. Lyle sighed and said he'd hoped it wasn't. He devoured a corner of toast with a slice of prosciutto and cheese. "So you were the one sending those text messages?"

Magnus refilled his teacup. "Indirectly of course. So don't go getting any ideas. But yes, the words, the deeds, consider me the author."

I poked at the plate of food, but my stomach wasn't in it. "You're a piss poor writer, though I'm sure you loved feeling powerful. That's what this is all about isn't it? A power trip."

"Don't act so smug, young lady. You think you can reveal my motives with your psychological mumbo-jumbo."

"I don't need to reveal anything. You're a Polaroid." I ran a hand through my hair. "You've exposed yourself."

Magnus laughed. "It must feel so good to be clever."

I scratched my shoulder. "What did you stand to gain from all of this?"

"Ah, the dreaded motive." Magnus patted his wife's rump as

she placed the teacup and she swatted him in the back of the head, rushing away with a blush. "It's simple. She grew weary of losing. When we met, I assisted her in a number of her pet projects—pun intended." He winked. "But then there was the business of the Old Mill development. I honestly had no idea she would take umbrage to it, but not even our warm friendship could deny me my plans." He paused to prepare a plate of food. "Though I will give it to her. The injunction she filed has real elegance. I might've broken it apart in a decade, but who wants to wait? Which left negotiations. And I'll be damned, pardon my French, if Marva herself didn't provide the inspiration. We enjoyed a long chat and determined that given her fatigue—such tiresome work, all her activism, and she'd grown bitter of the meager returns compared to her husband's accidental celebrity for stumbling on some useless sleeping medication—we determined that if she was made a martyr, her cause might spread. People have a way of gathering behind a victim. We arranged the paperwork, developed a plan, and set to work. Regrettably, Marva struggled with cold feet, but I assure you, when she left me this morning, she had recommitted to our shared success. Her signed confession implicating Ransom should arrest any doubts. Don't you agree?"

Lyle dispatched several olives and washed them down with a cup of bourbon. "Wow! You really know how to pick it." He stood. "So listen. I'm screwed if I'm nothing else, and don't ask me how we got here because if you did, I'd say my partner must've smoked some cosmic hash and seen the future, since she sure as hell didn't roll up her sleeves and work to get here, but however it happened, here is where we are, and you're the one thing standing between Marva and tomorrow. I don't want to talk about how everyone hates her. She might be the original bitch, but she's our paying bitch, and we're not letting some rich prick and his buffoons wipe her off the map."

"You'll watch your tone in my house." Magnus glared.

"I'll do whatever I want in your house." Lyle reached across me, stabbed at my purse, dug in the pocket for my cigarette and lighter, ignited the tobacco and inhaled, coughing. "How do you do this shit?" He handed me the smoldering cigarette. "See, I already called the police."

Darling-Dear appeared in the room, staring at the smoke drifting toward the ceiling, her face a catatonic mask of anger and confusion. Lyle always understood human motive, and I swelled with admiration at how he'd so quickly assessed Mrs. Adderpaine's weakness and exploited it. She marched into the living room, her hands in claws, her face a mask of rage.

Magnus stood and raised his arms, stepping in front of his wife. "You're bluffing. Why would you call the police?"

"Because I woke up in the back of my own car in a strange place." Lyle turned a hard gaze on me. "Or maybe I just figured no one in the godforsaken mess would bank on simple logic, because god forbid anyone would accept that sometimes you can't control every last fucking detail."

"Where'd you come from?" What else was there to say?

"The backseat, where else, huh?"

43

THE WHOOP OF A POLICE SIREN ECHOING NEARBY preceded the crunch of rubber on gravel outside Magnus's house. A moment later, Mike Shotz ran into the receiving room. He stopped and rocked onto his heels. The cigarette hung between my lips. Lyle had stood and was facing the foyer. Darling-Dear shrieked and threw her hands in the air, surrendering. Magnus laughed.

Shotz pointed at me. "We don't have much time."

Magnus rubbed his belly. "Pardon me, officer, but I have *not* invited you into my house."

"I'm not a fucking vampire."

"But you do abide by the code of police conduct?"

"Lyle, can I come in?"

Lyle nodded. A smile captured my lips. Magnus's faded. His face twitched.

Shotz turned to Lyle. "But listen, I'll take care of this. I was trying to tell you when you hung up. Your giant escaped."

A stone weight fell on my chest. "He what?"

"We busted through the front doors just after you two morons vacated and found Ransom in a heap on the ground covered in fucking duct tape...Nevermind the details. The big guy managed to give us the slip. We found a wad of tape all balled up, tossed in a bush in Ransom's backyard."

"How?"

"Hell if I know. But if you—"

"Bravo!" Magnus interrupted Shotz, red blooming on his cheeks, his hands clapping. "Bravo! Bravo!"

Shotz unclipped his handcuffs. "You better get out of here."

Lyle vaulted for the door, and I was up and following him with the teacup still in my hand. A splash of bourbon spread on the shag carpet. Lyle fired the engine. I stopped long enough to tell Shotz Magnus had a white envelope. "Get it. Don't let anyone see it."

He nodded.

Racing outside, I crumbled Marva's written confession and gestured to Lyle. "Borsheims!" He shrugged, but I pleaded, "Just drive." He jammed the transmission into reverse and hammered the gas before I'd fully sat. We squealed with a bumper-scraping crush onto the street. I put my lighter to the ball of paper as we sped through the neighborhood. Noxious smoke made me cough, and I rolled down my window. I dropped the flaming ball on the floorboards. My fingers stung from the heat. I stomped out the flames. "What time is it?"

Lyle was grinding his teeth and wringing his hands on the steering wheel as he pushed the car past seventy. "You've got eyes." He swung across the double yellow into oncoming traffic to pass a Ford Fiesta, and swerved back into the right lane as the horn of a pickup blared. Its driver had hit the brakes hard enough to burn rubber, and the smell flicked me in the nose as we raced past.

With ten minutes to the hour, I wondered if fate meant for

Marva to die, regardless of all we'd done. She was likely parking at Regency that moment.

Lyle looked both ways at the intersection on Maple, as we'd come to a red light, he slowed slightly, then punched the gas and shot a gap between traffic. I closed my eyes and braced my hands on the dash, expecting impact.

A police helicopter thumped past the intersection at Dodge. Lyle wrestled the wheel and the brake pedal and negotiated between two sedans, jumping the edge of the median. He merged onto the expressway at eighty-five miles an hour.

We shot past cars in blurs of color, climbing the overpass. My vision restricted, pulse tightening, breath catching. Subtle déjà vu. Not like the memory of life relived, but like that of a life reintroduced. The sky was just so, the air just so. We were gaining on the police chopper and two cruisers, lights flashing, sirens blaring, in the left lane. They were tailing a gold Geo Metro. As we crested the rise where the expressway opens onto the overpass I pointed, panicked, terrified, because I knew, and I knew I knew, but I couldn't stop myself from the foolishness.

"That's him! Laser! Laser!"

Lyle let his foot off the gas.

"Pull off." I tapped Lyle's shoulder. "They've got him."

Lyle pushed past the police cruisers. "That's what they thought before." He pulled up alongside the Geo.

Laser was hunched, behind the wheel, too tall for his stolen ride, and bare chested. Lyle kept pace, the nose of his car at the rear bumper of Laser's.

"Pull off!" I knew how this ended. "You don't have to die for this. I need you."

"I'm not going to let them screw—" Lyle's voice caught in his throat. "What'd you say?"

The shadow of the First National Bank building loomed

above the overpass, its skin of copper-colored windows. "Stop! Stop!" I braced my hands on the dash and screamed as loud as my lungs could scream. "Stop!"

Lyle briefly eased off the gas, but he still swerved to keep the Geo close. Our bumper nudged Laser's. A sick flutter spread through my stomach as Laser's car lost its grip on the road, described one perfect spin and slammed into the roadside barrier. Lyle had hit the brakes, but his frame bit into the Geo's cheap plastic bumper, which arched us in a slingshot. Laser's car met the concrete barrier on the edge of the slow lane, but ours was pulled onto two wheels. The impact sent us airborne.

We slammed onto the top of the median. My seatbelt locked. Our car rocked once on the concrete wall, balanced for a fraction of an instant, long enough for me to see the blood-spurting force of impact on Laser's body.

You might not believe I saw his dead eyes or the way the police cruisers shrieked to a stop, avoiding further collision, but I did because I'd seen it before, though always ever in my dreams, all I'd known was the feeling of disembodiment, the floating free of sailing through the air, which is what happened when Lyle's car tipped over the median leaving dead Laser and his stolen Geo Metro above.

We plunged through the air no more than two seconds, but those two seconds were the longest stretch of focused time I'd ever lived or have since. I counted all one hundred twelve thousand, six hundred fifty-seven hairs on Lyle's head, memorized the stains on his front teeth which shone through his grimaced lips. The flecks of yellow shot through his blue eyes and the red mole at the intersection of his forehead and hairline, the scrape on his right hand at the outermost knuckle of his index finger, the one nail he'd failed to pare with all the others, which were cut to the quick, the way his collared shirt draped over his chest, how the top three buttons hung open revealing a thin spread of hair over his sunburnt chest, the finger-width strip of whiskers that were several days growth longer than the rest and the dimple in his chin, the scent of bourbon and salami, a silence though his whole face muscled toward a rictus of shouting, the foolishness of a woman who thought she could save anything, just anything at all.

44

I WOKE IN A HOSPITAL BED WITH A ROARING HEADACHE. Invisible bugs crawled beneath the surface of my skin, and an unwelcome euphoria sang in my blood, a drugged euphoria. I blinked away the whisper of a dream: me in an open field of tall grass with the sun low in the sky and someone just beyond the horizon, unseen, but longed for.

A heart monitor beeped its rhythm nearby. My hands flexed and relaxed. A burnt rubber odor clung to the inside of my nose, reminding me what I'd lost. I was alone in a room for two. A faint breeze of forced oxygen misted my nostrils. In my left arm, an IV pumped fluids.

I felt my face with the tips of my fingers, discovered bandages on my chin and cheeks. My left eye throbbed. I encountered soft stubble where hair had been shaved from my scalp. In the center of the bald spot I counted a seam of stitches that ran from the brow to the crown. I wiggled my toes, bobbed my knees. The body seemed to respond to my brain's commands, and I wondered how much pain I *should* be feeling. Other than the stitches and bandages on my face, I found only an elastic wrap on my left shoulder.

Then sleep.

I woke in a hospital bed, alone in a room for two, with a lapping headache. Ice flowed beneath my skin, and a dull sigh trickled off my lips, a drugged sob. I blinked away the laughter of a dream, a great black dog bounding over sand, lunging into the water. He was the spirit of Lyle and his image would be my closest friend in slumber for years until I plunged into the unknown, the full consequence of all that had unfolded still before me.

The faint breeze of forced oxygen tickled my nose. A nurse padded into my room. She checked the IV bag, flicked the tube and met my eyes.

"Oh." She hesitated. "You're awake."

I blinked. The voice was in my throat, but I didn't want to use it.

"How are you feeling?"

I offered a slight nod. She rested her hand on the plastic arm of the hospital bed.

"Are you in pain?"

My lips parted, and a whisper of "No" escaped.

"That's good. That's good." She told me to sleep.

I did.

I woke in a hospital bed with sharp pains of emptiness in my stomach. Invisible hands wrung my guts, and a trickling growl hummed in my throat. I blinked away the darkness of dreamless sleep, and with one hand pulled the puff of oxygen away from my nose. The heart monitor measured a separate time, my pulse faster than seconds but not fast enough. I was alone in a room for two.

A remote at my hip had a single red button in the center of its body. I depressed the button and a soft chime echoed. A peach colored light in the hall outside my room illuminated. Some minutes later, perhaps hours, a nurse appeared. He was tall with dark skin that reminded me of advertisements for Caribbean vacations.

"Look at you." He smiled.

"No mirror."

"Glad to see you have a sense of humor."

I hadn't meant to. "Could I have water?"

The nurse nodded. He asked if I was in pain. I said no. He said he would check with the doctor and see what he could do about my thirst. Before he retreated I asked if he knew what had happened to the driver in my car. I knew the answer, but wanted to hear it spoken. The nurse stood with his back to me, and only slowly turned.

"He was dead when the paramedics arrived."

Slowly, over days, the pain increased. I'd broken three ribs no bandages could heal. The wrap on my shoulder was holding gauze in place to keep a palm-sized burn from infection. The doctor told me I'd had forty-one stitches in my scalp. I'd passed all motor function tests, and every scan had indicated no nerve damage or hemorrhaging.

There's not much to say about Lyle: dead on impact. They always say that. Maybe he broke his neck and felt nothing, or maybe he fractured his skull and his heart beat frantically for minutes, trying to supply enough blood to his brain, which bulged through a crack in his head.

No one knows what Lyle's last moments were like, because he was dead by the time help arrived, but I think I know better than anyone that death is rarely instantaneous, and even when by the hand of a clock, it is sudden, the mind has a final say, which is rarely pleasant. Life is a force that refuses to be beaten but always fails to win.

The food they served me during recovery was offensive: salt-free kidney bean soup, sugar-free gelatin, white rice. I convinced a night nurse to talk to my doctor about nicotine patches. The doctor maintained that the majority of successful quit attempts came cold turkey. I told the nurse I had no intention of quitting and the only result of cold turkey was painful headaches that Dilaudid only sharpened.

After six weeks in bed, a team of physical therapists set out to rehabilitate my body with torture they called PT. Twice a day some college-aged man and woman would file into my room, manipulate my legs and feet, bend my knees and elbows, instruct me to breathe this way or that, and help me into an EZ Stand. The exercises grew more complex with time, but at a certain point, they stopped hurting and started boring.

"I'm not a geriatric patient."

A guy with spiked hair who called himself Tandi laughed and said anyone who'd broken twenty bones and ripped her scalp open had to go through the same process. "You're more stubborn though."

From the day I was cleared to eat solids and drink milk, Susan delivered my meals several times a week. The most I offered her in the way of recognition was a wink, and even that seemed to put her off balance. I still believe she recognized the complexity of my being in that hospital room, the way she kept one eye on me while she prepared my tray and slid the bedside table over my lap and asked me if I needed anything else. She never relaxed in the room with me. Once, she even asked what it was like to die. "I mean, you flatlined." She cleared her throat. "Was there a tunnel of light? They say you were dead for three minutes. What's after this?"

If life is defined by a beating heart, and death by the heart's failure to beat, then nothing follows this life, because I couldn't distinguish between the flatline and a dreamless sleep. I measured my response. "It was peaceful."

And maybe Susan never understood what I'd gone through, though I believe she knew my experience had exceeded the failure of my heart. She lingered in my room, like a star-struck fan. She and I had searched for the same meaning, and though I'd found nothing conclusive, she seemed to sense I'd met the mystery. Every drug store she robbed, brought her face-to-face with mystery, but none had introduced her. She knew that.

About a month into my recovery, prosecutors visited me with a list of questions and an audio recorder. I declined comment, save to say my partner died a hero attempting to save Marva. Given another chance, I would've exposed her and let the courts have their way with her, but you can't know what you don't until you do.

Taxpayers footed my hospital bill, on account of the public service I'd provided, and in the wake of my testimony a steady flow of fan mail arrived. People called me a hero for my role in the capture of a solicitor, Magnus Adderpaine and his contract killer, Larry Surlman, whose crimes were numerous.

When the hospital approved my release, I still required the use of a wheelchair, which the doctors told me could be anywhere from six weeks to six months. Just outside the hospital's main entrance, beyond the sliding doors, beneath the shaded canopy, I met the cool breeze of fall. Lyle should've been there to drive me home, but instead, I called a Lyft. The driver helped me into her backseat, folded my wheelchair and tucked it into her trunk. Lyle should've been there to drive me home.

45

SOME DAYS I ROLLED MY CHAIR THE TWO BLOCKS FROM my apartment to the office and rode the elevator to the second floor, parking by the window, learning how to breathe and soaking in the scent of our shared workspace.

My mind projected his last hours on the window glass. I would try to manipulate the outcome: capture the steering wheel, cover his eyes, shield his body with my body. When nothing worked I went further back, wrapped my arms around his shoulders before he ran out of Magnus's house, but he slipped through my grip and dashed toward death nonetheless.

46

You don't pay detectives to solve a murder, you pay them to prove a life's worth keeping. Sometimes the revelation is wise. Blood spills, but everyone lives happily ever after. Other times the solution is a blunt instrument, and the guilty win. What people want is the knee-slapping laughter, consoling wisdom—there's a purpose for everything—a speck of hope.

Marva arrived at my office one snowy afternoon in late fall, just as I was preparing to wheel the two blocks home. She said she wanted to pay me in person, but felt it might be best not to disturb me in the hospital.

I thought of Lyle. "You could've sent flowers, huh?" I always thought of him.

She shrugged. "You don't strike me as the sentimental type."

Perhaps I wanted her to say how grateful she was that I'd saved her life. Maybe I wanted an escape from the barrage of regret, but if that's the case, I was unprepared. I cranked one wheel and opened a path for her to step past. She aimed for the kitchen, and when she returned she held two glasses of Magdalene, neat, full to the lip. I sipped from the glass she offered.

"Do you have a cigarette?"

We smoked. Some time later, Marva leaned over the armchair where she sat and seized her purse. She produced a thick white envelope. Its heft nauseated me. She said there was a little extra, to account for pain and suffering, and that's when I knew her story would redeem nothing. I should've sent her into the cold and invited her never to return, but instead I thanked her, which is a testament to my lingering numbness. Either that or I still believed I might find a justification for having let Lyle die.

"I knew when we met, there was something special about you. You irritated the hell out of me. That's always a good sign. You always hate the people you're most similar to."

I wanted to tell her we had nothing in common, but I wondered.

She continued. "What you did, it was a real stroke of genius. And I have to admit, everyone underestimated you, me most of all."

I shaped my cigarette ash on the side of the ashtray. "I'm used to it."

"But I've been dying to know. How did you know about Laser? We didn't even review my case. I didn't have a chance to tell you anything."

I drew on former lives because if there was one person who didn't deserve the truth, it was Marva DeLonghi. "We have an arrangement with Jake's. Remember the bar where you met Lyle? Our booth was bugged. You'd be surprised how many walk-ins found one or the other of us there. If Annie sees one of us with a client, she texts the other, and we can call into the feed." I was making the shit up on the fly, and it was far-fetched, but Marva's eyes said she was lapping it up. Lyle always said, Throw it on the stoop.

After a moment her brow wrinkled and she drew on her cigarette, hollowing her cheeks to the extreme. "I don't remember mentioning anything that would've suggested Laser's involvement." She exhaled.

"Big guy. Grant Wood. American Gothic look-alike."

She thought that over, and her shoulders relaxed. "Right." She drew the vowel out with satisfaction. "Doesn't seem like much to go on though."

"You think detectives ever get much to go on? You're the one who said you underestimated us."

"Still, that's pretty impressive. If I'd known you were that good, I think I would've lost a whole lot more sleep between then and now."

I glanced out the window. "Not with Ransom around."

She laughed. "I wouldn't touch his shit with a ten-foot pole."

"Oh?"

"Any drug that's supposed to grow hair, but instead makes people pass out is suspect, if you ask me."

Sitting with Marva made me feel dirty straight through to my appendix and I wanted her gone ten minutes ago. I bolted my drink and lit a fresh cigarette. "Well, anyway, I'm sure you didn't come down here to shoot the bull, so let's get to it."

She traced a figure-eight on her knee. "That's a strange phrase."

"Which?"

"Shoot the bull."

"Breeze. Whatever. A high school friend of mine, Emory, he used to say it."

"Well."

"I mean it. You paid me. So unless you got something you want to say, I think we're done here."

Marva gave a wounded expression. "Maybe we are done here."

"Looks like it."

She stood. In the way she lingered, I knew she couldn't leave well enough alone, but the more she persisted, the less I wanted anything to do with her. It's the difference between a cold and a flu. Spend one day puking your guts out and wake up the next day ready to pounce. Or spend three weeks with a stuffy nose, chapped lips, runny eyes, aching muscles, and a throbbing headache. Marva was definitely a cold. "I know Magnus told you things."

"Lot of people tell me lot of things."

She circled the chair she'd been sitting in and leaned her elbows on its back. "He probably told you I hired him to kill me."

"Sounds about right."

"But he maybe didn't give you the real story."

"Telling the truth can be such a burden." I wanted a bag of cheese puffs, but the office was bare of anything save liquor and ice. "But honestly, I don't care anymore. There was a time when knowing the whole story meant something to me. Things change I guess."

"Oh boo-hoo. Let me get you a tissue." She gave a breathy chuckle. "You're better off solo. The way Lyle talked. God, I doubt he knew what color my eyes were. Don't tell me he didn't make passes at you. I'd hardly sat with him before he started undressing me in his mind. You're liberated."

I'll give it to her. She had a knack for knowing her audience. Because most women loved Lyle's attentions. It's a testament to the oppression of our culture that women root their identities in the affections of men, but where Lyle and I were concerned, she understood nothing. I'd seen beneath his bravado, even from the beginning. Sure, his behaviors gnawed at me most of the time, but he'd once said something I never forgot, even if it was a crock of shit. He said men were oppressed by men too. How did I think it felt to be a guy with other guys fawning over women knowing if you didn't drool at the hottie walking down the street, that if you didn't whistle and place bets on her cup size, the other guys called you a queer. No one wanted to be an outsider, and not everyone was strong enough to be that: a bad excuse, and a worse world-view, but not without its grain of truth. "You better watch it."

Marva rolled her eyes. "Fine. Give it time. You'll see."

I clenched my fists. My right hand searched for the knife that wasn't in my pants pocket.

"The important thing to remember—" she clicked her tongue —"is that I really did start out wanting to die. Keep that in mind because it's hard won. I'm convinced you can't really change this world if you've never sunk so low that you really and truly want to die."

Where death was concerned, she had no idea. I was eight times her superior in that category and I knew at bottom, no one wanted to die in the final moments, which meant whatever *hard fought* truth she thought she'd won, it was a lie, and basing your life on a lie was bound to lead nowhere good. "Then I'm convinced you're insane."

"Until I'd given up hope, I lacked the courage to act. But when I knew what had to be done, what had to happen if I was ever to enjoy life again, every day was suffering."

"Listen to you. As if your suffering was so much more profound than mine."

"I'm not the one crying over one dead lowlife."

In times past, Marva would have fallen dead with a blade in her brain before she'd spoken the last syllable of "lowlife," but as I've said, I wasn't my former self. If nothing else could prove I'd lost, that I remained hunched in my wheelchair was conclusive. "I want you out of my office. Leave. And don't you ever, ever contact me again."

"It's too late for indignation, but I forgive you for not knowing that yet. It won't be long before you'll realize you're responsible for everything that happened."

Still more proof that I never learn, I should've told her to eat shit and die, but instead I said, "Enlighten me."

"That's exactly it. That's why I came. To free you. Now it might be hard, but what I'm going to tell you will give you the courage to live again, because I'm pretty sure you're not far from where I was just before you met me. If you don't already have fantasies of ending your life, it won't be long. You can see it in a person's aura. And I'm pretty sure if you got there before I got to you, you'd have gone through with it. Lucky for us both, Magnus accepted a plea deal."

47

"I'd been bored. Married into money. Got lazy. Started drinking. Yada, yada. Then I woke up one day to an article in the New York Times about the bees. Everybody knows about the bees. Dying in droves. Pesticides. Loud noises. It terrified me, but unlike the masses, it awakened me to something long dormant in my soul. From childhood I'd always been sensitive to oppression. Where most girls where perfecting their mascara, I'd been perfecting my skills in debate. I won state with my debate team, even travelled to D.C. to participate in the national competition and did extremely well. Met George W.

"In college I met Ransom and he fawned all over me. Said no woman he'd met took the world so seriously. Stupid me, I believed him, but he was just like all men, except instead of charming me with comments about my beauty, he massaged my ego with poems about my intelligence and whit. The next thing I knew, I'd dropped out of graduate studies to have an abortion because we both agreed kids were for other couples. Years passed and I just got further and further from caring. Every comfort was at my fingertips. I distracted myself with trips to France and South Africa, with all the finer things. You might be thinking I was weak, and you'd be right, but I found myself when Ransom stumbled onto his stupid drug. I peered into my soul and I saw the depth of my disgust. People were falling all over themselves to fund his research while rats were sleeping to death in his laboratory. I wanted to make a difference, a real difference, and I told my husband, and he said whatever made me happy, which was his way of saying, don't bother me. And do you know what happened? I poured myself into causes that mattered, and what I found was that people talk and talk and talk, but nobody wants to *do*. They'll show up at your rallies and your protests. They might even write a check to your foundation, but when it comes to making meaningful changes to their lifestyle, they refuse. The same people who held signs on street corners condemning the uses of pesticides were filling their grocery carts with GMO vegetables and cornfed beef. The easiest thing in the world, to give up beef, and no one would do it. The easiest thing in the world, to quit buying fucking Round-Up and no one would do it. They'd drink your wine and encourage you to fight the good fight, then they'd all go to Stellas and chow down on cheeseburgers and fries, congratulating each other on making a difference. I wanted to die, because no one would listen. I wanted to die.

"Then Magnus came along and I felt reborn. He was the first person I met who got what I was trying to do. I told him about how cows produced methane at startling rates, and he turned vegetarian in a day. I told him how cars produced so much CO_2, but how electric cars weren't much better because they charged on electricity produced by coal, and he went and built a thousand acre solar farm. People were paying attention to him, and he was calling me onto stage to tell my story. I felt like I'd won, until he told me he'd bought that stupid development at Old Mill. He said, 'Come on Marv, it's one little inconvenience,' and he tried to convince me that since he was going to be using the land to develop fixed cost housing for the poor and state-of-the-art community resources, it was really a carbon tax, more or less. I asked why it had to be Old Mill. I said there were countless other developments, but he said no other one would do. He had this whole team of researchers who put together their bids and he knew what he knew. It was about money, about recognition. Old Mill was a very public location, and it was a kick in the teeth to TD Ameritrade, who'd been eyeing the land for a decade, and who he'd outbid, and wasn't that just grand? So I broke ties with him. End of story. Just like that. And I wanted to die, but I really wanted to die, and I tried to do it, but I couldn't. Not on my own. So I pled with Magnus one more time, and do you know what he said? He said he was sure there was a solution to our problems that was mutually beneficial. He said the fight for sustainability had always been more my thing, that our interests had dovetailed, but that if I'd lift my injunction, he'd be sure to maintain our partnership. I said he could fuck our partnership and go to hell. At that point, he said I could have it my way. He'd outlast me in court. He compared our bank accounts. Keystone XL, Trans Mountain Pipeline. He had interests in both. And he said he'd give it to the protesters, they'd actually held out longer than anyone expected, but we all knew how it would end, and that was ten thousands versus big oil. How did I think I'd hold up, just little old me against the Adderpaine empire? I knew he was right. Knew it to the bottom of my bones, and that's when I decided it was time. If I was going to lose the battle, at least I could start a war. That's how I said it to him, and he liked the idea. He said he didn't care where his money came from. If people got behind renewable energy and land-sharing with wildlife and responsible farming, there'd be enough money to go around. Maybe my dying would spark a movement. He doubted it, but he was more than glad to play along. I knew he was the devil. He had more fun planning my death than I've ever seen anyone have doing anything. And right up to the night I met Philipe Ruskov, I was willing to die to salvage some crumb of what I'd fought so hard to gain.

"Sure. Somewhere in the back of my mind, I'd had fantasies of outmaneuvering that asshole. I'd done plenty to implicate him in criminal controversies. But like the Old Mill development, without something sensational to light the fuse, he'd have more than enough power to legally bury anything I brought against him. Then, after I met Ruskov I saw the way out. I woke up from my death wish. So I spent a month building the papertrail. You've seen the news right? And I stalked him until I found Laser. That's when things really got going. I trailed that son of a bitch to the strip club and put my cards on the table. He was as vile as they came. He said he looked forward to killing me, to putting my head in a bowling ball bag. You can't appreciate how hard it was not to insult him for being so boring, so unimaginative, but I did. I let him feel powerful, because that's what all men want. And I led him to his own downfall. I asked wouldn't he rather have my head and Magnus's in bowling ball bags. Wouldn't he rather enjoy seeing my husband behind bars for the murder of his own wife. Wouldn't that all be so much fun. It's hard to believe there are men like Laser in the world, but he was so aroused by the prospect that he didn't even want money to execute the plan. He said he'd dreamed of killing Magnus from the start. I told him the first step was meeting Ransom. He had to win Ransom's trust. At the same time, I told Magnus I was having second thoughts about his plan. I maybe hinted at causing trouble and suggested I wanted him to take care of my husband too. I told a story about how research labs were cruel to animals and that my husband needed to pay for his selfishness. We conspired to frame him. From there it was easy. Though I have to give you a lot of the credit. I had bought this souvenir brick from the Riverfront Park fundraiser, and I'd meant to pass it to you as a piece of evidence to get you on Laser's trail, but you didn't even need it because of your bugged booth. Bravo, again. Here was me, thinking I'd need to go into hiding for months after I slipped Laser at Christian Noble, thinking, even with all the evidence I had implicating Magnus in a plot to murder me, I'd have to wait out years of court trials and testimony and probably never really get to enjoy my reward properly. Then you come along and light the whole thing on fire. Laser's dead and Ransom's in jail for conspiring with Magnus to have me murdered, and Magnus signs a plea deal. The most powerful man in Omaha and he signs a plea deal because you involved one crooked cop. Can you imagine what would've happened to me if they'd found Magnus with my money or that lousy signed confession? Well, I kiss your feet Luke. I really do, because you're just as calculating as me.

"I didn't know, the day Laser died, what you were going to do. I sure lost sleep wondering, because you had me too. You could've told your little police buddy what I'd done, and I thought you maybe might, which I didn't know how I was going to deal with, but you didn't say a word, which is how I know you'll one day thank me for freeing you from that dumb, horny bastard partner of yours. He was in the way and you knew it. One of those people who can buy a lap dance and look himself in the mirror the next morning and actually believe he has moral conviction. But we're the ones with moral—"

I'd heard enough. I'd heard more than enough long before I spoke: "Get out. We're not the same, and I loved Lyle. I loved him, and because of you, he's dead. That's not what I wanted, no matter how it looks."

Marva's eyes grew wide, but a smile played at her lips. "Don't lie to yourself, honey. But you're right. I've said my piece. I did it for me, the same way you would've done. Someone, just one person needed to know the truth. I'm glad it was you."

48

MARVA, FOR HER PART, MADE GOOD ON ALL HER HOPES. Every media outlet wanted her story, and she relished the opportunity. She brought fame and attention to a dozen lost causes. Christian Nobel Furs was heckled out of Regency. They quietly reopened a store in Rockbrook, but the clientele never rebounded. 20's Showgirl closed, as advertised, and exotic dancing became a footnote in Omaha's history. Employees at TD Ameritrade celebrated the victory Marva won of protecting the pond—turned wildfowl preserve—where Magnus Adderpaine had intended to build his community center. Editorials frequently cited his downfall with glee. *Absolute Power Corrupts*, they headlined. Marva's involvement in protesting his planned development led to a mayoral campaign some years later.

I despised the stream of referrals she sent me: eco lawyers looking for investigation into corporate practices that oppressed the less-fortunate; employees who contracted occupational diseases from exposures to suspect chemicals; homeowners faced with imminent domain. None of these causes were wrong, they just took me away from the muck of the alleys where I belonged. I rejected them when I could afford to, and spent my time at Jake's or Burke's, me and a tumbler of Magdalene, despising the reflection of me that mirrored the woman Marva recognized. I'd let my own friend die so I wouldn't have to.

But one winter, several years on, I looked up from a fog of bourbon into the eyes of a familiar face. She was frantic, pleading for help, eyes swollen, nose pink, lips trembling. Her hair was a mushroom cloud, nuclear explosion. *Help, help, help.* She wore an orange jumpsuit, the number on its pocket: 047468113.

I reached for her hand, but mine passed through hers, and as it did, she faded. Certain I'd not hallucinated, I dug in my pockets for something to write with, found the nub of a pencil, and scratched the jumpsuit number on my beverage napkin.

I called Shotz, who wanted to take me to dinner. He felt he shared responsibility for Lyle and said so, though I didn't explain how he'd also played a key roll in assuring Marva's victory. We were both guilty, which accounted for the sustained silence that had spread between us, but I said I had other things in mind.

He texted me a few hours after we spoke, long past midnight, but at an hour that still found me wakeful. The inmate number belonged to Debbie Lenvil.

I'd recognized her ghostly face, but refused to believe my eyes until Shotz delivered the news. Debbie had been my cellmate in another life, or was it an earlier version of the same life? I'd once promised her assistance. She heard voices and dreamed dreams, and she projected dreams and spoke to strangers thousands of miles distant. Debbie communicated with the dead—though it turned out—never the dead I wanted to hear from most. She said he was uncommitted, and I hope I know what she meant.

On the first day of spring following a strange winter of sleep, marked by binges of fitness and eating and reading and Netflix, I called the Nebraska State Penitentiary and scheduled an appointment to visit Debbie.

The fastest way to the prison would've been straight up Maple to I-680, but instead I detoured south to Dodge and hopped on the interstate near the overpass. I hadn't been able to revisit the scene of Lyle's death since, but as I passed the spot, I chanced a brief glance, and I don't know what I had expected—a memorial? —but the surge of energy in my stomach was all that spoke to what happened there.

A little further on, as I merged onto 680, I drove past that pond where the only detachment of migrating Sandhill Cranes east of Grand Island rested on their journey to Texas and Mexico. Someone I adored had died so those cranes could keep their pond. I raised my flask of Magdalene to them, took a pull, and lit a cigarette.

In the parking lot at the prison, my hands and feet numbed. All the blood in my body gathered in my chest, and though my heart raced, it was as if the veins curled in on themselves, forming a protective case around my ribcage. Visiting Debbie would mark the beginning of an irreversible journey, as much the end of a thing, as the beginning of something new.

The prison guards searched their hardest for my dignity before letting me into the visitor's room. They patted every surface of my body and found no weapons of self-respect, no idealism, no fatal good will. When they were certain I was as hopeless as any inmate should be, they led me to the room where I'd once sat opposite Marva DeLonghi.

That first moment with Debbie was filled with manic energy. She was the sort of woman who rejected tact. She leaned into her aluminum chair and smiled. "I remember you."

By every strange twist, the only consistent theme had been my solitude through cycles of life and death. I may have expected my visit to reward me with memories of a time before Lyle was gone, but what Debbie gave me with those three words was so much larger. Perhaps the guards could've found a shred of self-respect after all. That Debbie carried an imprint of me through those tunnels suggested I still had the chance to make right the path. "Then you know what I have to do."

49

Debbie said Marva had to die violently. Pick your moment, not your weapon, was her idea. She rifled in her jumpsuit, producing a small glass cylinder. My throat caught. She said, "It's not free. I give you this, and you promise when you've finished your trials you ensure I get out of this place."

I nodded, and she must've read my next thoughts because I didn't have to ask how she'd gotten the medicine. "In prison, you can get anything if you pay enough. And it worked last time, gentle as lamb's wool. Raise a toast to Ransom when you take it. Poor man."

Reaching for the bottle, I felt the grip of time winding down, but Debbie withdrew her hand. "You'll see I'm set free?"

When I agreed she described what I would have to do. Her mystery began in North Little Rock where I would investigate a string of bank robberies, eventually exposing Rabbit Harrelson's crew. Harrelson would be funneling the stolen money to an account in Hamburg. Flying to Germany, I would discover the trail of a woman known as Der Scheidungskünstler: she married men, took their money and pets and left them impotent. I must work with the German police in exchange for a lead that would send me to Nepal, chasing a crippled monk toward a base camp on Mount Everest. From his hands, I would obtain the artifact proving Debbie's innocence.

"Oh. That's all?" I said.

"Perhaps you can find someone to write a book about it when it's over. Might make for a fun beach read."

Debbie said Marva never deserved the gift she received, but since the universe had bargained with her by whatever means, at least I should get an opportunity to have my reward as well. But Marva had to die violently if I meant to return to the beginning. From there, Debbie believed I could save Lyle *and* Marva—and of course, herself. She handed me the vial of Vivifica. I received it in silence.

Though the visitors' room stank of sweat and bleach and mildew, my nose seemed to gather the cool scent of cigarette smoke and a ham and cheese hoagie. I couldn't know for certain that I would see my old knife again, but for the first time in so long, I hoped I would.

ACKNOWLEDGMENTS

It is a pleasure to thank the people and organizations whose encouragement and kind assistance made this writing possible:

Eastern Washington University, especially Gregory Spatz and Samuel Ligon, two writers and mentors I deeply admire. Annie Bomke Literary Agency. Without Annie, this book would have been a disaster. Her patient and numerous edits are responsible for the semicoherent work you're reading. J.P. Valliéres, John Gimbel, Joseph Salvatore, Ryan Switters, and my growing band of Twitter friends. And most importantly, Ashley, to whom this book is dedicated. Without Ashley, I tremble to imagine and hope I never must.

A handful of local establishments are mentioned throughout the book, but in many ways their existence is fictionalized to suit the needs of the author. For all errors of representation, I take full responsibility. Please, if you're ever passing through Omaha, stop at Dos De Oros for the finest tacos I know of, and tell them I sent you.

ABOUT THE AUTHOR

Jody J. Sperling is the author of numerous works of fiction including novels and short stories. He has also published nonfiction. When not writing or reading, Jody can be found recording his podcast, TRBM, a show to connect writers with readers and vise versa. He lives outside Omaha with Ashley and their four boys.

Please leave a rating and review of this book on Amazon or Goodreads, or Facebook whether you loved or hated the story. Reviews are our lifeblood. Click this direct link to the Amazon review form if you read the ebook.

 twitter.com/jodyjsperling

ABOUT THE AUTHOR

Jody J. Sperling is the author of numerous works of fiction including novels and short stories. He has also published nonfiction. When not writing or reading, Jody can be found recording his podcast, TRBM, a show to connect writers with readers and vise versa. He lives outside Omaha with Ashley and their four boys.

Please leave a rating and review of this book on Amazon or Goodreads, or Facebook whether you loved or hated the story. Reviews are our lifeblood. Click this direct link to the Amazon review form if you read the ebook.

 twitter.com/jodyjsperling

ALSO BY JODY J. SPERLING

The Seven-Figure Marketing Mindset for Novelists

The 8 Ball Magic of Suzie Q.

FORTHCOMING - PREORDER NOW

The 24/7 of A Russian Named Ruskov

The 6 Sorrows of Shohei Matsui